Drape the Couches

DAVID GALVIN

DGP

MMXII

This edition first published May 2012

David Galvin Publications DGP

Granary Cottage

East Melbury

Shaftesbury

Dorset

SP7 0DW

ISBN 978-0-9563-681-7-1

CONDITIONS OF SALE

All rights reserved. No part of this publication may be reproduced, stored in a retrieval system, or transmitted in any form or by any means, electronic, mechanical, photocopying, recording or otherwise, without the prior permission of the publisher.

This book is sold subject to the conditions that it shall not, by way of trade or otherwise, be lent, re-sold, hired out or otherwise circulated without the publisher's prior consent in any form of binding or cover other than in which it is published and without a similar condition including this condition being imposed on the subsequent purchaser.

Cover picture by Simon Hackney artwork

Synopsis

Destined to last twelve hundred years Rome again finds herself at breaking point. One man and one man alone, Caesar Diocletianus, has to act quickly as barbarian hordes cross his frontiers and internal revolts spread. In appointing the aggressive Maximianus as co-ruler, he defiantly splits the Roman world in two. One is to rule in the East; the other in the West.

However, without their sanction or authority, a third claimant quietly sets about taking his chance at seizing the throne. In declaring himself as their brother and a saviour too, would the lowly born but rebellious Mausaeus Carausius' reign be able to succeed in the far off province of Britannia or would he eventually fall prey to the gods of Rome?

What marks him out? He has stolen their fleet.

Contents

Chapter I	DRIFTING AMBITION
Chapter II	WHAT AM I WORTH?
Chapter III	A JOINT CAUSE
Chapter IV	ACOLYTE OF MITHRAS
Chapter V	SEA OF SWORDS
Chapter VI	PAY FOR WAR
Chapter VII	BRITANNIA
Chapter VIII	IMPERATOR
Chapter IX	FRIENDS AND ENEMIES
Chapter X	THE DARKEST LIGHT

CHAPTER I

DRIFTING AMBITION

Oceanus Germanicus slapped against the wooden side of the first merchant ship's hull with its wet hand and slapped again whilst Aeolus the wind filled her sails with sufficient breath to carry her inland upon the rising tide to her berth. The two ships weighed down with their cargoes were slow and vulnerable, yet the passage from Britannia had proved safe from any pirate attack for they had been accompanied by a twin prowed warship now turning about for the journey home, the seas around it churning with white foam where the oars bit into the shallow depths off the quiet coast of Gallia Belgica. In the mid afternoon breeze her pennants fluttered and sunlight bounced from an array of rounded shields upon the deck denoting its war like purpose whilst the large ram at the prow forced its way onwards through the blue green waters. The small crews of the merchant ships cheered wildly in thanksgiving for the protection offered by the ship of Portus Dubris and in their return a silver horn sounded with the marines lining the sides of their warship, a Liburna, and raising their swords in salute. Every safe crossing meant normality slowly returning to this part of an empire that had seen Britannia and the north western provinces taken from their legal masters over a period of a generation by usurpers within the army. Civil war had brought numerous conflicts wasting the lives of countless men and the enemies of Rome had not been slow in their exploitation of the strife within. Towns had been burnt to the ground, treasures stolen and people forced from an ever deserted wilderness where the restless tides and the reassuring appearance of roman soldiers in their forts came and went in equal and desperate measure.

From the deck of his small pilot ship, Mausaeus Carausius looked out to sea. Across the flat horizon no other sail matched that of the warship flapping gently in the clear sky and the waters were empty. Considering the time of year Carausius thought that was strange for the channels he had been told had been cleared of their dangerous foes and a series of coastal forts across the narrow sea given to providing protection both for the islanders and shipping alike. Trade in these summer months ought to have been brisk before the onset of winter and the closing down of the safe passages to Britannia and more boats could have been out. It was as if somebody knew something. He raised his hands against the sun, turned west and watched the Liburna sail beyond them with its oars out of the water and wished it well. For their own protection they were now meant to be met by the Classis Germanicus who protected this wide river mouth and all routes along it to the port inland where the cargo ships would discharge their goods safely; only nobody came. There was no fleet escort to be seen. Deep in tactical thought, he watched as the invading tide slowly covered the drying sandbanks that had been exposed throughout the morning and realised that they couldn't wait any longer. To sit at anchor was perilous and would be a draw to any pirate out on the ocean looking for an easy kill. The low shallow beaches were empty too and no roman soldier appeared from the pale grasses to hail them or give them courage. Instead a silence hung over the small swaying craft only to be broken by the captain of the merchant ship looming over him and calling out.

'Are we to move?' he shouted.

'There's nobody here.'

Carausius snapped into responding.

'Prepare to follow and don't stray off my course for I know this river well, so trust in me. Let your sails up slowly and do not go too fast. Once we are in the channel itself then the way is easier to see. Do you understand?' He yelled.

'Yes' came the obvious answer.

The experienced seaman wasn't a fool either.

The river pilot, in the pay of the merchants of Ganuenta, was used to making decisions. After all the safe arrival of cargoes was of utmost importance to the business of the port and following barbarian incursions and destruction it had taken a great deal of trust for them to return and trade from there. Many had lost their wealth and had seen their goods being carried off into the deserted and hostile marshland long before the bewildered appearance of any organised roman relief force had arrived. Yet he had carefully considered the predicament in a manner that he always had done so. They were in a rising tide; there were friendly forces in the river somewhere that would be armed and there were land forces available backed up by many cavalry units if only they could be alerted. As the scapha, the light scouting boat, gently rowed up the river estuary followed by the lumbering merchantmen he noticed movement on the bank and instinctively alerted the man next to him.

'Did you see that?'

'See what?'

'I saw a flash like a shield and then it disappeared' Carausius said, pointing.

'Row to the middle of the channel and don't stray towards the bank.'

He enjoyed the command given to him and on a fine summer's afternoon his spirits were high in being able to combat any threat upon him or his responsibilities. On either side of them grew a scrubland of low alder that came close to the mixed shoreline of river mud and shingle and behind them came the flatlands of peat or sandy soils and ditches full of endless mosquitoes where the wind blew strongest. This was his homeland and he knew that the military commanders had thought it not worth defending in any force. Instead a raised network of roads built of crushed sea shells linking fortlets would be sufficient to raise the alarm and greater forces be organised for a counter attack if the Saxons or Franks came again; but it was all too slow this response and in the absence of any substantial building stone with which forts could be soundly built, Carausius often wondered what the Romans saw in holding this land at all. It was merely a convenient border but one full of desperate men looking to fight in their service. For him personally, taking to the river wasn't a difficult decision as there was little left to do on the land without the constant fear of sudden attack, and if the worst came to the worst he could always evade danger by sailing away instead of running. A boat he knew would always outpace a man with a horse and Carausius would willingly give over his fates for settlement by the goddess Nehalennia for it was in her that he had long believed.

'Look. There's a figure on the bank' and he pointed again like the straightest of sun rays at the solitary figure.

'He's too far way to hear me. Who is he? Look, the man with the cart! I can't see anybody else. Can you see the man on the bank? Look right!' and he called loudly out to the larger and taller merchantman following closely behind with instructions to scan the low waterline for danger and attack.

The cargo ship responded with the reply that nothing else was visible and that he must be alone. They weren't going to stop and urged Carausius to continue. With the river now meeting the incoming tide, small whirlpools began to develop around the changing colours of water and through these the bulky ships easily pushed their way. For the small pilot craft rowing too was becoming more comfortable with the crew looking forward to the safety of the river itself and away from the vagaries of current, tide, wind and shifting channels. No day was the same and the inland port appeared a safe refuge from which to work with the provinces of Britannia without risking the full force of Oceanus. Only in a few remaining memories had the stormy waters taken on more land and submerged them, fortunes lost and people forced to flee their homes and it was into this changing landscape that the Franks had arrived unwanted. He was mindful of that fact and acknowledged that one man on the side of a river wasn't exactly their army. Everybody relaxed until they spotted the woman frantically waving, thigh deep in mud from the nearest bank.

'Quickly; Head towards her!'

Carausius ordered the lighter, swifter boat to change course and move out of its channel.

'It could be a trap Master. Is that wise? What's another body in the river to you, either dead or alive?' his trusted friend and advisor spoke.

'I don't know Galerius,' he answered and then at sixty paces or so from the figure stranded in the mud he threw himself into the cold salty waters and began his swim towards her.

The current he met was stronger than he had imagined and Carausius soon found himself being washed away from where he could last remember seeing the woman, although he could hear a faint voice crying out above the sounds of his own rapid breathing. Despite the summer tunic and the wearing of leather sandals on his feet he calmly remained above the choppy waters emerging from the ordeal on a beach a little downstream from the boats that he had, without thought, recklessly left behind but in the afternoon warmth the river pilot quickly regained his strength and breath and realised that he had to raise his right arm above his shoulder before allowing it to fall. Galerius, if he could see, would understand Carausius' instructions to let the anchor go and wait. He watched him obediently mirror his own actions and the oars lifted from the water. A moment later, two splashes alerted him to the fact that the merchant ships too had stopped. To prevent themselves from turning on the tide and facing the wrong way down the river they now had to lower their sails. If they did turn, then that could be disastrous as Carausius had no means of pulling them about and there was the ever present risk that they too could bump and become stranded upon the submerged banks of sand. How long was this ridiculous mission destined to last on one of the most vulnerable edges of the empire? Galerius himself rubbing his forehead wondered and watched as events developed slowly upon the shoreline.

Carausius had come out of the water and waded up the beach where it looked to be firm shingle and with every careful step he walked to the edge where there was confidence that he could then run in safety through the sharp grasses to where he had seen the woman's body trapped in the mud. She was still there crying and the waters of the ocean were rising about her.

'I'm going to die!' She wept repeatedly.

'I'm going to die here!'

Above them the man with the cart watched on oblivious to wanting to help and stood impassively looking out into the river before Carausius, having scrambled to him, shook him and shouted for some rope. There was no reply; the stranger possessed no words that could be understood and through the matted strands of wet hair, salted skin and clothes that were clinging around him in the warmth of the day Carausius began to question what he was doing. He had embarked upon a mission that he had to finish. He again looked closely at the stranger before starting to shout and wondered where he had come from as his appearance was Frankish; his face carrying different features from his own. The Franks had been allowed to settle in the wastelands of the river margins on land that no-one else wanted and he could be one of them. Fortunately he carried no weapons that Carausius could see and so he feared little for taking whatever he needed from him there and then. In his cart was the evidence of a salt worker – shovels for digging peat and wood for evaporating the water. There was also rope. Taking a bundle of wood, he quickly ran to the edge of where the woman was crying, stuck in the soft mud of the beach and carefully he laid it out before lying down and pulling another piece from behind him to lie on until he was within reaching distance of his quarry. Throwing her the rope, he told her to wrap it tightly around her waist and backed away the way he had come, the end of it in his hand. He stood up and looked out upon his real purpose and responsibility of that day to see that the smaller pilot craft had abandoned its position and was gently floating away from the larger ones. The wind had caught the merchantmen at anchor and was pushing them around. In their proximity to one another the risk grew of a collision, albeit at slow speed and the greater danger that they both would get stuck on a sandbank.

Carausius ran back to the cart but its owner had fled into the quiet tracks of the marshland scrub and was now nowhere to be seen. Without concern he tied the rope quickly about the axle and forced the mule to accept its work and walk forward. As it did, the rope tightened and the captive woman fell forward before being pulled roughly over the wood he had laid out to rescue her. Momentarily she lay still before shakily standing up and washing the mud from herself in the approaching waters. Carausius had stopped the cart and was untying the knot.

'You have saved me' she shouted above the sound of the wind and water.

'My father will be forever grateful.'

Carausius running down asked...

'Who are you? Were you with that man and the cart?'

'No' she said.

'My name is Helena Messalina and my father is a merchant in Ganuenta. I don't know where that man had come from; he hasn't been there all the time.'

'I am from the town myself and my name is Mausaeus Carausius.'

He looked dismissively upon the well dressed young woman before him and then quickly back out to the unfolding events in the river. Galerius was taking responsibility with command and that had bought Carausius a little more time to question the young woman.

'Why are you out here? Do you not realise that it is dangerous?'

He wanted to shout at her but couldn't. Her yellow dress was stained with salt and mud, her shoes lost to the sands but a pleasant smile filled her face. Helena explained that she had travelled out from Rigomagus to visit her father and take an active interest in his business. Her real reason though, it transpired, had been to come and view the very edge of Barbaricum itself and having been given a slave and transport with strict instructions as to where and where not to go, she had found the allure of travelling to the coast too irresistible to ignore. The slave she added had decided to run for help at his mistress' distress.

'And had you died, do you think that he would have told your father?'

'I don't know' she naively replied.

'I hadn't considered the danger.'

Carausius forgave her there and then trying quickly to formulate a plan that would see her safely back despite the more pressing matters to attend to. Out in the river channel both ships had now swung around on the incoming tide and one had crashed into the other with a force that sent it spinning out of control. On the steering deck Carausius could see the frantic efforts of the crew splashing and trying to physically pull the ship back on course by use of the long oars there for that purpose but they failed and the ship, firstly rising over the shallows, was then pushed onto a more permanent strand where she settled out of the safety of deeper water. The second ship too fared little better and its fate was sealed by crunching uncontrollably upon another well known but by now, hidden danger. Only the pilot craft remained free of the river's ensnarement and it struggled to row quickly to the bank where Carausius had watched his mission fail.

Galerius shouted from as close as he could come.

'We need help. Can you swim back?' but Carausius was unsure as the boat represented a smaller target than the beach had when swimming in the current.

Certainly Helena couldn't be expected to swim out there. He sat her down and quickly explained what was going to happen.

'We are going to go for help' he said.

'Firstly I need another larger ship to pull these two off the sand and secondly I need to alert your father that you are out here. The safest thing that you can do is hide and stay out of sight. Not all ships in this river are roman. Remember that and we will come back and fetch you. Don't try to walk back, as the countryside can be dangerous. There are no villas this close to the coast, they are far inland, and therefore nobody to give you refuge. If a roman patrol comes along then so much the better but I wouldn't expect it.'

With that Carausius marked in his mind where he had left her and then started to wade back into the waters for the short but strenuous swim to his boat, crew and problems.

'Wait...' she shouted in excitement.

'Listen to the waters, Carausius. Listen to the waters upon the beach' and she repeated in a low rhythmic chant

'CA-RAU-SIUS, CA-RAU-SIUS, IM-PER-ATOR.'

To this she added...

'Look! From behind the low clouds Roman Jupiter lights up the sea towards Britannia for you!'

However, it was in that distant finger of silver upon the green sea that the warship had become a faint dot and no longer their protector.

'You will come back, won't you?' she yelled but Carausius, struggling in the cold water failed to give her an answer.

Safely aboard the scapha he quickly regained command and waved his hand at Helena on the beach to get in and seek cover. Where she was standing in her yellow dress proved she was too exposed yet Carausius was finding it difficult to care much more about her. After all, he had saved her life and he didn't understand her prediction for the future which he hadn't fully heard, or so he thought. His priority was to get another ship organised and one that could pull the two stranded ones from their temporary incarceration. He bade his crew return towards them and issued instructions at a distance that their men were to take every precaution against attack and not to fall asleep. It could be tomorrow before they returned. With that the twenty hardened rowers set off upstream with the low afternoon sun beating down remorselessly upon their chests and faces. Even with the tide carrying them as far as it could before it began to struggle against the out going waters of the river, the work was physically hard and the views reduced by the flat empty fields about. To a man they just fixed their stares at the bottom of the boat and all pulled together. Then just as they were to round the first bend in their journey and lose sight of the merchantmen, an eagle eyed scout shouted out that several small low ships were rapidly entering the river with many oars but no mast and following the exact channels they had just used. Carausius called them to a stop and as his craft floated gently in the current he watched the situation unfolding behind him powerless to intervene. They were pirate ships and none of his crew carried any weapons aboard. Like sea wolves they had surrounded their prey trapped upon the sandbanks confident that they too could manoeuvre at will and get close. Meeting with token resistance they climbed aboard and soon bodies were seen thrown into the waters below until Carausius had counted all the crew. A rope was quickly tied against the side to hold the pirate boats tight and then goods were passed down into the arms of those not engaged in the fighting.

'Franks.' Galerius said.

'They've watched us come into the river and waited but wouldn't risk an attack with the warship there. Of course, with no mast who would have seen them?'

He attempted to sound sympathetic but Carausius thought otherwise.

'They wouldn't have risked an attack if we hadn't stopped either' he shouted.

'Two ships looted and their crews lost to pirates' and he slammed his hand hard against the wooden side.

'Row on, before we fall prey to them as well' and as the strain was taken up no man could ignore looking back and seeing with his own eyes the fate of the ships stranded where they had left them.

In an hour they would be entirely picked clean of the best cargo and the pirates gone laden with goods. Their young commander, the river pilot had made a catastrophic mistake.

With only reed torches to see by the light of dusk made tying up alongside the artificial quay at the port difficult and with tired arms and legs, came the bad moods. A crew, usually buoyant at the safe return of another cargo, were keen to be off and leave Carausius to explain the absence of any shipping behind them in the quiet, darkening rippled shadows of the river. One by one they quickly sidestepped the owner, Numerius Septimus Clemens, before gathering again behind his back like women and electing to slip away into the night to discuss their own captain's fate. Septimus put out a hand to pull him ashore followed by Galerius.

'You'd better go Galerius' Carausius told him and Septimus, keenly aware of the friends' short conversation, sensed trouble.

'You've either lost my ships or Neptune claims them. Which is it to be Carausius?' He asked worryingly.

'For the river is empty of my cargoes.'

Septimus that day had had his own problems. Barbarian raids to the east had spread panic in Ganuenta and that in turn had deprived the area of available troops who had gone off in support of the river fleet. He looked tired at having to constantly secure his warehouse against thieves and wasn't now in the mood to hear poor excuses of further losses upon his wealth. Every merchant in the town had at one time or another considered leaving and trading elsewhere but following attack after attack, they were persuaded to stay by the all too rapid appearance of the emperor and his armies trying to shore up the damaged province and keep it under roman control. Unfortunately, this time he wasn't to arrive as further inland bands of peasants, deserters and looters had joined forces and were plundering the rich villa estates at their mercy. The Emperor Lord Diocletianus' protection was required everywhere and the bandits knew that; the army couldn't appear and all provinces in the west were suffering, except Britannia whose safety seemed guaranteed by the seas. So he repeated his question as to where his goods and ships were and then felt too overcome for a response, for that day his daughter had also gone missing on the coast. To the dying sun of the evening he whispered out...

'Sol Invictus; who will you send to deliver us vengeance against this darkness?'

Carausius, with his head lowered and too humble of birth to join in this appeal, felt the shame of the day's losses and watched a wealthy man having to invoke the powers of the god Mithras in order to recover them. At the same time an empire had failed to protect him too yet it would resolutely be back to demand more taxes to pay for his security. He had also failed him in his neglect and begged to be allowed to return the following day to negotiate his future. His mind couldn't help wandering again to seeing the warship proudly sailing across Oceanus and towards the safety of the island province of Britannia, whilst Septimus however remained defiantly there, on the rough wooden planking looking at his empty berths and expecting their ships and cargoes to be coming back with the lonely darkness drawing about him.

CHAPTER II

What am I Worth?

A ray of pure light illuminated the way to Septimus' warehouse and a white cockerel strutting and scratching about a villa garden called out that it was early in the morning. Market stall holders putting their awnings up against the glare of the sun acknowledged Carausius as he slunk past unaware of whether or not yesterday's news of his losses were going to be widely known. On the docks men were busying themselves unloading wicker baskets of fresh fish, mussels, and reeds and on their tables lay an assortment of brightly coloured almonds, cherries, chickpeas and plums all locally grown. The larger more expensive goods had to be imported and it seemed that even these were arriving in fewer numbers because of the dangers, not of the seas but of the pirates sailing at will upon them. Carausius knocked hard upon the wooden door of his master's building trying to ignore the sideway glances of the market stall holders and waited to be admitted like he always had been. He looked down in embarrassment at the unusually long delay for the key to be turned and kicked at the dirt for amusement before turning, with his back to the whitewashed cob wall to face his inquisitors.

'Have you seen Septimus Clemens?' he asked them meekly.

'No' came the reply, almost as if he had, but didn't want to say so for Carausius had earned himself a reputation as Septimus' shadow and loathed doing anything wrong.

His work paid well and that had sparked jealousies within the town. To a man they all enjoyed seeing him squirm waiting for sentence to be passed, when eventually the stout wooden door with iron braces was soundly unlocked.

'Carausius...' a very tired Septimus slurred, after which he closed the door having admitted his errant river pilot.

'Master, can I get you anything' he said wanting to be of immediate help.

'Some water perhaps...?'

'Over there' and Septimus pointed to a jug of wine.

'Fetch me that!'

Standing close enough to smell his stale breath and to catch him if he fell, Carausius added...

'Is that wise? It is early and the heat of this day will only cause you to make bigger mistakes and then people will say that you are a drunkard. Water is better' and he quickly went back out into the market square with a jug to draw from its fountain before returning to again close the prying world out upon their conversation.

'I didn't sleep last night either' he chose as his opening line trying to ingratiate himself and atone for the losses that were his fault the day before.

'It was too hot and the mosquitoes were taking my blood for an orgy. That, and the snoring of the crew in their quarters next door, and nobody could sleep' he sniggered.

Septimus though hadn't listened to a word he had said and instead was staring behind him in silence. Then he tilted his face to one side.

'What do you think they are doing to my daughter now?' he asked quietly.

'To sail upon the sea is a risk and all I can do is offer to Nehalennia that my ships are safe and that my risk is rewarded. My daughter however, is not a cargo to be lost. My only son is in Germania Superior as we speak, fighting the Alemanni and is to this day still alive, I hope and pray. My goods I can make up for again but it will take time and how much time do we have, Carausius? How much time is there for each one of us? How much time do my children have?' at which he broke down and started to cry.

A fresh cup of water was immediately brought to his lips and an awkward silence accompanied the slurping noises following. Septimus looked a beaten man; Carausius unable to help hadn't realised who Helena was.

'I was thinking last night of a way I can rid the river of these thieves. I'm sorry; I know that it won't bring back your daughter. Will you listen to my plans as it is going to need the army to help us with soldiers and their artillery? You, Septimus have the confidence of the local commander and he too may be keen to win a small victory against the Franks. You know that they will never come in enough numbers to fight a complete war and so every death of theirs, however unremarkable, has to be taken from them without risking the lives of our men. My idea is that...'

Septimus had heard it all before in his career as a merchant and sighed. He was forever being told that the emperor is in Bonna with his three legions and that nobody is to leave the towns and run away. The attacks are only temporary and the enemy will shortly be routed and destroyed when they choose to fight. Men are needed to stay and work the lands before they collapse into ruin and food becomes even scarcer to obtain. Food for the soldiers; that is what everybody understood by the land is not to fall into ruin. The soldiers must come first. However, he couldn't fault Carausius' eager mind for a solution. Standing up and gently touching the dust on the straw packed crates of terra nigra waiting to be exported, Septimus felt the need to point out a few facts of his own.

'Mausaeus; I may call you that? This is really your land. We Romans have settled here and as you know that settlement hasn't been without fault. Your tribes have benefitted from our arriving as have we from the strength and bravery of your men in the army. However, everything is not what it seems. What do you think my ships were carrying? Wool, iron, wheat, and a few precious pearls maybe? You would be right but there was a greater cargo hidden amongst them at the bottom of five false barrels – silver' and Septimus threw an antoninianus coin at him which he graspingly caught.

'Would you trust that coin to buy you anything in a year's time? No, of course not! Feel its weight. The amount of silver is getting less and less as the empire struggles to find new resources to pay for its wars. There's hardly any wealth in there at all. I have, Mausaeus...'

He lowered his voice.

'Allies in Britannia that will exchange my goods for pure silver ingots, and those ingots I smuggle out in the bottom of barrels to smelt down in order to produce silver dinner plates and candlesticks. I can then sell those back in the island for gold. People will trust the weight of my goods and I have an excellent reputation. What would the fiscal officials say at my smuggling activities? They may look inside my barrels at Londinium, but who can say that they are not what I claim them to be? So unfortunately my losses yesterday were greater than you may think and yes, I am a thief too.'

He helped himself to a handful of chickpeas and cheese from a small black bowl and moved away from the conversation.

'I never tell you what the cargoes are and you never look, do you?' he said from a distance.

Mausaeus Carausius' eyes had suddenly been prised open at the extent of his dealings but he vowed to keep the most vital of information to himself like a lifelong friend. That vow was quickly to be tested by a thump at the door matched only by the nervous beating heart in his chest.

'Numerius Septimus Clemens? Are you in there?' Somebody in obvious authority shouted.

'Open up, immediately!'

Septimus could hear local people denying the soldier's interrogation and trying their hardest to thwart him in his duty despite his use of horses to push them away. Whoever it was outside, was giving orders for foot soldiers to clear a path through the market place with their spears, reiterating again his demand that the door be opened at once. On hearing the second crash against the lock, Septimus shouted...

'Alright: alright. The lock is seizing up. Wait! I'm coming.'

The door opened upon a small gathering of known and unknown faces and the sword bearing Decurion, dressed in his red leather strips, leather knee length trousers and burnished square chainmail shirt sitting astride his horse. From his iron and bronze open faced helmet a red plume of horse hair fell as a crest and beneath the peak above his eyebrows looked out a man of serious intent.

'You will open the door when I say so next time' he shouted, obviously aware of his unwelcome presence there in the market place where despite being jostled, he continued...

'I have something for you' and he beckoned two soldiers to drag the captive along the warm sand and gravel surface of the street and drop him at Septimus' feet.

The crowd moved back at the danger amongst them, with the prisoner, a Frank, kicking and lurching at them having been pulled roughly along via iron chains around his neck and ankles before being kicked to the ground in front of the merchant and his warehouse full of secrets and spices.

'There...' in the silence the Decurion said from his horse and addressing everybody for business that day had stopped entirely and gathered closer to him.

'This is why you pay your taxes. Look at the thief we have caught. A barbarian that knows nothing of creating his own and instead has to steal from us. Your ships Septimus; he has stolen from you has he not? Remember that when the tax collections are due! All of you listen well, for the armies of Rome are constantly victorious! Where we caught this one there are others ready to take his place but we will need you to be patient so stay here and do not fear for the future. His like can never take these roman lands!' and with that, he signalled to one of the auxiliaries standing close to put the man to death.

Swiftly a narrow leafed spear head was thrust into his back without him being aware and he fell uttering his language into the street, the partially naked body then being dragged to the river's edge before being thrown in, free of its chains. A trail of red marked his passing: the body swirling gently in the lazy current to float downstream leaking blood.

'Oh, and Septimus' the Decurion continued, 'there is another gift for you' at which he waved his hand for it to be presented.

Septimus panicked at the summary justice he had witnessed and backed away a little but he needn't have worried. Through the gap in the crowd ran the yellow dressed figure of Helena Messalina.

'Father!' she shouted and fell into his welcoming arms.

At the Decurion's leaving and behind his employer's new found joy, Carausius took the chance to venture from the blackness of the store room and walk the short, bloody distance to the river bank. There he looked at the lifeless body floating face down and although not certain that it was the man on the shore, it was still a Frank. Where had been the fabled roman justice that morning? He thanked himself that summons hadn't been imposed upon him for after all, he lived within a civilised world; a world that could forgive the loss of two ships and their crews. With that weighing heavily on his mind he returned to Septimus and his joyful reunion with his daughter. The day's instructions were now to lock up and go home as his master was to celebrate his good luck with his wife, and Carausius if he so cared was free to join them later to discuss whatever plans he had formulated for attacking the pirates at their heart. It was as if the war had been won, for everybody in the market place went about their business with renewed vigorous confidence and were doubly keen for the soldiers on patrol duties to return off duty, and spend their bronze and silver coins at the earliest opportunity. In discreetly nodding through the crowd of heads to Carausius, Septimus urged him to keep his mouth shut about the silver and that message he understood.

Evening came and with it the first of the biting insects. The villa retreat of the merchant wasn't outside the town at all, for he thoroughly enjoyed all the benefits of urban life and like the emperor had repeatedly said, there was safety to be found there. Not everybody agreed however, as it had no walls and could be open to attack at any moment. Many feared that the attacker would be the unpredictable water itself. Still, it was safer than being beaten or killed by rogue bands of peasants roaming the land. In the street Carausius slapped at a mosquito feasting upon his neck before approaching the villa entrance where a slave met him and after asking after his business with Septimus, admitted him. The merchant, his wife and daughter were relaxing in the summer room where the sun was providing its last warmth of the day except for beneath a thin vine planted to provide some darkening cool shade. The plant, of poor quality, was struggling to thrive in the salt laden coastal air. Incense choked the room as a precaution against the mosquitoes and it was through this haze that Septimus got up to greet his guest, whilst in the western sky Sol Invictus was slowly setting with only an hour or so of the day left for business.

'My wife, Sabina' he said introducing a not unattractive woman of middle age.

She moved quietly and without fuss towards Carausius through the sweet smoke of their room, allowing him to kiss her smooth hand before retiring again to her seat.

'And my daughter...' he continued, beckoning Helena Messalina forward.

The woman in the blue dress had bathed and changed and now smelt of the best perfume, unlike the heavy smell of the river mud only the day before. She too accepted Carausius' polite kiss before showing him to a seat facing her family. Septimus clapped his hands and through a narrow doorway a servant carried a silver jug from which he poured a rich draught of wine into a goblet on the table there for him. There were to be no other guests that evening and it was as if he was giving the impression of having grown tired of life after celebrating the safe return of his daughter. Septimus spoke fondly of his trust in the gods but wished that the authorities too would take their responsibility more seriously than they had. How many more times could they save him? How many more times were the tax men to fleece him? He longed for peace and stability for himself and his family yet was unsure as to where to find it. That, Carausius felt was what was emptying him of his strength and was keen to put his ideas quickly forward as to the solution. Sitting between his wife and his daughter and holding both their hands in his lap, the employer waited patiently for him to speak. Messalina though, smiled and asked that they first thank Carausius for saving her when he did. Without his bravery she would have succumbed to the waters and undoubtedly drowned. The family therefore acknowledged him, although without too many questions, which seemed odd as her father had lost two ships, their crews and cargo because of him. What had his daughter told him about the day's events? His quiet forgiving eyes gave nothing away even in the peaceful tranquillity of his own home. The only mention Septimus made, was of needing to salvage the ships which, if they hadn't been damaged by fire, and that he disputed for it would have raised the alarm, could be used to shore up the river bank where it was washing dangerously away. That to him was the end of the matter. Who knew of the hidden silver Carausius quietly wondered and what was Helena Messalina's half heard prophecy? Impolitely scratching at the bite on his neck he leant in towards them and began to detail his plans for a change in their fortunes before darkness forced the meeting to its late end with the ashes of sweet incense, cold and powdery grey in their bowl spilling flecks into the air at his leaving.

A few days later Numerius Septimus Clemens arranged for both he and Carausius to travel the short distance to Helinio where a meeting had been organised with the local auxiliary commander. It was an opportunity to discuss the increasing lack of naval support in the neighbouring waters where Saxon and Frankish boats were roaming at will and disrupting the valuable trading links with Britannia. The army relied upon keeping those links open for both grain supplies to the armies of Germania and reserves of men for Britannia. The two were interwoven and the security of the Western provinces very much dependent on them working together. Septimus couldn't understand why the governors of Britannia Superior and Inferior weren't doing more to attract the emperor's attention and plead for the Classis Britannia to be reformed in full and therefore patrol the narrow waters on a more permanent basis. Perhaps they were frightened of admitting that they no longer had the confidence of their master in their posts and would therefore be replaced with somebody who had, or perhaps the merchants of Londinium were happy at not seeing competitive cargoes arriving from across the waters and wanted to keep the profitable market place to themselves. Either way the narrow waters of Oceanus were being filled with the boats of their enemies and if the auxiliary commander was unable to fully co-operate it was because of trouble elsewhere. The barbarian tide in Gallia Belgica was unfortunately spilling over faster than he could mop it up. He would, Septimus knew, pass on his concern to his superiors who inevitably then in the grander scale, promise resources at a later date. Action was required now, however small scale, however limited.

At their journey's end to Helinio the two were admitted into the small wooden fort built on a low promontory looking out to sea and back again inland. The cavalry unit stationed there were out on patrol and a detachment of foot soldiers had returned from theirs. There had been no sightings of the enemy and all appeared quiet upon the frontier, although Septimus was sceptical about their reports. He knew this land well and how easily disaffected soldiers could melt away into the marshes to form their own bands of thieves preying upon an increasingly frightened population. A rumour of attack and defeat could cause widespread panic and it was the unfortunate Decurion who was left to deal with this threat as well as the real one of Frankish incursions. Discipline at times was lax and the prospect of serving on a dangerous and remote insect infested frontier, without comfort, was unappealing. All resources were being given over to the larger forces watching over Fluvius Rhenus and most anticipated that the poorest of this land would eventually be ceded to the invaders for their settlement in a bitter mistrustful treaty. However, before that happened, the merchant wanted all he could get before he too was forced to run away. Keenly watching the small troop unbuckle their swords and then remove their iron helmets, Numerius Septimus Clemens steeled himself for what he had in mind to say about his fears and losses. Nothing today was going to deter him from demanding action from a seemingly disinterested army, the head of which in that district was quickly and with purpose striding towards him.

'Be quick. My time is short' said Manius Tullius Fruscus, the horse rider that had delivered Helena Messalina safely back.

He again appeared aggressive in his manner.

'I've reports to compile. Is something wrong?'

He eyed the unruffled appearance of Septimus as evidence that it wasn't and returned to the offensive.

'Is your daughter stronger now?' he asked.

'Yes, thank you' replied Septimus.

'I am most grateful to you.'

'We cannot devote our time to recovering those that have chosen to ignore the obvious dangers arriving from the seas. You may give an offering that we were there to save her at all; now why are you here and who is he?' Tullius enquired, pointing at Carausius.

'I am here to speak on behalf of the merchants of Ganuenta and this is our river pilot, Mausaeus Carausius.

He also helped save my daughter's life' Septimus said without going into further detail.

'He has a plan to trap the pirates and we need your help with men. I can provide the boat.'

It all sounded so easy and because of that Tullius Fruscus turned upon him with his vengeance. He watched as a group of his soldiers continued to place their shields in the small barracks before he rounded on them both.

'I barely have enough men to patrol this area and those that I do have, I question their loyalty, and you expect me to lend them to you! Have your fears made you idiots?'

The men whose trust he had questioned looked at him with suspicion and cursed loudly enough to be heard. Tullius Fruscus' right hand tightened on the pommel of his sword before he continued his attack upon the weakest there..., namely Septimus and Carausius in the hope that his aggression would ward off a sudden violent outbreak from his men.

'There is a river fleet that patrols the water' he growled.

'I am a soldier. If you want protection then go to Colonia Claudia Ara Agrippinensium and talk to the commander there. Farewell then!' and he grabbed Carausius by the arm in readiness at ejecting him from the fort.

His men laughed and cheered at the rough tactics being employed and then moved in for a chance to put their weight behind their leader before Septimus chose to cry out above the noise.

'Mithras may you protect us' he bellowed and a silence immediately fell upon everybody.

Without caution he continued nervously on...

'Listen, I have silver, good silver and if you will follow me this one time then I promise every man here reward for his bravery.'

A mutinous quiet hung upon the small fort on the edge of the empire until broken by a rising tide of muttering greed.

'Silver, that is what he said.

' Good silver? How much has he got? What do we have to do?'

All men were suddenly united in their curiosity and Tullius Fruscus in releasing Carausius' arm wanted to question the merchant's unrequited offer.

'Why did you say that?' he asked.

'You now have the attention of my men more than I do.'

Seizing the opportunity of repairing his damaged image before them, he invited Septimus into a small intimate room where the remark could be discussed further but before the door could be shut the merchant asked that Carausius be present, not only because of his knowledge of the rivers and the plan that was his, but more importantly he knew where the good silver would be coming from and Septimus didn't want it to be known by anybody else.

With the three of them in private discussion the army of Rome was quickly bought off by a merchant from Ganuenta, yet nobody outside of the fortress was to know of the pact and the silver was to be delivered as soon as possible following the ambush upon the Franks. Tullius Fruscus for his part had heard stories of commanders inland providing military assistance to wealthy villa owners against bandits in return for payments and considered that his decision to provide aid as nothing more sinister. He wouldn't risk placing himself in this position again, and therefore had to be confident that the military plan was going to be a success and for it to be so they had scheduled it to take place in two day's time at the next available ensnaring tide, weather depending.

Septimus and Carausius were helped onto their horses with the guards politely opening the gates for them to leave. The prospect of money had raised their stature as had the idea of hatching a plan: Soldiers it seemed like to plot for it gave them security, the chance to kill first before being killed and a sense of purpose which the everyday boredom of patrol didn't. The merchant himself, however was happy at the outcome and with the short ride back to Ganuenta before them he leant across to his pilot and asked him why he hadn't considered a military career, as even Tullius had agreed that the ambush plan was a good one. Carausius had no answer at hand and admitted that nothing was ever certain until finished. Even then, there could be mistakes.

'What might they be?' Septimus asked.

'I'll tell you that when we've finished' smiled Carausius.

The warmth of the fine dusty day continued into the evening and Septimus was keen to stop at the temple of Mithras outside the town where he and the other merchants worshipped alongside the occasional serving army officer. Carausius however, because of his rank, was refused entry and like a slave remained outside holding the animals. He watched as Septimus descended the stairs into the small, stone built cave like structure where he would encounter the god of the unconquered sun offering up to him for a successful victory and also to give thanks for the safe return of his daughter and the safety of his son who was still at war far away. Towards the darkness he blindly went, past the acolytes of Cautes and Cautopates and through the veil of incense where at the temple's far altar his god appeared through a sunburst of light behind the carved figure of Mithras. Septimus bowed in reverence uttering his prayer and then slowly backed away having offered up a suitably magnificent gift for a favourable future. Through the gloom he could sense others sitting upon the benches provided for solitude with their god, and god like they too moved in shades of colours difficult to distinguish. Neither was there shape or form but nevertheless they were there, sharing that intimate moment of belief with the merchant. A few moments of contemplation later and Septimus emerged into the evening light taking a little time to allow his eyes to settle upon it and refocus whilst in the far west, a blood red sky was cooling in readiness for the night ahead.

'Farewell Carausius, you may go' He appreciatively said.

'Report to me when the tides are right on the next day and I will pass your message to the fort. If this enterprise succeeds then I will faithfully promise to introduce you to the Lord Mithras as an initiate. Sleep well.' and off he rode into the smoking oil lamps of Ganuenta and towards his own faith in the unknown.

Good weather two days later allowed Tullius Fruscus to be as true as his word, with lightly armoured scouts being ordered to quietly make their way through the dune grasses that bordered the empire and Oceanus Germanicus. Wearing no chainmail but only a tunic of brown cloth, leggings and soft leather boots they moved swiftly amongst the low mounds of sand seeking out their prey. Meanwhile, in the river channel, the tides were turning and the merchant ship of Septimus' could be seen struggling to make it into the safety of the river mouth. A breeze blew off shore and she had no sails. A Frank with a bright shield had noticed that too, crouching low to see if any other shipping was due to come to its aid but the seas were empty. On the decks he witnessed the cargo of barrels stacked up hopefully with their silver content and counted the crew desperately trying to row in against the tide. This could be a good day to steal from the roman merchants and he went to move off signalling to the waiting ship full of thieves, like himself momentarily hidden from sight. He stood up but then immediately fell, clutching at a dagger wound deep in his lower back. Another knife ripped into his chest and he dropped the shield. A fresh pair of hands took over pulling the cloak from the savage before placing it over his own shoulders and then standing up to raise the bright disc high enough for the ship's captain to see. The attack signal had been given. Through the sight finder of the ballista hidden amongst the sand, the soldiers of the fort at Helinio watched their ship slowly come towards them.

'Hurry up' one whispered to himself.

Another joined in.

'Row harder you dogs or else you will be caught. Even with the wind behind our backs what use will our darts be if you are too far away. Nobody wants you to die. Come on! Hurry up' he too urgently muttered.

From behind the curve in the river's mouth to the sea the pirate ship slowly emerged but she too had to fight the outgoing tide. In her sights was a lone merchantman packed with cargo and travelling the slower. Tullius Fruscus' scouts could see the crew frantically thrashing at the waters with their oars in an attempt to make ground and pull alongside. Little by little they drew closer before the roman ship chose to veer off towards the beach.

'Follow it' the Frankish captain shouted in his excitement and disregard for the channel.

'We've trapped her; she's ours.' Except he ran aground.

Rushing to the side of his ship he looked in bewilderment as eddies of water bore witness to the outgoing tide.

'Quickly' he urged in panic, 'free us with your oars as poles. Now push!'

But it was to no avail. The boat spun around momentarily looking out upon the safety of open waters before fastening itself hard upon the sand and gravel bottom. The sound of barrels being pushed into the sea caused them all to run to the landward side of their ship before hearing the command to shoot. Archers were now standing where the cargo had been and fired at will upon the stricken crew, initially too confused to offer any resistance. On the beach soldiers ran out to pull at a line thrown from the merchant ship and secure her before trying to avoid the darts of the ballista bolts as they tore burning trails across the clear sky heading towards the dry timbers of the Frankish ship. Soon she was ablaze and her decks empty of visible life. It was all militarily over except the enemy ship would be properly attacked when the tide had receded thoroughly and if found, no prisoners were to be taken.

In this small war no Roman, soldier or citizen had lost his life and to a man they all saluted Mausaeus Carausius as he waded through the shallow waters to the beach. A flat bottom decoy boat had done its work and looking down from their low vantage point both Tullius Fruscus and Numerius Septimus Clemens accepted the river pilot's guile in being able to fool the enemy although Carausius himself knew that the ship could have overturned at any moment and everything lost for a second time. In this trial of vengeance and though he had won, Carausius knew that there would be losses to come. He accepted that as his fate, as much as he had to accept the silence of the waters tugging at his legs.

CHAPTER III

A JOINT CAUSE

Septimus, regarding himself as a good employer, wanted to thank Carausius for his ability to turn a failure into a success, thoughtfully recognising his twin dubious abilities at strategy and revenge. There had been an overwhelming outburst of confidence again in trading, as it appeared the greed of the Saxons and Franks could be tempered with foolery and deceit and because of that he was to host a meal in recognition of what he thought to be his victory. The most important local merchants were invited, the army commander Tullius Fruscus and of course, Carausius as special guest.

The preliminaries to dinner were taken up by questions to the Decurion. What was the new threat from across Fluvius Rhenus and why did the army not have a sea going fleet to counter the pirates? His answers were the same as he had given Septimus – travel to Colonia Claudia Ara Agrippinensium and ask there! Had somebody offered a little inducement towards their protection then his reply would have been a lot different, as commanding a force of happily paid soldiers was preferential to commanding them in the prospect that one day the legitimate imperial watered down coinage would arrive from a distant mint in an attempt to satisfy their needs. Fruscus' problems would begin when his men had spent that money on wine and women and wanted more. However, that wouldn't be his ruination tonight and he felt free to enjoy the company and fish around for proper clients requiring mutual support. Relaxing in a fresh tunic of dull yellow tied about his waist with a thin leather belt and wearing open toed sandals he looked forward to the meal to come. Septimus, he already perceived to be a generous host.

'Guests...' he called out.

'If you would like to follow Acilius, my slave, he will guide you to your places' at which the pretty atrium emptied in orderly fashion and headed towards the triclinium where, after the religious ceremonies were dutifully obeyed, the first course waited to be served.

Carausius naturally anticipated being at the best table and was bitterly disappointed when shown to the lesser one. However, Helena Messalina was placed alongside him, which would have been adequate compensation for most, but the true merit that he felt he deserved for the victory had been stolen by his employer who was already with Tullius' help, reliving the recent action with his other friends. He could hear them laugh at the demise of the pirates and was completely oblivious to a dominant woman at his side until she poked him hard with a stiff finger.

'We've all dropped our oysters...' Helena Messalina said from a food stained couch.

'Answer me…, what's the best way to deal with a slippery enemy?' at which she mimicked a shell for a ship and attacked it with small iron knife on the table.

Picking the sea flesh out, she offered it to Carausius' mouth and he let it slip down savouring the saltiness as it went.

'Slave, wine over here' and she ordered for her dining neighbour's beaker to be filled to the brim, at which there was an open objection.

'Careful, a little water as well' Carausius said.

Helena continued with her talking but he wasn't listening. Throughout the next course of white fish cooked in coriander and seasoned with sweet vinegar he attempted to raise his voice so as to be heard on the more important table higher up, yet his host simply turned his back upon him regarding it as a social rudeness. Tullius, although enjoying the rough watered wine had made it his intention of staying the course until later when the best wines would be served by Septimus and the conversations more secretive, more businesslike. Whether Carausius was present or not wasn't for his discretion but he had developed a quiet admiration for the pilot's skill and knowledge of the local waters and wanted to learn more. His own mutinous predicament in Helinio could flare up at any time and who knew when his fickle men would throw down their arms if confronted by a concerted sea attack from the east? As a career soldier he had been chosen to be posted on the frontier as a bolster to any such threat. His responses were land based cavalry ala mixed with lightly armoured scouts, yet with these he could do little to win a decisive victory as by the time he had reached the enemies' chosen battlefield, they had simply sailed away. Tullius required more resources; far more than were available. He raised his silver beaker in Carausius' direction and mimicked a salute at which the sailor instantly relaxed. Helena Messalina though, having gone slightly cold at his lack of attention would take a lot more persuading than that. With a prawn in his fingers he beckoned jokingly that she took it and thereby return the favour of her feeding him. A few prawns later and feeling slightly more comfortable in her presence, he quietly asked her...

'Why had you reason to call me 'Imperator'?'

Helena smiled with a sideways glance.

'Keep you voice down, fool. Don't you know there is a new emperor fighting for us – Caesar Gaius Aurelius Valerius Diocletianus Augustus?' she whispered.

'He defeated the old emperor Carinus and has now titled himself Britannicus Maximus in his memory. Seeing you prepared to save me from the water opened my eyes to what an emperor has to do. In the light of the gods and as my father's employee you are here to protect me, aren't you?'

Her innocence failed to match her knowledge of court affairs or politics though and she took another morsel of food.

Carausius' utter disappointment shone brightly through his weak smile. To think that a woman he had never met could have provided such a prophecy was ridiculous, and he was angry at himself for his arrogance in having believed it. He was there to protect her father's shipping from loss and nothing more, but how she came to know so much was intriguing and after being pressed upon the subject Carausius learnt from her that any new usurper had to be ruthless in declaring himself as the legitimate emperor by any means at his disposal. Helena had picked the story up before coming out to Ganuenta and was keen that her father knew, as her brother was fighting on the borders of Germania Superior and Raetia alongside Diocletianus. A new emperor could also mean new taxes and it wouldn't be long before his relief on the fresh coinage would be declaring a joint unity with his subjects in the common good of securing peace for all concerned. That was until he too was deposed in his turn like the rest. As a means of making amends at hurting Carausius' feelings and not realising how much he had believed her simple trickery, Helena offered to meet him in secret in the garden following dinner. There she suggested a womanly promise of more. Carausius was difficult to fool a second time, and as he turned to see Numerius and Tullius cementing their friendship and preparing to leave the room before the evening's entertainments had finished, his anger rose at his perceived treatment by her family. Not only had he saved Numerius' daughter and given Tullius hope that the enemy were fallible, neither had made a true effort in his eyes to secure further loyalty by deed or financial reward. Helena, secretly rubbing against his penis beneath a light tunic was rapidly giving him reason to want to take his immediate share in flesh.

'Carausius you animal, you are hurting me!' she cried.

'Gently, or do I remind you of a whore?'

He for his part pumped harder at the warmth on offer straining his neck to bite at the fulsome nipples that stood out from their cloth retainer. His hunger for her was intense as she wriggled like a toy doll in his grip until eventually with a sigh loud enough to wake the town he let his warm seed spill out and over her legs. He was finished with her until the next time and calmly got to his feet brushing the soil from his knees. Helena was slower getting up, taking a little more care about her ragged appearance as she had to return indoors and possibly encounter her parents, never mind the slaves clearing away after the meal. As she pulled her clothes about her and with the oil lamps of the house being extinguished, Carausius left the garden like a snake to the voices of Numerius and Tullius exchanging their mutual vows of meeting again in the temple of Mithras. It appeared that a new friendship had formed around him and one which may serve to have benefitted all in the early months to come. He, it now appeared, was sought after and a day later in Septimus' office by the quay that was confirmed without any need for ceremony or ritual.

'Carausius, come in and sit down' Septimus beckoned, at which he did, making himself comfortable on a small bench of light wood.

He looked hard at the face of the man opposite him that was momentarily busy with documents before raising itself to look back at the river pilot. This man's daughter had recently given herself easily to him, so what else was on offer now? He forcibly wanted to put the following demands into the merchant's mouth and they were to include sharing profit, becoming an initiate of the Temple of Mithras and of course an alliance with the merchant's business interests considering that his own son could be pronounced dead at any time whilst away fighting. Somebody had to care for the family. Septimus, having taken his time, eventually looked up.

'I trust you enjoyed my evening hospitality' he said.

'My daughter has been silent since we last saw you. Have you fallen out? She can be extremely fickle and she won't tell you this, but in being unable to conceive has shown an emptiness for men that gets her into trouble; as you know to my cost.'

He refrained from mentioning again the loss of his ships but Carausius knew what he meant.

'However, I have a proposal for you that I would like you to consider' he went on, at which point Carausius leant in closer for the intimate business details to be revealed that would of course be of some interest to him.

Septimus immediately came to the point.

'This is what I want. It would involve leaving my daughter to her uncommon thoughts where my wife and I could take more responsibility for her. We know that we've neglected Helena Messalina but what I plan, and I have Tullius Fruscus' support in this, is that you are allowed to join the army as an equal ranking officer backed up by my finances. Carausius, my offer is that I would meet your expenses, provide you with good armour and in doing so I could be guaranteed knowledge of military planning through you. Think of it as still working for me if you want. What are your thoughts on the matter? In these dangerous times I see it as a safe and strong offer.'

To Septimus' pride and horror he burst out into raucous laughter. He could happily leave his daughter alone if that's what he wanted, but why didn't the old man just say so? Was sending him off to the army the solution to anything? Septimus wasn't his father and Carausius wasn't about to be the dutiful son either. A soldier's life didn't beckon for him and he wasn't going to obediently serve on the most desolate of frontiers, forever watching out for the arrival of enemy ships and then not knowing where they were to make landfall and strike next. It could be his life and for what? It would be like trying to catch a shadow racing across the land only to witness another ray of light to your left or to your right equally demanding the capture of it. No, Carausius felt happier on the vague but familiar river currents and wanted to remain there albeit with more in the way of reward and recognition from his employers. Septimus had to try harder in charming his unwilling employee with the need that the emperor had for loyalty and sacrifice in the face of constant danger. If his son could do his duty then so could Carausius in seemingly more favourable circumstances. A concerted attack wouldn't be coming from the sea as the Franks could not mass enough ships or men and there was infinitely more to risk by serving in Germania Superior. This was an easy posting if not devoid of comfort and luxury but when that too failed to convince the riverman, Septimus angrily revealed his last throw in the game of chance.

'Mausaeus' he ponderously said.

'I would offer you my daughter yet I sense that you've already had her and there will be others, no doubt. It isn't the pleasure of the flesh that keeps us is it? It is money. How much do you need? One hundred coins, a thousand? What is your true value? I saw you looking at the savage in the river. Others like him die for nothing, except the miserable clothes they live in and yet you decline to join their sacrifice of death? Who do you live for Mausaeus? Who is it that rules over you? Is it Nehelenhia or is it Caesar Diocletianus?'

The merchant was struggling with his temper and was all for throwing his employee out when Carausius opened up, forthrightly choosing to speak his mind.

'Where is the profit in my becoming a soldier?' he said, the laughter now gone.

'If you coerce me then I'll simply run away. We both know this isn't fit for my retirement; this fragile empty land. Find me something better and I will go. Offer me the protection of Lord Mithras too.'

His thoughts were briefly interrupted by the image of the roman warship returning to its safe anchorage in Britannia. Dismissing that, and for good measure, he concluded that he wished a small estate in the province there, close to the sea hidden from both Saxon and Franks.

'Britannia' Septimus asked.

'What do you know of Britannia and why would an island with so many broad rivers be any safer than living here?"

Carausius, baulking at his tactical naivety quickly corrected the lack of knowledge that armies can't land everywhere and for every sail spotted riding across the sea there would be a column of horseman following and every beacon would be lit in the nearest of forts to warn them off. He quickly drew a map on the floor with his foot to show that he wasn't to be deceived when it came to military planning.

'The island is also full of silver plate as well as empty beaches' he menacingly added.

'Nowhere is ever going to be completely safe from a shallow bottomed boat.'

Septimus immediately understood the unsubtle reference to his business activities, although not fully comprehending Carausius' desire to serve in another province.

'We have a deal, then?' He said.

'Tullius and I will honour our part and you? My daughter could be yours and we united if you forget about my cargoes? Come…' and he stood up preparing to embrace the man rising himself to meet him.

'Keep your daughter' Carausius said. 'This is business' at which the two men met and coldly clasped hands.

Septimus had his man but at a price higher than he had bargained for and Tullius, his sailor soldier. Together they would agree a date for Carausius to begin his military career and as money bought most things then it too would swiftly buy his promotion, although Tullius Fruscus was to be ignorant of his merchant friend's planning. So then began Mausaeus Carausius' new life as little more than a mercenary fighting for the wealthy class. Negotiations in return had bought him something, but he felt the early pangs of resentment at having to be there at all, and it was only a friendship that was to grow between Carausius and his mentor Tullius, that prevented him from running away from the seemingly onerous obligation now thrust upon him. Throughout the early months of his training news constantly spread of more revolts from within the disaffected province of Gallia Belgica where the rising tide of Amandus' and Aelianus' peasant army was threatening to sweep all before it. The roman strategy of defence in depth was facing the threat from across Fluvius Rhenus and hadn't concentrated upon protecting the rich heartlands in the rear where bands of refugees, deserters and slaves alike had taken to plundering at will. Any attempt at bringing them to battle had failed because, like the Frankish and Saxon pirates striking the rivers and coast they too could simply vanish afterwards having no strategy or base. All they could see was a burgeoning province soft for picking clean with the legitimate and illegitimate emperors fighting amongst themselves and someone failing to exterminate them. Roman generals came and went but it was the decisive appointment of Marcus Aurelius Valerius Maximianus as Caesar that was to turn the tide in Rome's favour. Charged with sweeping them away by Diocletianus, whilst maintaining the safety of the western borders, was his responsibility and this policy of vicious warfare enabled men of suspicious qualities to rise above their senatorial counterparts in vying for important army commands. The old ways were conveniently pushed aside at the point of a blade with unfamiliar family ties trying to gain the ultimate in prizes – control of the empire itself or at the very least, profitable parts of it cloaked in purple, silver and gold.

It was upon this new order that Carausius lay in waiting upon his first battlefield like the she-wolf that had suckled Romulus and Remus so that Rome could have its first city. From his vantage point he looked into the valley below and waited for his time to come. Keeping low, Tullius Fruscus crawled towards the edge of the same hill. His heavy woollen cloak helped muffle the sound of his weapons and a helmet lay in a grass hollowed bowl to prevent it from rolling away. An anxious face bore the evidence of a recent skirmish, carrying upon it blood, yet he was in a buoyant mood as the acrid smoke from the burning villa and its farm buildings wafted up and spread towards their hideaway. Below, figures momentarily ran for their lives before being cut down by their attackers if not raped before. There was no sign of a picket from the savages on the loose and their lack of any discipline shone through. No sooner would this house be burnt to the ground then they move a little further on and attack the next helpless villa in this rich fertile land seemingly safe from the more feared pirates far away on the coast. What voices that could be heard pleading for their lives had now fallen silent with their twitching bodies now still, leaving the plundering to begin in earnest and in unmolested quiet. Out of a tiled farm building a cart was drawn and sacks and amphorae lain upon it. Then, using little more than human effort, it was pushed and pulled towards the villa's main entrance where larger items of value were hastily being loaded up whilst men were despatched to find the draught animals with which to hitch it up and draw it away. One crazed one had been spared and it struggled to pull the laden vehicle over the prostrate body on the ground before eventually it won over with a blood stained wheel and lurched forward along the narrow lane from the house and towards the larger road a little distance beyond; a loose following of assorted horsemen and foot soldiers gathered behind shouting. Tullius looked at the sweet shoots of grass before him and spat, before slowly rising to his feet, the smell of burning sour in his nostrils, the smoke haze stinging his eyes and the sound of crackling timbers well ablaze in his ears. They were supposed to have been their protectors.

'Let's take them now?' he urged without caution.

'We have the advantage of the slope and they will not be expecting us. We have enough men here to finish them off and add this number to the rebels that we encountered earlier. This could be a good day!'

Carausius however, remained more guarded. He realised that Tullius' eager aggression was motivated by the need for death alone whether it came in ones or twos. That wasn't going to be enough to spare the countryside from its ravages though and there needed to be more concerted killing. Maximianus would respond to the brutality, if not personally, then maybe in kind and recognition of the noble Roman cause. Carausius got up and watched through the smoke as the lone wagon struggled to escape, its heavy load lurching wildly from side to side. Who would he give the wealth back to if the rebels were caught and punished? Who was there still alive to claim it? Whose wealth was it? If he kept it, was he a thief too? He momentarily thought about the silver hidden in the bottom of Septimus' barrels before his attention was drawn to the assortment of dead bodies lying about the villa grounds. From behind his back Tullius patiently waited for the word that he needed to launch an attack upon the unsuspecting vagrants slowly and confidently getting away. Indecision was filling the mind of Carausius, with him wishing that Caesar was there to congratulate him personally upon his success but nobody in the imperial camp would be and instead a warm sun beat down and the land rippled in the distant fields. They had to attack soon or watch as the opportunity drained away with their lack of intent.

'This isn't as I would wish it Tullius, my friend. I have other plans that involve catching a shoal and not a single fish. Those plans remain for another day. However, if you and I can guarantee the safety of these men here then we will attack them. A pack of hounds chasing the stag needs to be rewarded, therefore, recognise the bravery of your men and share what profits you may find.'

Then raising his hands behind his neck, Carausius pulled his helmet tightly over his head before once again glancing down into the farmyard. Four or five bodies still lay in the dust. Drawing himself firmly into his saddle before beckoning his equal to mount his own horse he fiddled with the pommel of his sword, withdrawing it once or twice to ensure that it would come easily in his grip when truly needed before snapping it safely back into its scabbard. He looked back at the thirty horsemen behind him tightly gripping their reins, for all there sensed fear, with their spears in their right hands ready to thrust into the backs of those rushing to escape. Then with a prayer for his own safe return, Carausius the soldier, urged his horse forward and as it rapidly picked up speed before the others sweeping down the slope and towards the rebels, the ocean that once he had known now seemed a long way away.

The larger force struck home with the advantage of their speed, although they were easily spotted before reaching the peasant band. Tullius shouted for his men not to follow the stragglers on horses getting away, but to concentrate instead on killing those grouping together and with the least chance of escape. It would be unlikely that reinforcements would come as the Romans had the better resources in the shape of fortlets strategically scattered about and without fuss a superior cavalry force could be assembled and sent on to their relief. This was a regional skirmish played out most months but small or not, the Romans fought hard to rid the land of the rebels they encountered and Carausius, confident in his new command. He saw in the faces of those desperate men wildly swinging at him a loathing which at the time he couldn't match. Live or die, there would always be another roman general waiting to take his place with the need to constantly crush the false emperors. At every body that he hacked into, the trailing weeds of their deceit were deprived of life, shrivelled and painfully died. Around the cart and its valueless cargo bodies fell whilst Rome and her citizens in unprotected villa estates throughout Gallia ignorantly worked on a little safer. Then without ceremony the engagement was over. Tullius ordered the dead to be left there to rot whilst a small group of soldiers were sent back to the nearby farmyard to gather the few bodies and throw them into the smouldering remnants of the fire. Having done that, they were to rejoin the scouting party and prepare to form a guard, their compatriots looking to sleep the night on the land. It would be another day before they were expected back at their fort and if there wasn't any food available on the cart they had saved, then soldiers were to demand more from the nearest of villas without accepting any protest. Those left scouted about for fresh fields nearby that offered protection under a falling sun travelling slowly west and across other battlefields yet to come: Carausius led the way. As his horse picked its step through the assortment of bodies he silently thought of Septimus, for he alone had witnessed his fascination over the dead Frankish warrior in the river and hated him, for being here now was proving difficult: Carausius wasn't entirely killing barbarians – because of the laws of Caracalla, he was now killing fellow citizens.

Later that afternoon with everybody safely back together and an overnight camp found, Carausius gave permission for one or two of the horsemen to go down to the river nearby in order to wash their horses off as well as themselves. The heat of the day had subsided but a little, and barely was there enough wind to tease the scrub poplars that lined its edge. The rippled surface of the waters curved around from the south. Everybody was thirsty and without exception calmly waited their turn for a drink. Small fires were lit by others in the camp and the fumes of simple cooking fled towards the sky. From his vantage point

Carausius watched the men return, water dripping from their horses in sweaty laver foam. He greeted everyone back before allowing the next to go.

'Is there anything to tell?' he asked.

'No' came the reply.

Although in roman lands their forces were scattered widely with all scouting parties' orders to maintain military control by whatever means and then report back. In the event of more serious incursions then a measured response was required maybe with imperial backing. By avoiding the metalled roads, Carausius knew that bandits couldn't move easily at will but could strike rapidly instead where their taste for adventure took them and then disappear into the tangled growth where agriculture had found no place or reward. This was his battlefield not the unencumbered views of the Ocean; the safety of towns and villas, not ports, his new responsibility. Leaning over the saddle, warm from the day's work and with his arms crossed he looked far out into the vulnerable distant land and saw its wealth open to any man strong enough to seize it. Suddenly his horse pulled its neck up sharply from the grass at the figure approaching him, causing Carausius to instinctively snatch for the reins. He looked down and saw one of the cavalrymen keeping as low as possible as he approached.

'We'll need to put the fires out' he whispered before going on to explain why.

'There is a boat coming up the river and it isn't a roman merchant. On each side there are fifteen men rowing and the sail is down. It looks to be low in the water and heavy. No one saw us.'

'Is everyone back from the river?'

'Yes.'

'Good. Take my horse' Carausius said slipping off and handing over the reins before keeping low himself and making for Tullius lying quietly asleep in the warmth of the evening sun.

'Wake up' he urged.

'We have more work to do. Put all the fires out quickly and get the men to stay here until I return. You! Come with me' and he selected the nearest armed soldier to accompany him down to the river's edge.

Upon waking Tullius did as he was told, quickly smothering the juvenile flames with cold damp earth. Further orders were issued and everybody kept down whilst the horses were removed out of sight and into the woods. Upon the quiet waters of the river strong arms forced the oars to bite in deep with the desperate need to find a safer and less exposed refuge. Even with the sluggish current in their favour the crew strained at every pull as the boat slipped closer to where Carausius was hiding, his hand again clammy upon his sword in renewed fear. This was as close as he had been to a river borne raiding party inland and as the boat swept across the water, preparing to take the bend before it, he feared that the murky waters staining the river where the horses had been drinking would reveal their presence. He needn't have worried, for as it splashed by the Frank on the prow was looking out intently for the shallow waters that could have trapped them momentarily. Only a spear's throw now separated the two and Carausius, trying hard to suppress the urge to call them to battle had to stand up. He remembered the ease at which the ballista had killed the pirates in the trap upon the coast and although without such arms, sought out another easy victory. He shouted like a barbarian would, and after hurriedly rearranging themselves upon the boat an arrow was fired in his direction but it whistled away before sinking shaft deep amongst the grey mud and reeds. Another quickly followed from the wall of shields being raised on the deck, and the soldier accompanying Carausius, in not following its flight, fell to his knees from being struck hard in the neck. Through the darkness of his closing eyes he glimpsed the shields moving to the rear of the boat and listened as the harsh voices barked across the water. Who in that brief moment had stolen his life? Who was it getting away from Roman justice? Carausius crawled to comfort the man, but he had quickly faced his death and departed. He could only watch in anger as the boat increased its stroke and chaotically headed off downstream, but then, once out of range, got up and ran back through the reeds and gravel to Tullius.

'Quickly, get somebody to follow on this bank' he ordered.

'If they stop and land, then retreat. Do you understand? How close is the nearest garrison?'

He spoke rapidly but Tullius lacked the urgency of responding to the direct order.

'Vibius has died for nothing' he said bitterly under his breath.

'We could have watched the Franks and then struck at a better time. The Ocean is to the north and there was still time to plan such an attack. He was a good man Carausius and is going to be difficult to replace. You alone have killed him.'

A lack of confidence quickly arose amongst the troop from this damnation.

Yet little was to be gained from arguing there and Carausius' offer to see that Vibius had a proper burial fell like the arrow that had missed him, upon waste ground. His body however was recovered and put over his horse before Carausius gave the order for everyone to abandon that evening's post and start to make for home in the surrounding gloom. By finding a road it would take them a little longer but would be safer and as the final rays of Sol departed the skies the pirate ship accompanied by its vigilant followers crept for the mouth of the river and its own particular refuge. Their raid, so far a success could still be at the mercy of the Romans who if they could, would reclaim the stolen wealth and cut them to pieces before the river met the falling tide of Oceanus. Only they didn't.

CHAPTER IV

ACOLYTE OF MITHRAS

A thin slice of sunlight shone upon Carausius' face, irritating him in the darkness of his temporary sarcophagus, and with his arms tight against his side there wasn't the room to defend his eyes from the brightness creeping in. Above he could hear muffled voices and as they impatiently moved about, then grains of soil fell into the void below scaring him into thinking the whole structure was about to give way and crush him with its weight. His eyes stung from the falling dust and cursing his own helplessness he tried to remember the acolytes of Mithras placing him there after having first removed his blindfold. All he had seen were the facemasks of the followers and felt their tight grip upon his shoulders as he was bundled quickly into the tomb, eyes to the sky, before experiencing the semi darkness of death as the slabs were drawn across him. It was a small shallow hole, the length of a man where the air stank of the damp earth and loose stones wedged themselves into the skin of his back. He was desperate for it all to end, when the boundless sky would again be revealed to him in all its vastness. Feet shuffled about and with their partial activity viewed through the narrowest of openings, Carausius could sense a new concern – above they were lighting a fire.

The sensation of an increasingly warm surface, mingled with the stale cold air close to his face and he wanted to shout out for rescue like any man would but felt there wasn't the room to arch his back and cry for it all to stop. Is that what they wanted; the priests, for him to break and admit his submission as a weaker man? Desperately he tried to pull his arms to his mouth and failed. The fire, growing in intensity, couldn't warm the earth sufficiently to cause him discomfort and it became apparent through the struggling anxiety that this was a trial and one which he was expected to pass. Nevertheless, with his back to the solid earth and the occasional spark falling down to die in the darkness Carausius couldn't help fearing for his own life. The one man who could aid him was powerless too, yet silently relishing the tribulations that a true follower had to undergo as he in his time had done so. No harm was ever going to be inflicted upon the flesh but it was important to assess a man's reaction to the mortality of his own life and through that gain a closer bond to his god. Just as important was the social elevation that Carausius would enjoy as a new worshipper and with those closer ties he would mix comfortably with both the mercantile and military elite throughout Gallia and beyond. However, in this moment in time he would have questioned that: Nehelennia had been his goddess, with a hound at her feet and apples upon her lap casting her protective veil over the travellers of the stormy waters of Oceanus. To have found himself entombed in the earth was as far away from the familiar sound of the river as he could have imagined. The sailor it appeared had now turned into the soldier and one struggling against change in his narrow chamber of tribulation. How simple life was plotting the daily course through unpredictable currents, where to face danger was to face the goddess, and how complicated it all seemed now in this structured path to divine acceptance. Why was he there? As his body began to stiffen and nerves twitch with immobility his mind ran ahead to what he was going to do with his much anticipated freedom.

Then with the movement of the slabs came the earth gently cascading in and Carausius' eyes grew ever more reddened and sore. He turned his face to one side unable to really see the two masked men pulling him up and onto his feet. For a moment there was a stumble and for a man of thirty years and a few more he felt old but comfortable at the blindfold again being tied across his watering eyes and readied himself to being led along. All too briefly he witnessed the Lion, the Raven, the Bride and Soldier looking impassively at him unable to recognise his sponsors that day – Septimus and Tullius. Septimus, the merchant of everywhere had arrived in Juliobona via the safer route across water to Gesoriacum and then by road to Samarobriva following the cavalry patrol's return, where he bade Tullius to arrange the Temple's new initiation ceremony for his former employee. A generous donation and feast would ensure a good turnout of followers and it did. Carausius could sense them there, milling about him in total silence and then very softly he was urged to move forward by a gentle tug upon the arm. Although oblivious to the light, his nostrils became keenly aware of the smell of pine cones burning close by and the sweet scent of bracken upon the floor. His group stopped suddenly and hands pulled at his hair as the blindfold was removed. For a moment his eyes recognised nothing; then little by little as they grew accustomed to the light he saw where he was. Before him stood the shrine emitting a dull glow and at his sides remained the two supporters who had led in him. A priest moved to the head of the small procession and after asking Carausius to repeat...

'You will see a young God…in white robe and scarlet cloak and having a crown of fire'

He pulled the shroud from the stone image to reveal the red and white painted Lord Mithras in whole, emerging from an egg, with blade in hand and surrounded by the signs of the Zodiac. From his carved radiate crown, rays of light shot across the darkened room to strike the faces and walls of everything there. A hand slapped Carausius hard across the back: It was Septimus and his voice was instantly recognisable through his mask.

'Drink this' he said, carefully handing over a beaker of wine almost in recognition of Carausius as his son.

A small piece of bread accompanied it.

'Be strong, there is more food to come.'

The initiate did as he was told, although the confinement, darkness, reeking pine smoke and now drink were taking their toll upon his senses. He mumbled the lines to the new god and didn't take a lot of care over placing his offering upon the altar either, to the distain of those closest to him, who could be heard apologetically muttering above their own prayers. Carausius, needing to get out and into the refuge of daylight, was glad when eventually two men gently held him by the arms and guided him safely past the twin figures of Cautes and

Cautopates, standing immobile as the party filed up the shallow steps. A sky of the deepest blue met them and a fresh breeze carried little fear upon its wings. The Earth they stood upon was temporarily at peace with its men and its gods for it had gone well.

Juliobona sat quietly near the coast and although never safe from pirate raids, today it seemed the only place to be, for amongst the congregation had been a navarchus with experience of the seas between Belgica and Britannia and the legate of Legio XXX Ulpia Victrix away on leave and holding estates in the area. It was to the navarchus that Carausius was instantly drawn. A wiry, reactive man like himself with the instant ability at seizing the opportunity, he attracted attention with his tales of the coastline and the island not so far away. News was always important especially news of the Franks and their allies. No-one dared openly question the imperial policy yet military decisions were taken hastily on the back of failures and as a result capable men were choosing not to fight for the legitimacy of Rome, but against it. Merchants were running out of goods and the markets to sell them in, where people fled from burning towns and Rome failed miserably to quell the fires raging out of control all over. Many silently prayed for a better future. A new leader; yet they lacked the personal bravery to instigate that change so huddled together in small groups, and it was within this temple of Mithras that Carausius could sense his own greed emerging. Those here today were in positions to help him, as long as he could repay their faith and trust as Numerius Septimus could tell them he had, and after quietly bringing his conversation to an end with the sailor he walked across the grass of the sanctuary towards his mentor arms open in religious peace. The two gripped the other man's forearm tightly and chose to head for a quiet spot where they could be momentarily alone to talk; Septimus being the first to speak…

'It is good to see you for you are now with us. Are you recommending yourself to others Carausius, for you appear completely at ease with those around us and Tullius tells me of your military progress? Have I made the right choice…are you my saviour? As you see…'

Waving his hand in a circular fashion to capture it all in and then continuing,

'This could all be yours. Am I not as true as my word?'

His flattery and patronage had physically put a sword in the hand of Carausius but the emperor needed to know that he was killing with it and not the merchants of Ganuenta, who if stories were to be believed were now being forced from their homes not by the advancing swarms of Saxons but by the ravenous waters of the ocean. How much longer could Septimus trade on his diminishing wealth and how much longer would he be able to buy the kind of protection that up to now he was enjoying? He, of course, wouldn't be totally ignorant of the calamities befalling those inland, as day by day it became a struggle between the world of the gods and the natural world of mortal men. Carausius thought back to the dead piled up at the villa and the easy slaughter that followed. In his mind he could smell a rotten carcass and in his ears hear the last bloody curse of a dying man as the sword cut in. The wealthy merchant standing there before him didn't look it, but he was as frightened as the rest of them, terrified of losing it all and Carausius was his only hope.

'I cannot fight for your acceptance or those of your tolerant friends' he answered.

'To be here today is more than I deserve and I pray that Lord Mithras gives me the courage to find the right words. You have supported me and then ask me questions of the army, but let me answer you that the struggle is going to last well beyond my years. We lack numbers and without the speed of more horses to cover the ground we have no hope of progress. Your lands regrettably also attract the raiders who do not discriminate between us. What more is there to say?'

Septimus, feeling that he hadn't paid good money to hear bad news again turned upon him.

'I cannot supply the whole army but I am putting silver into your hands. Promise me that you will take your escorts around my estates and that you will watch my interests. If you capture the raiders then cut their throats, as I do not want them as settlers picking over the goods that I once owned. Ignore the emperor and do what I have told you to do. We will support you as we support each other in this temple and the better times will return.'

'It is the will of Oceanus that forces you to abandon your land so you needn't worry about the barbarians' Carausius answered.

'Look to move elsewhere.'

He too could be forceful, adding...

'Has your son not got the rewards from Diocletianus in his heart? Therefore let him do your fighting for you. I will do what I have to do and the money that you are providing is giving me what I want for the moment but what happens when it runs out? When will all of this be taken from me? You rub your warm hands in spices and become rich; my hands are covered in blood. My price for protection Septimus cannot be guaranteed, for one day I may want more, much more!'

Sensing that the legate instead could be of more mutual benefit Carausius said his uncertain farewell and moved off. Then uttering under his breath loud for him to hear as he walked past, the merchant spoke...

'I've a son fighting a losing war, I've a daughter with madness of the mind and now you leave. Curse you Mausaeus Carausius; Menapian' and like a shower of spears his words fell upon the former employee making quickly for the unsolicited protection of the legate's company.

'Now I see that you've emptied his purse you try for mine…am I not right? He said; uncomfortable in the presence of an initiate who it seemed had offended his very sponsor.

'You are losing your friends and influence' and with the rituals coming to an end the commander, a man of some strength and bearing, was keen to be off.

'Excuse me' he said curtly, before walking to his litter and the short journey home.

'Carausius, come!' called Tullius.

'We must go too.'

The evening was to bring a storm over Juliobona where Jupiter chose to strike the earth indiscriminately with his thunderbolts and the ground hissed with the cool moisture rising. Inside the safety of the tavern two men looked into their clay beakers of ale and barely spoke. The day had freed one of them to speak his mind whilst the other was unwittingly now going to become a victim of that freedom. The war was still continuing many miles away and both were relieved to be able to relax. Tullius, the born soldier, had berated his friend enough for his treatment of Septimus, acknowledging however, that to be able to think clearly a commander needed to act independently of anything or anybody. The merchant and his constant demands for security had become burdensome, weighing Carausius down and he moaned about having to carry an anchor and swim at the same moment. It couldn't be done and so to save himself the anchor had to fall into the soft river mud and be lost. Tullius understood the reference all too well.

'We can fight on' he said optimistically.

'Win more glory for ourselves. I know that the keys to success are no longer selfishly held by the Senate. In fact it is they that seek out the emperor wherever he happens to be and beg to follow his orders. The sword, strength and courage will win us a fortune. Soldiers are required everywhere, good soldiers like you and I. Avenge Vibius' death at the river by killing the raiders in enough numbers and there will be opportunities worth taking. Rome will pay you well to guard her but you have to take the chances that fate provides. Are you prepared Carausius, for this is the moment? We can take a little of Gallia with us and provide for ourselves at the same time, making demands of others as we go.'

Tullius wouldn't have spoken so had he not seen the manner in which the allegiance to Septimus had been broken. His friend was now unshackled and dangerous enough to take a risk, any risk at all.

The call for more ale was sharply interrupted by the door of the tavern swinging open before being closed again by the force of the storm. On the step there stood a soldier draped in a heavy woollen cloak with a hood drawn across his face. He removed it, and shook the water from himself before announcing to any ranking officers there that they were to report to the theatre of Juliobona at first light and receive an update of the military situation. These orders were issued by Julius Magnus Aurelius, legate of XXX Ulpia Victrix and were to be obeyed. He then left as suddenly as he had arrived, leaving behind a conspiracy of whispering at to what was happening in the countryside around. The need for drink diminished and the two men, officers in the army of Rome made for their bunks surprised but excited at the rapid news and the action that would come from it. This was another break for Carausius; the opportunity to avenge Vibius, but as his friend quickly fell asleep in the bed next to him and the lightning softly played across the walls of their room, he struggled to get some sleep himself. In the discomfort of his straw mattress thoughts raced like clouds across the sky and wouldn't settle, for all he could see were the blue sails of the Liburna making for Britannia, clashing swords and Helena Messalina, in her yellow dress whispering 'CARAUSIUS, CARAUSIUS, IMPERATOR' upon the beach.

Rain puddles lay like glass upon the floor of the theatre caused by the comings and goings of performers where they had dug out shallow grooves, but everybody tried their best to avoid them by huddling close to where the ground rose a little. A soft wind, heavy with moisture blew from the ocean yet little rain fell and the sky was grey. Cloaks had been worn but with the indifference of the weather they were unclasped and left neatly packaged up upon the low walls surrounding the arena they were standing in. If it did rain again then they were close at hand. Carausius, his mind as dull as the sky with lack of sleep, felt slightly better at only having a tunic and light cuirass to wear and noticed several others trying to wake up too. These few he acknowledged as being there in the tavern the night before and like the reliable soldiers they were had obeyed commands and attended. Only the legate was missing, but by their prompt salute the taller guards on the gate provided the entrance for him walking at a brisk pace and followed by his centurions as he made for the centre of the arena.

'Everybody come here...' and they followed.

'Shut the gates' he commanded raising an arm in their direction.

With hands on their swords to stop them from swinging to and fro the small group encircled their leader for instructions and now suddenly unconcerned by the water around them.

'Listen well, all of you' he began.

'Lord Maximianus wants to force the Bagaudae to battle. As you are aware they have no strategy. This is ours: The Caesar Diocletianus cannot spare enough men to aid him and therefore we need to use all our resources wisely. The fleet for what it is will try to prevent pirate aid from the seas and that will allow me to concentrate my forces in certain areas where the enemy are known to be strongest. I do not want any effort spared or any individual villa protected, because I am wise as to some of your dealings. If the land is darkened through warfare then it will under Rome's light, recover again through peace. Any man caught not fighting for the cause will be punished. My centurions have your orders and to join us we have two legions – XXX Ulpia Victrix.'

At which a small cheer went up.

'And XXII Primigenia. Lord Maximianus is expected to leave his fortress and push West and North to support us. We have the means to win this war!'

With that he dismissed himself, but before leaving gave one more sign of encouragement for them to take away with them.

'Whatever we recover' he said.

'I understand will be shared.'

He was then gone, but before the centurions could ready themselves for their speeches the moment had fallen as few were concentrating, thinking instead of the commander's last promise – that there would be a share of spoils to the victorious and brave.

'This is it my friend; this is our chance' said Tullius.

'After we've listened to the sandal plodding army we can make other plans. Horses are the answer and they know that. Before Maximianus arrives from Augusta Treverorum we have time to find glory for ourselves and our cavalry!'

He was going to be difficult in this situation to control, but like everyone else, he had to lean into the circle and take his orders, which were to rejoin his unit at Durocortorum where an attack was being planned against the rebels. Two legions would arrive from the east with the cavalry pushing against them from the west and if the rebels made for the coast then the navy and marines would be standing by to cut them off there. If their forces scattered undefeated then the war would drag on hunting them down and Diocletianus would have to demand his soldiers back to cover the Persian frontier in the east. This was an offensive that was destined to seize roman territories back and everybody knew their orders. If villas were to be seen burning then they had to burn and if people cried for protection then they had to be ignored. The legions, their victory and their soldiers had to come first.

Very soon the roads to Durocortorum witnessed evidence of that policy. Stragglers were pushed to one side as at first small groups of cavalrymen trotted past them in their saddles to be joined along the way by scouting parties recalled to harvest their knowledge of Belgica. Spies were left out in the open countryside to report back, as no one could fail to realise that again an attempt was being marshalled by Maximianus to clear the province of trouble and restore the land to its legitimate conqueror. A small army had quickly swollen to several thousand horsemen all concentrated upon the area between Durocortorum and Bagacum. Their orders were to establish camps, liaise with the scouting parties but not to make contact with the rebels in case they dispersed in suspicious fear. Weapons were to be readied, tack was to be securely maintained and forage was to be seized from wherever. No one was to disturb the army in its preparation. This was the ideal opportunity to campaign against the invaders and drive them out before the autumn turned quickly into winter, where desperate men would be forced to take even more risks with their lives amongst the fortunes in war. Their dead could be left to rot where they fell to serve as a reminder as to who was victorious and their blood allowed to wash from the rivers upon the shores of distant lands as a warning to others. Roman eagles were to be as invincible again as they always had been.

Julius Magnus Aurelius without the full might of his thousand strong legions had drawn up an early trap that would involve spreading the cavalry like a net before the oncoming Augustus, but the plan had its flaws. How could he know the precise location of the army and without reserves the rebels could easily escape through gaps in the cavalry screen? His logic had originated from the pages of a textbook and lacked the guile required to fight an enemy devoid of strategy itself. These were men on the run from authority and who would stop at nothing fighting for their freedom. They didn't pay the taxes; they stole them. They didn't desire an empire; they took from it. Carausius and his men sighed at the rumours developing from the news that they were to be used in this way. One battle would settle it, one battle where there was no disputing the legitimacy of roman arms yet their leader lacked the authority to pursue it. Instead this would lead to countless nights billeted in small towns followed by chasing across the featureless countryside in relentless pursuit of men hiding their weapons and then retrieving them again as another rebel leader emerged promising more than the last one had. There would never be an end; only the constant reminder of the beginning to this struggle and something had to be done. In not being alone in his thoughts, Carausius sought permission to approach the legate with another plan before he was due to begin his patrols towards the oncoming Maximianus.

'My Lord' he said, entering the small room of the villa where Magnus Aurelius had chosen to settle his more senior officers under the half demolished, yet watertight roof.

'I beg if I may be allowed to, present another solution to your troubles here...' and he tried to continue.

'How dare you! Who let him in?' A centurion cried at the ease at which the rebel like Carausius had gained an entrance.

The guards on the door were silently witnessing another fool challenge the feeble military mind of their leader and enjoying it, that is until they felt the wrath of their superior beating them about the chest with his stick.

'Idiots!' he said.

'Do you want to stand in the first cohort when we attack because I'll see that you do?'

'That's enough' spoke Magnus Aurelius.

'I recognise this man. Follow me...' and he collected two trusted centurions to accompany him into another room where Carausius was also to follow.

'Now, tell me what it is that you are worried about. Why do you question my authority in this matter? An initiate of Lord Mithras has to follow the rules set out for advancement and cannot fulfil his own destiny at the expense of others. Are you seeking glory or do you mistrust my guidance? Which is it Carausius? I've noticed it. Are you to turn against me, too?'

'No, my Lord; my duty is to you in all matters. I heard you speak of giving the brave their due rewards and I am also keen to find my place and settle after the fighting is over.'

'In Gallia Belgica?' he questioned.

'I am not certain, but I would wish to return to the sea at some time...'

'Legate...' a centurion interrupted.

'Perhaps the Decurion will hurry to tell us of his plan?' and he rolled out a parchment map for Carausius to study but he needn't have bothered.

'We are to cast a net and I think that is wrong.' Carausius spoke without any authority at all yet showed little fear in the face of his superiors. He continued with his reasoning.

'My plan would be to...'

'Your plan...' mocked a soldier distantly aware that he had been responsible for letting a raiding ship escape from the river nearby.

'You missed the opportunity then, what has changed? Is the legate a fool that he cannot follow instructions given to him and has to revert to following you instead?'

At this point he withdrew his sword pointing it towards the one time sailor.

'That's enough!'

Magnus Aurelius gripped the man tightly by the wrist forcing him to return the blade to its silver embossed scabbard.

'Carausius will provide us with his arguments and then will leave' at which he moved forward.

'Hear my thoughts' he said.

'We lay a trap at Bagacum. The town is partially deserted and in ruin because of recent attacks but can offer us the temporary protection that we will need. Spies are left out to spread the word that the army is allowing the land to fall into ruin as Maximianus hasn't enough men to protect it. Those with anything to keep, money and goods will be encouraged to travel there and then wait their turn to be escorted to safer areas when eventually reinforcements arrive, but that could be weeks away. The greed of the rebels will draw them in, especially if we go before and lay waste to the villas in their way. Anybody foolishly resisting us will be left to their mercy. The cavalry will then be hidden out of sight and what available troops that we have will be disguised as peasants. Word can be spread that the town is defenceless and that the soldiers have been withdrawn. Their traitors will see our army leave.'

'What, dressed as peasants?' asked Aurelius quizzically.

'No.' replied Carausius.

'The peasants will be dressed as soldiers and it is they who will leave.'

'What's to stop the rebels attacking them?' asked the quieter of the senior officers.

'Nothing, except that I believe greed will force them to choose the town and its inhabitants rather than fight the army, and when they do attack, that is who they will meet. At that point we commit the cavalry to ride behind them and cut off their escape. By doing this we are drawing them to us and not hunting them in ones and twos. The entire victory can be secured in one complete day.'

'Well, Carausius' saluted Magnus Aurelius.

'A commendable plan, but we all must fight together. Centurion; get messengers to ride towards Augusta Treverorum. They are to interrupt Augustus Maximianus on his march and inform him of our revised thinking. It is crucial that he brings his reinforcements to Bagacum to meet us and at all speed. Spies are to be sent out and to spread the word that everybody who wants roman protection must make for this town and this town only. Nothing must be left for the rebels at all. All riches and their wealth are to come with them but I expect a great many to bury their belongings and hope to collect it later when the danger is past. Not only do they risk losing it completely but it remains lost to the treasury if they are killed. Anybody witnessed doing this is to be whipped and their property confiscated. Am I understood?'

The two centurions saluted him before reaffirmed their orders. Carausius was told to leave and wait for his. The meeting had finished on this unpredictable note.

Martis was selected as the month to begin the attack, and as Magnus Aurelius had wanted, the stragglers around were driven towards Bagacum like sheep. What animals that hadn't been taken by the army for their needs were hastily shackled to carts and forced along the roads at unnatural speeds. If the plan had involved comedy and fear together, then it was working as the living crawled over the dead to find shelter. An unpleasant tide of peasantry and wealth was falling back from the countryside and rapidly lapping up against the broken walls of the semi deserted town until there was little room to drop their belongings and get some sleep. Stories of bandits attacking at will were spread by the Romans in order to inflict a little more panic, and therefore speed, into their citizen army whilst stragglers and the infirm simply lay down and awaited their fate behind locked bedroom doors. Villas and farmland were burnt easily in the dryness of the late summer heat with there being nothing left to steal. If they wanted the rewards this time then they had to come and get them. The plan was appearing to work. A few however chose to ignore their plight and were punished accordingly, shouting to those running away that there wasn't another army coming to save them and they had heard it all before. Carausius watched impassively as these people were taken outside, forced to reveal their hidden treasure which was retrieved and then beaten for their lies. One such recipient of this treatment was a Numerius Septimus Clemens who had chosen to ignore the army's request and now stood to lose in his foolishness. There, outside one of his villa estates, he was knocked to the ground by a horseman unaware of his status before being dragged by the remnants of his fine clothes to the place where he had buried the farm's profits. He thought that he recognised Carausius amongst the thugs witnessing his disgrace with soldiers dismounting and allowing themselves to search his house for other tokens of wealth. These wouldn't be seen by the Procurator but would instead find their way throughout the brothels and bars of any town still flickering under the flame of civilization. With his jaw broken how could a man complain but utter a few chosen words to Mithras before having to witness his daughter being chased out the rear of the house and across a rutted field to where two soldiers lay upon her. Not wishing to involve himself and show favour, Carausius turned away and made for the next orange tiled farmhouse across the fields. By Saturni the first part in the destruction of the Bagaudae had been accomplished and after watching the last of the soldiers throwing a burning torch into a thatched barn roof he ordered them back to Bagacum. Stories were now reaching him that the rebels weren't too far away and if in enough numbers, may be confident of winning a decisive battle over the Romans stationed there. Against the backdrop of a dying and deserted countryside he rode at the head of his column; at his horse's side the ragged army of citizens seeking Rome's protection slowly ambled with scarcely enough strength to pull itself along. On the horizon lay the dubious safety of a fallen town.

What guards that had been posted outside on the road found it increasingly difficult to separate the migrants coming towards them at all hours of day and night until at last the flood receded to a trickle making it easier. At this point the exchange of soldier and citizen was to take place and begrudgingly items of clothing were removed. Weapons however, were not to be given over and Magnus Aurelius had promised that their military disguise ought to be protection enough. They were to leave that night and carry with them enough shields to make believe that it was a Roman army getting away under cover of darkness leaving the town defenceless. A tired, depopulated and unarmed mass did as it was ordered, whilst its army hid behind the crumbling walls and waited for the dawn to come. Behind them and off on the road towards Samarobriva marched the financial sheep of Rome ready for shearing at a future date and amongst their ranks stumbled Septimus Clemens and his forever ailing daughter. To add authenticity, marching commands were given that were to be shouted at every other pace along the way at least until the tenth milestone had been reached, and when eventually these cries died away from the stillness of the early morning sky, every soldier's pulse feared the coming day. A messenger had arrived back from Maximianus. The news was good. He had understood the change in plan and was marching accordingly to their relief but they were not to expect a rapid arrival as the potential to be ambushed was high and Diocletianus had forbidden any relaxing of army discipline on the march. Troops were too valuable a commodity and to lose them was to risk death at the hands of the emperor. They could expect the two legions to rescue them in three days yet the messenger had seen bands of men already on the move and estimated them to be far closer. Panic swept over the small force of foot soldiers that had been told that their cavalry were close by and ready to attack at the rear of the enemy. How were they to know that they hadn't already fled? What lies were there being told? In trying to regain trust and hold the situation in check, Magnus Aurelius laughed that he hadn't fled and would be fighting alongside them although, he like most of them knew, accepted that the change in planning was of Carausius' doing and he wasn't there. The events were to get worse.

Carausius was close by and had like all good military planners, chosen the highest ground where he could survey the land and repel attacks at the same time. He had seen nothing and in the absence of camp fires his men were wary of the changing colours of night. A password was asked for and given and the scout brought into the tent where the attacks were to be co-ordinated, before everybody moved off into the random chaos of battle. The youngest there feared death; the oldest had seen it before and offered little moral support. Good luck pendants were carefully held in trembling hands whilst the gods of everywhere received their prayers and men quietly moved amongst their horses wisely selecting the best of both. Some jumped up and down in an attempt at making their mail armour more comfortable; others had simply forgotten how long they had been wearing theirs and instead fiddled with the leather ties that held their helmet cheek pieces shut. Inside the tent, the scout stuttered over his news.

The rebels were not easily tricked: That had been his message. A retreating army signals that they have little worth fighting for and therefore, are demoralised and effectively running away. Even under the cover of night they are vulnerable as they have made no contingency for their safety in the form of a temporary camp and are looking to place as much distance between themselves and their pursuer before being caught and forced to fight. Therefore, it made sense to attack them first and if successful, return and ransack the town afterwards. That was why Carausius and the other commanders had not seen them coming their way. They had simply gone around the trap set for them without them knowing it. The scout then went on quietly and privately to recall the fate of the column fleeing from Bagacum. Whoever escaped the carnage was fortunate in luck and deserving of life but not many were. The rebels had smashed their way into the false shield wall column and instantly recognised that these were not soldiers but women and men carrying the insignia of the army. Their fury knew little mercy and the pathetic band of stragglers were cut to pieces on the road and in the ditches alongside. However, with there being little of financial value to reward those doing the killing it had been decided to thinly cut a man's artery and put him on the road back to the town, where if he hadn't passed out with blood loss he could warn the army of its own impending fate. The roman trickery had aroused their treacherous anger as men who had been prepared to die once now had to face their own mortality again. The weakest amongst them couldn't do it and gorged their swords into the groaning civilian bodies as retribution. A strong commander would have regrouped and attacked at a time of his choosing but there were too many leaders amongst the rebels who wanted to steal what they could and then get away before Maxiamanus arrived with the relief force. The time for battle was now and the short lived life of the survivor on the road, its omen. That's where the messenger stopped. Carausius was to mobilise his force and try to surround the traitors as they sought an early victory. Speed and surprise were to be everything when the small force of infantry was trapped and fighting for its survival. With the attack concentrated upon Bagacum, the fields and roads would be quiet of enemy forces and the Romans could move at will. All cavalry were to canter and although the night had not yet broken to day there was sufficient light supplied by the tired huntress moon to aid them along their way. With five hundred men under his command, Carausius sought to lead them forward without the need for any encouragement. Rescuing their comrades was more pressing now than spreading the news of dead civilians in order to cajole them to fight harder and ignore death. Either they killed or the province would die and everything Roman with it. In the minds of every soldier riding to battle were the reasons that he had chosen to do so. They thought of themselves first and then dismissed the thought as if it had never mattered, and instead prepared for the fight.

Bagacum looked quiet as the cavalry arrived, with little sign of further destruction upon its already beaten walls and in the east the sun was lighting the sky. Carausius was mindful of the acolyte Cautes and quietly spoke a few words of incantation so that none could hear him before riding alongside Tullius to seek confirmation of orders.

'It would be foolish to enter the town' he said, citing that they would be better off attacking with mobility on the outside.

Tullius agreed, and they decided to split the main force into two. One would circle the town in one direction and the other likewise but the opposite way. This would give them freedom to ride at both enemy flanks at the same time. Carausius pulled on the bit in his horse's mouth and pushed hard with his leg to get the animal to turn about. A swift kick with his spurs helped overcome the animal's resistance to orders and he galloped off.

'Turmae one to eight to follow me' he shouted.

'Vexillarius and Tubicen; to the front and lead. Let's go!'

The excitement of hunting down fellow men raced through everyone's veins for the Romans were the far superior force and whilst the death of Vibius on the river bank had never really been forgotten or forgiven, the men had grown to trust Carausius' judgement. He had arrived amongst them as a river man, not a soldier, paid for by Septimus who was keen to have his property defended by an army that was indifferent to the wider issues of the day and wanted to take their share of what silver was on offer. This wasn't lost on their leader either, as he rode in a comfortable wooden framed saddle and wore a helmet that fitted correctly, embellished with Mars, the protector. By his side hung the spartha, the cavalry sword that he knew was of quality and wouldn't snag in its scabbard when called upon to be pulled free and bring instant death in a swing. The merchant had been good to him when it mattered but at this moment it was far from his thoughts. Carausius pulled his horse to a stop and ordered his men to fan out to the side of him, as no more than two hundred paces ahead the ragged indiscipline of the opposing army showed itself. He paused briefly to take stock of what he was witnessing. Small groups were clustered together and racing towards the semi demolished buildings housing roman soldiers and being led by one or two of the braver amongst them. Upon being repulsed, they retired until another braver than the last went forward to resume leading the attack. Carausius could see clearly that they had no real strategy other than try to win small isolated skirmishes and were not presenting a concerted front. That wasn't to say that the Romans were finding it easy either, as archer after archer tried desperately to pin down individual targets and many were missing and wasting their arrows. The shouts of command could occasionally be heard before the voice fell silent in choking death and the battle move a little bit further forward. It was apparent that although heavily outnumbered, the Romans were holding their ground but needed relieving and quickly. In the light of the approaching day, Carausius was surprised at how many traitors had been seduced by the lies the scouts had spread about wealth being taken into the town and like rats, these men required killing. With the order to attack given he silently raised his spear with his right hand, clutched the reins and shield with his left and pushed his horse into the front of the line. He didn't know any valiant quotes to shout so instead nodded to the man next to him to blow the horn and off he raced.

Waiting to throw the spear seemed like ages and the horse was proving difficult to manoeuvre in a straight line although it had been rehearsed over and over again. With his hand raised, a target revealed itself and foolishly Carausius let the weapon fly more out of wanting to get rid of it rather than securing a kill. The man swerved and the missile fell past him although another rider's caught him in the chest as he moved to defend himself again. Carausius rapidly went for his sword, which although was bouncing around off the side of his right leg, came free with ease. Another man came forward with a shield raised before hacking at the horse's chest. It grunted an indescribable moan before carrying on under the pressure of excitement and a primitive will to stay alive. Its rider swept low as he raced past and delivered a deep wound to the side of the assailant. More men were coming to meet him now and rapidly he moved to avoid the killing blows. Soon his horse collapsed beneath him and he found himself fighting on his feet, luckily being thrown clear of the stricken beast. As a leader he was marked out, yet at close quarters there wasn't the discipline to kill him evident in the faces of his enemy. The bravest had met him on the charge in towards them, and now all that were left were the simplest amongst them in their array of disjointed stolen armour and blunt weapons. These were too frightened even to run away and hoped instead for mercy if they fought hard, but there wasn't going to be any offered. Under the peak of his helmet he glimpsed the battle going on around and rapidly found the time to issue orders to the trumpeter. Above the heads of the fighting men and horses he saw the flag of his unit flying across the battlefield, safely in the grip of its rider, and that gave him the strength to ignore the lack of sleep and food, the weight of the armour and the perils of fighting for his life on his feet. One by one as his opponents reached out to despatch him he managed to evade them and instead take their breath. Tullius' forces had now joined in and the danger was quickly receding with the rebels in full retreat. What shouting that remained was coming from the roman side imploring their troops in Bagacum to remain where they were and not come out, as there was the real possibility of being mistaken for the enemy in their ragged civilian clothes. Today was going to be a cavalry victory and as Carausius glimpsed Magnus Aurelius saluting him from the edge of the town with his arm raised, he realised that with a sense of purpose that Vibius' death could now be forgotten and his spirit no longer seek its vengeance. Free now and with a complete victory in his mind, he set about hacking down the weeds of disaffection and driving them towards the rays of a new day rising above Maxiamanus' army slowly approaching from the east.

CHAPTER V

SEA OF SWORDS

A purity of decaying snow laced the limestone hills surrounding Augusta Treverorum where Maximianus and his court celebrated not only the defeat of the Bagaudae, but also the twin victories over the Germanic tribes, the Alamanni and the Heruli, who had crossed Fluvius Rhenus and into Roman lands the previous autumn. In recognition of these successes, Diocletianus had decreed that Maximianus share the throne with him, but as ruler of the West, raising him without suspicion to Augustus. There was however, an underlying reason which was that it allowed the senior emperor to dictate imperial policy and the junior one to wage violent warfare in its name. This was a responsibility ideally suited to Maximianus, eagerly waiting for the final rapid melting of the winter snows and the planned attack upon Germania Inferior through the crossing at Mogontiacum, where the eagles of Rome could once more trample the barbarous soil beneath their wings. All throughout that long cold dark season, the one thousandth and thirty-ninth following Rome's accession to its empire, men toiled hard in the army's fabricae churning out an endless resupply of weaponry and warm clothing. Behind solid wooden doors fires sparked as muscle and sweat skilfully went about its business. In stable block after stable block, tired horses were replaced with fresher, stronger ones, ready for the ardour of campaign shortly to begin and capable foot soldiers were raised up to cavalry status to ride them. Smoke was constantly seen drifting skywards from the many busy temples and workshops alike for Diocletianus had decreed that the favoured pagan gods, Jupiter and Hercules, would revive all their fortunes in war and were again to be jointly worshipped. Other alien religions refusing to support this faith would be crushed.

Pulling his purple cloak warmly about him and having had sexual intercourse with another officer's wife, Maximianus marched out of his room to inspect the preparations for war accompanied by his bodyguard. Behind, in the soft comfort furnishings of the last banquet were his best men quietly talking amongst themselves about the elevation to Augustus of their leader. Many pondered their opportunity of attacking a weakened enemy for its legitimacy could bring them all fame, yet also the danger that followed it. Maximianus had conveniently forgotten the peasant revolt of the previous year and wouldn't be handing out awards to his followers as it could appear disrespectful, acknowledging the killing of roman citizens by roman soldiers. In palace truth, he had claimed the glory for himself of quelling the rebel uprising and what wealth that had been recovered he also took. It wasn't the prerogative of any man there to say otherwise and amongst the silver plate and finest engraved glassware of the dining tables nobody was strong enough to ask him for their share.

Far away, Julius Magnus Aurelius had also chosen himself to boast about rescuing the town of Bagacum until the legions arrived. Often, to reassure themselves that the day of the battle wasn't their day to die, soldiers talk and search out familiar experiences from others to share. At Bagacum few were left to salute the arrival of Augustus Maximianus as they had been dispersed to their temporary camps and knowing that a relieving force was approaching, Carausius too had been dismissed. The immediate fear was that the Saxons would use the opportunity to launch a sudden raid upon the coastline left unprotected by the massed forces inland. As a consequence of meeting few of the actual soldiers from that day Maximianus posted one legion to round up any rebels and then retired with his banners flying proud, safe in the knowledge that the threat was over. The proclamation was that he had won an important victory. However in the lengthening days, that threat was again in the minds of men talking about the emperor of the west and of the seas that next he needed to win back from the pirates. In the cramped officer's quarters of the coastal fortress at Gesoriacum, a meeting was being held to decide the Romans' next plan and it wasn't going well. A bronze oil lamp struggled to provide sufficient light against the natural gloom of the afternoon and everybody shivered in the cold of a raw northerly wind pulling at the window frames and shutters. Luxuries were non existent, and before the assembled few could each help themselves to a luke-warm fish dumpling served in a spicy celery seed and pepper sauce, Magnus Aurelius fussed over paying homage to Hercules with an offering of sweet incense.

'Mighty Hercules, I approach you' he said respectfully.

'May we trample our enemies as you struck down the lion with your club? Give us the right to rule the seas as Oceanus has'

And he delicately crumbled the sweet powder between his fingers before allowing it to fall upon the naked flame below the bronze figured altar. All too briefly it glowed, before failing to fully ignite and instead gave off a fragrant white vapour that swirled into every dark corner.

'Vesta of the hearth, give me light and warmth' thought Carausius, mindful of his own initiation into the cult of Mithras and how this little space reminded him of the gloomy temple there.

Ceremony over and with the sense that all the best officers of the west were now in Augusta Treverorum, along with their Emperor, Carausius felt emboldened to speak without fear of recrimination or danger as he had never spoken before. Magnus Aurelius, wiping his fingers clean of the recent powdery offering turned, at the mention of a reward, to face him. A tall man in his latter years, he had been chosen well for this role and defeated the question comfortably...

'Reward, Carausius? What reward is this? How dare you to ask!' he mocked.

'What extra were you expecting our divine Augustus to pay you? Never forget that it is you that serve Rome and not the other way around, for I've never heard of payment for killing citizens. If it is so, then tell me of it!' he joked and walked to the table where the food was waiting.

Carausius raised his right arm in protest with his palm out, and instantly bright swords were drawn from their scabbards behind the legate.

'I would be careful of your next move if I were you' he said and squeezed a cooling ball of fish between his fingers before taking it to his mouth and enjoying the taste of spices and white salty flesh.

'Let me remind you who put you where you are; Numerius Septimus Clemens. Where is he now?' he teased.

Carausius did not have the answer as the peasant revolt had spread people far and wide in its panic and it could be months before they dared to come back, if ever they did at all.

'Then let me tell you...' Magnus Aurelius continued.

'With my own eyes I have seen him here trying to trade from this port but where has his wealth returned from? We cannot know? All merchants have suffered great hardships and the emperor wants them to start again, feel secure at the defeat of the Bagaudae and also feel safe from pirate raids which threaten this entire northern coast. To that end Maesaeus Carausius, you are hereby promoted to take command of the fleet covering these waters. You can guard his ships and what he carries in them; he can pay his taxes and then, of course, we can pay you. You are to take this command with all seriousness as a great deal of trust has been placed in you, but let me warn you of the consequences of your failing. I am shortly to return to my legion and more soldiers shall be following me. Your friend Tullius Fruscus is to command the cavalry here, as Magister Equitum, and between you, the land and seas are to be kept open towards Britannia. However, any thoughts of mutiny will be quickly crushed, as we crushed Aelianus and Amandus and there will be little mercy shown if you attempt to use military power to your own advantage. Have I been understood?'

He then picked at his teeth and pulled a fish bone free before concluding.

'I have recommended you personally to Maximianus for this task Carausius, but do not allow yourself into being seduced as there are agents here waiting for your weakness to shine through. Now leave and report to the navarchus in his office. You will want to talk matters over with him, but before you go...' and he raised a small glass beaker of sweet wine in his direction, concluding

'You have many choices now – yet it is the gods, and no man, that will guide you towards the right one. Remember that. Farewell!'

Feeling resentment towards and cheated by the authorities he left, but what was there to do? His status had grown in the elevation of his rank, which was to command the northern fleet, and that pleased him as it meant a recall to the seas, but also included the renewed dangers of current, weather and tide. There he could easily perish at the convenience of Maximianus.

The war against the Franks and Saxons wouldn't benefit him any more than serving back in the mosquito ridden frontiers would. Nobody would ever salute his name and what victories would be reported back to Rome? Who was the last feted commander of the fleet? Carausius didn't know and when asked later that day, the navarchus didn't know either.

In his blue tunic and heavy cloak he was to be found clutching a beaker of ale, and when pressed upon his duties for the day, replied that the weather would make sailing dangerous for him and his foe alike. Therefore drinking and gambling a little was all there was. Carausius could only agree and after presenting his credentials, sat down and joined him, whilst the worst of the weather beat against the walls and tiled roof. In the harbour below all craft were safely tied up whilst those that weren't rode at anchor in the lee of the hills. The tide wouldn't change for half a day yet and there wasn't expected to be any call to sail, other than watching a foolhardy merchantman trying to cross the narrow straights to Britannia during a periodic lull in the storm. They however sailed at their own risk and were not the prerogative of the fleet.

'But I've seen ships accompanied from the island before' Carausius said, recalling his saving of Messalina in the river mouth.

'Not from here' replied the navarchus.

'They are part of the old fleet of Classis Britannica. A few warships and scouting craft are all that's left. It isn't the force it was and to allay the emperor's fear of the island governor having three legions plus a fleet at his disposal, they withdrew it to here. Those ships are purely a token offer and supply vessels to the wall of Hadrian only.'

'But why then is the island safer than here?'

'Commander' the navarchus said respectfully, 'it is because of that very reason. You know of its many rivers and harbours that are guarded by forts; stone forts at that. It is easier for the pirates to wage a war here in the seas off Gallia, make landfall and then ally themselves with the rebels. In Britannia there is no escape route, other than the seas which could swallow their ships, and no mercy shown to invaders that fail to escape. The crossing is dangerous, the fighting is perilous and the escape hazardous. We are easier pickings for them' and having said that went to the large wooden chest containing current maps of the coasts and forts along them.

He laid it out flat over the table where the two men spent a profitable rainy afternoon pouring over strategy, tide and planning, before the lateness of the hour called Carausius to his bunk. In the morning he would inspect the harbour, ships and crew whilst the navarchus was left to organise a small office of mapmakers and clerks at Gesoriacum, for there was the growing impression that the war for which he had been sent to wage, was going to be won on parchment. In his mind new strategies began to emerge of defeating the pirates and he laughed inwardly at Magnus Aurelius' notion that the gods were to be thanked for his cunning. Only he would be accepting the praise and no one else.

In the morning light the seas were calmed of their fury from the day before and had returned to their routine task of filling the river estuary, with ships dancing quietly at their anchors. Alongside the quay, wooden hoists were busy pulling their cargoes up and onto the decking where labourers toiled to load them into carts and then lead them away the short distance to their appropriate warehouses. The fort sitting above on its higher ground impartially watched this activity, and apart from being called upon to search the occasional ship they remained neutral to the merchant's business, scanning instead the flat ocean for evidence of other shipping. When the alarm did sound they would dispatch a light, blue sailed warship with an armed crew frantically rowing to escape the currents and get out in to the open waters where they could chase their foe. Often, they were too slow and the evading pirate sails would grow smaller on the wide eastern horizon stretching before them. Against a backdrop of white clouds sailing quietly north above his head and the circling of sea birds, Carausius left the barracks and walked down to the hill to inspect his navy. The omens seemed good, for he was instantly met by the centurion of the marines who saluted promptly.

'Welcome, commander' he said.

'We have a ship ready for your approval' and led him to it.

The two climbed down onto its rough wooden planking where Carausius was momentarily startled by the crew loudly saluting him. Then barking orders, the captain called them to push away from the side and make for the open waters of the harbour mouth. They were closely followed by a second ship and when asked why, he was told that they were embarking upon an exercise for him to witness and comment upon. Although a sailor himself through choice, there were things that he needed to know about fighting naval warfare and when clear of the harbour and any obstructions the mock battle began. Throughout a not unpleasant early afternoon, with light winds and a shallow swell, the two ships manoeuvred for combat. As one boat prepared to escape, the other followed as closely as possible firing arrows at the tiller until it was forced into an ever wider circle to evade the darts. When it eventually exposed itself to being rammed in the side, the drum beat from the following ship increased in intensity and Carausius felt the surge drive them forward. At a safe distance the beat stopped and the rowers ordered to lower their oars and relax. The leading boat was then called alongside and Carausius shown how the marines would finish off the fight with their hooks, swords and shields. At the end of it all both crews were allowed to ride the slack water and rest, before catching the tides back home. There was praise from their new commander, who saw in their weather beaten faces a willingness to serve, and also an understanding that all were sharing a joint peril that could lead to their bloodless death through drowning. Carausius the sailor, had united them, but as the canvas fluttered gently and the steersman leant upon his tiller he implored them to be strong in their efforts and new tactics would be found for defeating the pirates. No man was going to be forgotten, and no ships lost. Their rousing cheer lifted the birds towards the sky and in the late afternoon sun with gentle white breakers chasing onto deserted beaches, the two warships waited patiently outside the harbour mouth to dock. On board, Carausius scratched at his beard and reiterated again those beliefs that the seas could be cleared, but before finalising these plans he wanted to visit the island across the water – Britannia. He ordered the ships to be readied for the short crossing which would be in a few weeks time. Beforehand was the need to ascertain who was commanding in the fleet and what their role was, and to this end, he summoned them all to Gesioracum to explain his tactics which had already rapidly evolved in his own mind. He believed them to answer the empire's constant worry about its insecurity on the seas and judged that the cavalry and navy needed to work as one. Therefore, Tullius Fruscus would also be required to be present and a messenger despatched to summon him.

At their meeting it appeared that the naval strength he had wasn't insignificant. There were six squadrons of ten ships apiece of Liburnae, the heavy lumbering warships and adequate numbers of the lighter, more agile scouting boats – the scaphae. With permission to build more ships already given, it wasn't going to be too long before the new commander of the fleet was in a position to attack the pirates out on the open waters and bring an end to their raiding upon the coast of Gallia Belgica. Further east was more problematic. The wide river channels of Fluvius Rhenus needed guarding evermore and the answer, Carausius felt, was in cavalry patrols. He therefore sought permission to raise more troops up to the cavalry and build more watchtowers along its banks, which then would be connected by roadways. Tullius Fruscus would be despatched there to oversee this work, but not before his friend had returned from his journey to Britannia. The marines of the fleet were to be housed in fresh barracks and provided with new armaments, as it would be they who were to do most of the upcoming fighting. All centurions were to make themselves known to Carausius as were each of the squadron commanders and by doing this, an inventory of the fleet was established. At the end of their meeting most were dismissed to return to their duties whilst those remaining judged as being loyal were taken aside and shown the battle maps for the war season ahead. Until then nothing was to change. The Saxons and their allies, the Franks, were to believe that by sailing west and attacking the rich countryside at will they could go unpunished as they had done up to now. The apparent defeat of the rebel army wouldn't serve to dent their confidence, as the Romans couldn't be everywhere at once and a warrior wasn't feted by his own people until he had plundered from under their very noses, returning home victorious and laden. For Carausius, soon to embark and briefly leave his plans behind, this was the command that he had wanted and on his terms. Confidence in him by his men was high; belief that the gods favoured him evident in the united shouts of acclamation from all the ranks, yet from behind his back no plot had yet been forthcoming. That was to worry him fearing the presence of agents within his staff. Who was it, holding the confidence of Augustus Caesar?

A few weeks passed and the person he trusted to get him across the narrow straights was true to his word. The Liburna and her twin ship departed from Gesoriacum on the early morning tide and as the warm dreams of sleeping men were still fresh in their minds. Once out into the ocean a gentle wind filled their sails and stars still lit the sky, followed by the navigators on earth below plotting their course. The ships easily rose, fell and swayed in unison throughout the journey leaving a smooth trail of whitened water behind as they passed. In the heavens pennants danced from the mast and on the decking stood the armed marines proudly behind their bright shields. Britannia was shortly to welcome her new protector. Carausius had never felt as supremely powerful as he did now. Up to this point his promotion had been largely due to the faith of a few men who believed in him. Numerius Septimus Clemens and Julius Magnus Aurelius in particular, but the emperor would be more demanding. Extermination was the solution to the Saxon problem and whilst he was far away killing in Germania he would expect no less from the newly appointed commander of the fleet guarding the western provinces. Numbers would ultimately tell their story, but silently as the oars bit into the passive waves and the walls of Rutupiae rose up from the island ahead, the man chosen to accomplish it was deep in thought.

'Sound the horns' went out a call and the order was instantly obeyed, although some notes faded on the wind and were momentarily lost.

Sails were brought down and the oarsmen skilfully adjusted the ship's pace to the harbour and wharf looming up. Carausius, from the prow of the ship watched it all efficiently happen as the boat swayed gently against its berth and ropes were let out to hold it firm. Once close enough a boarding plank was pushed out and the island of Britannia became flesh and blood to the sailor who had wanted to see it at first hand. Stepping ashore he was immediately greeted by another official dressed in military attire with a long sword at his side, leather boots, leggings and a bronze square plated mail shirt. Holding his crested helmet in one hand he greeted Carausius warmly and impatiently keen to explain who he was. Politeness allowed him to continue.

'Greetings Commander; I am Manilius Albinus, Praefectus Classis here in Britannia. My camp is Portus Dubris although I am often where the war takes me' he explained.

'I have servants waiting for us with food, which if we eat now will allow me to escort you into the province, so that you may witness its many and varied riches. Tonight I hope to make Durovernum Cantiacorum and then in another two days, Londinium, where the Governor of Britannia Superior waits to greet you along with the legionary commanders of Legio II and Legio XX. I have a trusted bodyguard and good horses. Do you ride?'

The man appeared efficient.

The food was simple but rich with sauces and had to be hastily consumed as the journey following the requisite offerings to Mercury, started in the middle of the day. Riding through the vast arch, past the granaries and out alongside the thick heavy walls of flint and stone, gave the newly appointed commander his first glimpse of what it was that Rome cherished in its most northerly province. It was clearly a land that had been worth the investment. As the sun reflected off the muddy estuary that had directed him here and as his ships and crews settled down to a well deserved rest, he looked forward to his future and tried not to think about affairs back in Gallia. Like Manilius, being sent to wherever the need arose, Carausius sensed that nowhere would ever be called home yet this posting appealed as being unbiased and unsullied by the hand of those trying to determine their fate over his. He was to be his own man and the reputation earned fighting the Bagaudae would serve as a harsh warning. In his companion though he saw a man eager to co-operate in sharing the burden of increasing strife and relaxed; however experienced he appeared. This was not an everyday occurrence escorting the commander of the fleet so their conversation began in the predictable official manner with dialogue of how the Saxons were penetrating the roman defences and what was being done to stop them. Information about Britannia was also freely given as Manilius was willing to explain that the tactics deployed there were similar in many ways. He spoke readily about using cavalry to back up the forts on the coast and how legions, once the mainstay of roman arms, were quietly kept in their permanent fortresses and seldom used. The urgent need was now to match ships with hooves. Only being this far from the real source of imperial power could he be so unafraid of speaking as freely. Little by little a picture grew in size of the state of affairs in the island yet as they continued along the broad military road towards Duovernum, Carausius couldn't fail to be impressed by the relative tranquillity of the countryside and the tidiness of the fields and farms tucked in amongst them. Agriculturally it was rich and its granaries bursting to feed the armies of Germania with their surplus. Again, the seas, a vital route for securing the safety of the island had to be kept free of invaders and although well inland now a sudden emotive anger swept over Carausius, temporarily helpless to prevent any thief at sea, now striking at will. The waves, his new battle ground and his alone, were calling him back; the island, suddenly no more than a temporary motionless trap.

'Manilius' He spoke loudly wishing to appear ready for his task.

'Can we ride on a little faster? The day is becoming longer and in my mind I need to rest. Order your guard to keep up' and with that, the party leant into a canter and onwards towards their night in Duovernum.

The town was reached in the late hours of evening where messengers were waiting to receive news for the governor the following day, but there wasn't any, so they were sent to their bunks instead. Likewise, no news had arrived demanding immediate attention and everywhere along the coast had reported calm and free from Saxon attack. The guards however would remain at their posts in case of emergency, taking it in turn to sleep a good night's sleep before undertaking the longest part of the journey the next day. Closing his door and imprisoning the dull glow from the lamp within the garish orange painted room, Carausius then locked it securely and soon was asleep on a wooden slatted bed, sword safely by his side and a soot laden wick slowly dying. Outside across the fields surrounding the forts and along the tops of the cliffs, tired eyes strained to detect an unpredictable enemy moving in the darkness, whilst in the streets of the town dogs barked at the wolves. There above, dancing through the blackest of skies, went the golden Fates of men to their dawn and ultimately onto their own beds.

Two days later the far ditches and walls of Londinium officially greeted them as they crossed Fluvius Thamesis by its bridge and rode on into the city making for the Forum in the northwest corner. Unsuspecting faces looked up at the new guardian of the seas and in his turn he quickly took stock of their demeanour as they went about their business. Carts filled the road and shops provided an ample supply of wares hanging up which were soon picked over by slaves out shopping for the evening meal. Money changed hands without bitter dispute and Carausius, surprised at the ease of it all, remarked of the lack of free markets in Gallia where all goods it seemed were being consumed by the army in its relentless fight for survival. Everything in Britannia appeared to be for sale and freely available too. Land, that precious commodity that everybody wanted, looked to be so with large vacant plots where no grand villas stood. In asking, he was told that the rich were leaving the cities and retiring to the dubious safety of the open countryside and their large grand estates. Once there, they easily shed their civic responsibilities and learnt to hoard their wealth where the emperor couldn't see it or steal it. Britannia had had her share of strife and the rich quickly responded to it, especially those who had backed the losing side in recent bitter internal struggles. Between the emperor and the Saxons nowhere was providing a safe haven in which to hoard money except the cold certainty of a hole in the soil and the vast jars in which it slept. What, with the river port lacking enough sails and masts to prove its commercial worth and the sight of empty warehouses, Carausius sensed an underlying purpose to his promotion. The province was doing all it could to fend off attack and little more, for beneath the calm veneer there lay a panic, the fright that soon all this would be lost forever and Rome washed away upon the next tide of blood to attack.

The man to briefly answer his questions would be meeting them in the imperial palace by the river's edge, but first it was to the stables to leave the horses behind and change into more appropriate clothing. Manilius had then wanted to travel in a guarded carriage but Carausius, having not seen a city before, wished to walk and view the streets at close hand. His host reluctantly agreed, knowing how short of time they were, but asked that they did not stop. Past the amphitheatre the small party went; quiet on this day and without ceremony, its banners drooped towards the ground, then on towards the Forum where an enormous building dominated the sky with its orange roofed splendour. Crowds of native toga wearing men milled in a sea of business ever keen to be involved in decision making and as far as the eye could see the roads were bringing in more through the five gates of the city. Under Sol's warming influence the empire appeared to flourish and if more evidence were needed of the value of Londinium then it came in the delicious aroma that burst into life from the many kitchens and the clanging from its workshops. The sweet smell of leather hung in the air too and the raw sewage that often blighted smaller towns was discreetly hidden in its drains. A rising tide had taken away the river estuary mud stench and various perfumed oils sparingly applied to native flesh had caught Carausius' nose. Beautiful women quickly filled his mind and had it not been for the intervention of Manilius, then he could have easily strayed into a brothel for the duration of the day. If it was female company that he wished for then something could be arranged later as Manilius himself was also a single man. Business though as always had to precede pleasure. It was the burden of keeping the Saxon tide at bay that Carausius needed to concentrate upon and without his trusted friend Tullius to advise him, he had to be alert for deceit or trickery. The twin emperor's were doing their best to repel the eastern incursion of their borders: Far away to the north they expected no less of their naval commander in his lonely duties too.

Having arrived not much later than anticipated, the group were admitted to the governor's palace. The man, short with a balding head and a beard waited in a polished marble room for them to enter and greeted Manilius and Carausius warmly. Introductions were made and legates of Legio II Augusta and Legio XX Valeria Victrix brought forward. After a simple sacrificial offering at the household shrine for their combined safety and that of the emperors, glasses of sweet white wine were offered and the men moved efficiently into a more private room secured behind its heavy oak door. Talk of the overall military situation would have to wait a little longer as the safety of the province now bordered upon defending its coasts and there had been serious attempts at finding the best solution to the problem. Carausius was to be invited back later in the autumn, when sailing would become difficult for most, and the attacks, as a consequence would temporarily cease. All four leading military men of contention were to maintain regular contact as best they could and share their knowledge of defeating the Saxons, a point which Carausius understood, yet in ignorance he had to enquire as to the whereabouts of the one missing legionary commander – the man responsible for Legio VI Victrix at Eboracum. It was a question keenly felt by all that served the province and in his reply the governor could not describe his ally as a lesser man due to the smaller force he commanded, but instead praised him in his loneliness of defending the furthest outposts of roman rule. This was a dangerous posting that few sought out, and had anyone ever been there, then they would understand that other than military comforts, few of any other sort existed. Therefore they weren't to expect him when dealing with problems arising outside Britannia Inferior. With two legions to the south and the remnants of the fleet there were adequate forces available.

Throughout the rest of that afternoon and early into the soft light of evening, the group talked on, keen to establish a bond of loyalty to a cause that would ultimately guarantee their own personal survival and that of their families. Carausius was encouraged to find a home this side of Oceanus where he could settle, and various river valleys were mentioned with fondness as having superb soils to farm plus good road links to the towns. He was warned of taking too much of an interest in local affairs as it could consume his time, as well as his fortune, yet nobody there could sense that he had none to speak of and had relied entirely on patronage up to now to provide for his promotions. A country estate would be fine, befitting his rank, but he couldn't buy it and as the conversation ebbed into the slow dreary hours of night this deception went unnoticed with the talk turning instead to the provinces across the waters and their respective fates. Finally, at the end of the now lengthy meeting, all men retired to their rooms led there by a slave brandishing a small lamp and as they each slept their separate dreams one man in particular felt the fallacy of his, although for now it didn't appear to be of concern either to him or to them; the money he needed would come from somewhere like it always had done.

The dawn broke with its usual bustle of slaves preparing for the guests to depart. Horses were thoroughly groomed and then saddled for the military commanders to take their leave and return to their posts, whilst guards milled about with efficiency not wanting to be ordered to other mundane duties through showing an unwilling aptitude. The last remains of breakfast were cleared away. Carausius, used to the soldier's life admired the steward of the house whose devotion to his master knew little fault as each guest had been individually asked if he had eaten sufficient for the journey ahead and if not, more could be provided. The Britons, he thought, although uncultured were obligingly loyal. A younger slave had dared to ask him if his mail shirt was too tight or his boots laced up correctly and didn't wince at being scolded for his impudence. In helping to sort the military clothing that had been sent over from the fort along with the horses, Carausius instinctively felt safe at the boy handling a sword and allowed him behind him his back to buckle it up. He returned to face him expecting nothing. The master of the seas smiled at such innocence and gently touched the boy's hair without rejection.

Manilius Albinus had suggested that rather than endure more overnight stays at dubious mansios they call in to visit a patron of the army at his home. He was sure that he wouldn't be there but that wouldn't stop them from being admitted and drinking his best wines. He could afford it, Manilius remarked, before sending on ahead a messenger warning the bailiff that guests would be staying a night or two and to prepare the house for occupancy. The estate was off the road to Rutupiae but wouldn't cause them too much in the way of delay at returning to the sea. He had heard scouts reporting back to the governor indicating that the island was safe at present and that all roman patrols were active along the southern coast between Anderitum and Portus Dubris. In any event they knew where to find the commander if his presence were urgently required. This was a small opportunity at relaxing before the lengthening days of combat ahead and ought to be readily taken. There would be slave girls available and the privacy that one would require for discreet infidelities coupled to a day's hunting for boar in the woods around. It was a reasonably comfortable house, used occasionally by visiting career men of social standing in return for their continued support and protection, but to Carausius it appeared familiar.

'Whose wine are we to drink?' he asked sourly.

Manilius couldn't be sure, as the exact ownership was disputed to this day, but the current owner had instigated new building works and that he was desperate to escape the ravages of the Saxons and be able to retire somewhere in dignity, safety and comfort too.

'And if I choose to retire in dignity and safety, will someone else drink my wine and coerce my slaves?' pressed Carausius.

'Come' answered his colleague.

'Are we to debate the rights and wrongs of our enjoyment of life? See it only for what it is; an escape from obligation and an opportunity to spend the money that the emperor would want to take from you. What harm can come from two nights away from your ships? If we ride on there will be time enough today to forget about...' but he didn't finish and suddenly instead felt urged to issue a warning.

He grabbed Carausius tightly about the forearm, having dismounted, adding...

'You may excuse my roughness, but you will listen to my words. This is an island wrought with fear. Long gone are the days of imperial strength when everybody bowed beneath the purple robe. There are two emperors fighting in the East and is that where you would wish to join them, you fool; in the endless forests of Germania? At least there is an enemy to fight! Nobody here knows whether the danger comes from within or without. We have had civil war and the towns throw up walls against usurpers as much as they do against the pirates.

Don't stand out from all others or else you will be accused of a plot against the way things stand. Good money is short, valuable goods even scarcer and still the army wants its share for protecting the vulnerable. Well, we are about to take our share.'

And he smiled.

'Don't make enemies of your new friends, for are we not all fighting on the same side?'

He released his grip before walking to his horse and having a slave help him back into the saddle. Angrily, Carausius followed, before leaving the opulent surroundings of the governor's palace and heading slightly south towards the coast and to his ships. Their guards, sensing the argument between the two men of similar military rank, rode back at a discreet distance and allowed the road's surface to dictate their pace for once they had left it to pursue the new route to the villa the disagreement manifested itself in speed. Keen to be the stronger rider and the first to their onerous pleasures, Carausius kicked his mount forward and leant easily into the gallop whilst Manilius warily stayed back. He had no way of predicting the sailor's reaction to their falling out but recognised that a man who risked his life to the unpredictability of the seas may eventually be the braver of the two. Calling a guard forward, he instructed him to follow the raging Carausius but to keep a discreet distance, guiding him until eventually his horse would tire and stop, which it soon did. When Manilius and the escort caught up, Carausius had dismounted and was staring far out into the distance whilst his horse breathed deeply. His host ordered everybody to halt and rest and after jumping down himself, carefully approached his offended guest.

'Please, accept my apologies' he said, having first ensured that no one could have heard him.

'This is my home and I hope my permanent posting: I have seen many changes. Some for the good, many for the worse and I have become blind to what others may see. Tell me about Gallia for no longer can the safety of Oceanus be granted to spare us. Come...what have you seen? Do men not help themselves?' and he held his arm out.

'Are you prepared to accept my apology and perhaps we may be friends?'

His pathetic honesty shone naively through and reflected off the bitter armour Carausius wore for his soul. Like a shaft of colour breaking upon the empty seas, the ray of friendship reached out and was then lost in the surrounding light.

'Yes, I have seen men taking what they want' he replied.

'I take what I want yet it doesn't satisfy me. Britannia, this island that all citizens across the sea would look to as their refuge, is little better. Look at yourselves!'

His raised voice drew the attention of the guard shifting to place its hands upon its swords.

'Where is the right to help yourselves? Where is the courage that Aeneas showed in sailing from his ruined city? Where are the boundaries of this empire that all fighting men serve? Why are we now thieves in our own land and little more?'

That said he felt empty and again mounted the tired horse and permitted the escort, a little wary now of his changing mood, to lead the way onwards and towards their requisitioned beds.

'He's tired of fighting' one of the guards muttered as he wheeled his horse around.

'No use here then' another said and adding...

'He wants to live off the lies like we do and then he'd start helping himself a little more!'

The messenger sent ahead had done his work well and rode up to them with news that the bailiff had been summoned and it appeared that the lady was away briefly but wouldn't object to the house being used. Nobody had seen her husband for months and it was rumoured that he could be dead, yet their son was alive and accompanying her on her travels that week. The bath house would be warmed ready for use and as the time of year hadn't yet fully turned to spring then the hypocaust too would be lit, although the bailiff was unsure of the safety of this seeing that the house had only just been renovated and repaired. He didn't wish to be the one responsible for burning it down! Nevertheless, there would be a meal prepared and time to rest with a day's hunting planned for tomorrow if they so desired. His master's house would be theirs to enjoy although the women on the farm had been sent away for the night to save any embarrassment in having to strike down a soldier trying to take advantage of the hospitality he might chose to seek there. All male company was what was on offer and the thought of it becoming tiresome for the guard. Some of the escort were for trying to ride onto the nearest town to find women although Manilius was quick in refusing to let them go. He showed adequate firmness in the face of opposition thought Carausius, unsure of where the nearest town was and doubly unsure himself as to where the coast and his route back to Gesoriacum lay. A warm night's rest would suffice without warning or danger and for that he had to rely upon Manilius keeping control. The villa they were staying at was off the main road and squatted quietly in a small river valley, too shallow and narrow to accept even the lightest of keels sailing upon it. An attack would therefore be highly unlikely and for that reason a night's rest seemed guaranteed. The pace therefore slowed to a relaxed one, with the guard concentrating upon idling, rather than watching, and without notice or care passed the face carefully hidden amongst the thinnest scrub that edged the track and who watched with great interest. Crawling like the animals he skilfully hunted for sport, he reported back on what he had seen to his mother as she remained tight lipped and a little fearful about their uninvited guests.

'Twelve of them, mother' he whispered.

'Two men look important; the rest the usual whoremongers that follow on.'

'Please, do nothing son and try to remain hidden out of sight. I am glad that your sister is not here; nobody will recognise you and we don't want any questions. I will allow them time to settle in the baths and find the wine and by then they will be too helpless to bother us. The governor can answer for their manners and our bailiff can bolt the door at night. Just give it two days for them to go. There's nothing to keep them here any longer and we can always go elsewhere.'

'Why do you think they have come?' the young man said.

'Is it father's business? Somebody may have some news of him. I must find out for you.'

'No. I promise that I will secretly ask, but nothing more.' She replied.

'You may have to accept that he is dead or missing. Now be quick for we need to find a neighbouring bed before dark for I am not sleeping here! Those days are past' she said, and off they silently moved through the woods.

Twelve men without the imperial authority to demand they get what they wanted arrived at the door of the main building and were met there by the bailiff. He snapped an instant order and a youthful male groom took charge of the horses, appearing as a spirit from nowhere. The soldiers, not having seen many people that day were surprised at evidence of life in the woods and hopes grew of him having a sister scratching around somewhere wanting a little money for lying down on her back. They were disappointed though and led instead into the main room of the building smelling a little of the tell tale hypocaust having recently being lit. Through their thick military boots they couldn't feel the warmth beneath their feet tentatively heating the thick mortar and tessellated floor so orders were given to remove them and sandals would be found in which they were free to move around without damaging the expensive panels by scratching their hobnails across them. As one, everybody removed their cloaks and threw them in a pile, expecting the arrival of a slave to gather them up, yet none came; the house was morbidly silent. All comforts were there – the furniture looking unused, the floors swept and clean with the painted plaster walls reflecting the beauty of a late winter sunset to the day, yet it appeared as if no one person wanted to admit ownership to such a fine building. Gone were the polished stone carved busts that normally adorned the rooms of country houses steeped in decades of ownership, with the ancestors looking on approvingly at the blatant increase in wealth and splendour. Here it was as if somebody was attempting to hide that wealth and also hide themselves. Manilius questioned the bailiff as to the rightful owner but was truthfully told that he occasionally 'came and went' and definitely wouldn't be arriving tonight. He was a man of some importance though, and could wield financial influence. With an empty house and the sole company of ten soldiers, the mood that evening was dejection. Having bathed but not really enjoying the company or stupidity of the fools he was billeted with, Carausius longed for home and familiarity. He poked at his food with as much enthusiasm, and whilst the others were keen to drink out of the governor's sight, he barely took a sip, until he couldn't take the boredom any longer and drank long and hard on the understanding that no-one would reproach him for having done so in the morning. Manilius had already suspected that weakness would overcome him and tried not to laugh at the ever decreasing wine in the glass flagon just in case it sparked a sudden rash argument from his guest. The only baiting that he told his escort to do would be amongst the bracken of the forest tomorrow when they could all take on chasing a wild boar with hounds, whilst the single indiscretion Carausius was guilty of was of accusing the emperor of abandoning them all, but no-one understood what he meant and so ignored him. Many things were said from many men in ignorance and very soon the sailor would be sailing away with his view of what his own command was and how best to cope with it. Manilius' views of Carausius had changed since their initial meeting at Rutupiae and he was finding him a man stoically resigned to almost fighting the Saxons alone without favour and resentful. With high command came responsibility, not towards the province, because that may not be your homeland of birth, but towards the men who maintained your position and likewise they remained entirely suspicious of every motive. To this end Manilius grew suspicious that Carausius could succumb to any insurrection as he fought with the doubts that were openly plaguing him. Somebody in Gallia had seen the promise of a good soldier there within and somebody who could devise their own strategy to win the war, yet Manilius wasn't a fool either and the endless coastline of Britannia with its vast rivers filling Oceanus, would prove an eventual overwhelming advantage for the Saxons and their allies to utilise, striking at will. Mercifully, at the moment, they couldn't attack in sufficient numbers and the roman shoreline fortress defences from Anderitum to Branodunum stood firm. Behind it however, lay a fear that whilst the seas were full of danger, so too were the ambitions of men who wielded imperial power in defending them from attack. It was only a matter of time before it was all to break down, Rome losing interest in the island and the cost of maintaining it for what? Gone was the prestige of wearing the toga and serving the imperial family. Instead rich men feared the army as much as they needed them and it was this that Manilius suspected Carausius of having dealt in – protectionism for his soul and his soul only. Jupiter and Hercules were not going to secure man's true loyalty and the court scribes of the emperor were not going to sing the praises of men prepared to help themselves either. These were dangerous times in which weak men were required to make sacrifices for their own safety's sake. The ten strong guard escort had secretly derided Carausius and it was with little fear that everybody crawled to their bunks for the night secure in the knowledge that the stranger was only dangerous in his thinking. Even come the morning and armed with a spear he wouldn't be any more dangerous, as he found out that he had few followers there prepared to agree with him.

The morning broke with a red sky but soon gave way to clouds and a light shower of powdery snow. Everybody was about early keen to try their hand at bringing down game and then enjoying the feasting afterwards. The bailiff provided the hunting spears with dogs and had also secured a few more unfamiliar local men who would lay the nets out into which the game would be driven; the land around being ideally suited as it contained many small valleys amongst the trees where they could hide before falling upon their prey. Carausius eagerly anticipated the day as he joined in the small donatives to Diana and Virbius who would both ensure good luck in the hunt, and as he rode off with the others he admired the collective human effort that also would bring the boar down. Everybody knew their place and although may have been at odds the night before all were now united in one cause. Across the soft ground they walked on their horses following the men with the dogs. They went ahead, the beasts straining at their leashes and crying out into the dark vast emptiness of the forest at the slightest scent they found. A shadow quickly moved and a flurry of snow fell from the lowest branches of a tree as the wild creature made its bid to escape and was chased by one of the dogs now unleashed by its keeper. Orders were given not to throw the spears unless directly challenged by the frightful beast, and if possible, all killing was to be done in the nets where high on horseback the human protagonists would be safe from being gored in the leg.

'Stab at them' Manilius reiterated, practicing the move sidewards himself from his saddle.

'Throw your spear and it's lost!' he wisely added.

He had hunted before.

Then with all warning came one of the wild pigs, sweat laden with its labours and turning to challenge the dog snapping at it, before again confidently returning to its forest refuge where it would all too briefly rest. The hunters needed to follow the action quickly for the dog would otherwise attack the boar and try to take it for itself regardless of the danger. Although trained to refrain from doing this, when pressed by an adversary the thought and discipline can leave in a moment's excitement, and although the owner of the estate wasn't there in person to award a trophy for bringing down a magnificent beast there was a lot to be gained from being there first alongside the dog. Carausius dug his heels in and the horse lurched forward. Momentarily his cloak spun across his chest making the use of his throwing arm difficult until after having swapped hands he confidently regained posture and rode on, spear tight in his grip. Before him the sloping ground had exposed a clearing across which a net had been strung and towards that he eagerly rode chasing the dog and pig. A foot follower shouted instructions that reverberated around the wilderness for the dog to cease its attack and this allowed the wild beast to lose concentration and run into the net it hadn't seen. The sudden and abrupt stoppage confused it and its anger mounted considerably as it fought to remove itself from the trap. Men either side quickly leapt out of its way fearful for their lives and pointing for a horseman to come and quickly finish it off. Carausius, spear in one hand and his reins in the other answered their call. He ducked below the branches of the hazel obscuring his view and then, when poised, fell upon the prey stabbing downwards as instructed trying to avoid striking his mount at the same time, which was intent on constantly spinning around itself and away from the danger that it had found itself in.

'Stand still' he shouted at the horse as flecks of blood spun into the snow from the neck of the wounded animal.

A telling death blow had yet to be delivered and until its last breath, the captured beast continued to try and frantically escape. Then with repeated thrusts the iron blade took its toll on the strength of the boar and it fell to its knees. Carausius could feel the softness of the muscles across its back, smell its fear and look upon its hairy skin as he stabbed at it again and again until eventually it had had enough and succumbed. Amongst the peace and the quiet of the bracken in the woods everyone claimed to have heard its last breath being given out. The remainder of the hunting party slowly formed around Carausius and the beast that he had brought down now showering praise upon him for his prowess, whilst into the bracken churned earth of Britannia its life seeped out. The dog wanting its reward lapped at the spoils and snapped at the pig's skin until restrained again being leashed and dragged off. Without reason Carausius looked at the man now busily bent over and slitting its throat, for he had yellow hair, that contrasted with the colours of the forest and his own dark clothing. Briefly they exchanged glances but when help arrived to haul the animal upright and tie it over the nearest convenient tree limb to drain it of its life, the moment was forgotten. It was back to the house the bailiff declared, unless anyone wanted to go on and try their luck. He had the men and another dog ready, yet having witnessed a good fight and then a good death, the others appeared satiated singing hunting songs to Diana for their supper on the way back.

It was into an empty farmyard that the party rode before dismounting for one last look at the boar tied to and straddling a pony's back. A request was made for the tusks to be made into a hunting knife handle and that was granted, although they were offered to Carausius first. He had no objections to seeing them given away and felt comfortable at being the centre of attention for this generous deed. His mood improved further at the bailiff saying that they hadn't seen such a beast for many years and that the kill was godly providence and well deserved. He would make sure that all the men gave to Diana and Virbius in recognition of the day's sport and Carausius, in equal measure, would offer a small piece of the cooked meat for them to enjoy. Manilius was more scathing at this, saying that it could set a dangerous precedent of men expecting a reward for doing what they were paid to do, but in not wanting to spoil the occasion tried diplomatically to reassure everybody that this was an exceptional fight and that the goddess would smile upon them for their continued favour. Warily approaching Carausius he beckoned that they all now retire inside and await the patient call from the kitchen that the boar was ready for eating. However, before climbing the few steps to the main door they were stopped by a woman slowly emerging herself and who was quickly identified by the bailiff as being the lady of the house.

'Soldiers of the garrison of Britannia, and I know you are that from my groom' she said curtly.

'You have arrived here uninvited, you eat from our table and then when it suits, you continue stealing from our land' pointing at the two men struggling to carry the beast behind the house and to the kitchen.

'What gives you the right?' she threw back at them.

The two slaves stood motionless, cowering and slowly lowered the carcass to the ground as if poachers about to be condemned with every gesture of her thin delicate hand.

'We are noble people, this family, under the protection of Rome' she went on, 'for which we pay our taxes and yet that isn't enough! She has to have more and we have to keep on finding more. It matters not how long you were planning to stay here? I want you to go and to go now!' She started to shout wildly.

'My lady, I would choose your words more wisely. Our very being here is protection enough for you and rumour has it that your husband consents to it' said Manilius Albinus.

'We guard the vulnerable by our presence so you are entirely safe.'

'Then who are you?' she demanded to know, descending the steps with her cloak tightly wrapped around her face to ward off the cold.

Both Manilius and Carausius sensed that she knew enough of military affairs to pursue the matter further, yet it was Manilius who continued to bait her with his reasoning. Advancing forward to see his protagonist's hidden features more clearly, he announced himself as the Praefectus Classis of Britannia whilst his colleague was Mausaeus Carausius, newly appointed commander of the northern fleet.

She laughed loudly before condemning Carausius as little more than a sailor who loved the pleasures of the land more now than he did the perils of sailing upon the seas.

'What of bringing the Saxons and Franks to their deaths?' she mocked.

'Were you going to lay in ambush and hide in our woods, hoping that they eventually walked past or were you planning to attack them in their squalid settlements that they call civilisation. As we speak my husband is raising his sails in Gesoriacum to bring valuable trade here but with every ship leaving port there are more pirates falling upon them that you are not killing. Mausaeus, the Menapian! From Germania Inferior I would recognise and are you not more of them than you are of us?' she taunted.

She was well informed. The barb stung Carausius' pride but he knew she was right. The Romans weren't clearing enough of the seas and he had been caught off guard and disarmed by a woman. Meekly he made his excuses for his visit to the island, stating official business, and wouldn't have come to their house had he known the repercussions. As for offering an answer to her complaints, all he could do was say nothing. Her family were one of many that would constantly moan at their treatment and there was little recrimination felt. At this time he didn't know her or her husband and made no promises towards future protection of shipping between Gallia and Britannia. The empire would stand or fall on many dangers, not just from the sea he concluded.

Picking the boar's carcass up, the beast was taken to the kitchen as planned, whereupon the escort party plus officers were reunited with their warm horses and told to leave. Before they did, Carausius had reason to turn to the woman on the step and enquire about her husband's business in Gesoriacum. He was wealthy, she replied; powerful, successful and wouldn't have wanted the army here unless it were an emergency. He wouldn't be frightened of exerting his influence over those who mattered if anything was said about today.

'What is your husband's name?' Carausius asked.

'We may have met.'

'You are to know that I am Faustina; wife of Numerius Septimus Clemens. He is my husband.'

CHAPTER VI

PAY FOR WAR

Preparation for war moved rapidly on with all available boat yards on the coast and slightly inland commandeered for the navy. Tullius had unfairly borne the brunt of his friend's anger and been ordered to bring reinforcements in with which the boat builders could be protected whilst they laboured to increase the numbers of craft in the fleet. The supply of iron and wood also needed to be guarded but as the province of Gallia Belgica slowly recovered from its insurrection there was a growing anger amongst the population that all resources were seen to be given over to this one cause. The army saw it differently and turned the labour of the merchants to its own advantage and then stole their produce from their warehouses to feed its troops as the seas remained closed and the weary spring drew on. The stores, particularly those of Numerius Septimus Clemens, were targeted immediately and when they ran dry Carausius let it be known that all his fleet would be chased if for one moment he thought that he could evade his duties and refuse to provide aid. There would never be a single silver antoninianus handed over by the army for these goods and other merchants would be treated in a similar manner, offered well below the market price. The prospect of a new revolt therefore grew with petitions being openly sent to the emperors but these cases were intercepted and burnt before being given the opportunity of sprouting their lies. Eventually Septimus, as head of the local merchant class had to calm the row and sought out a meeting with his old adversary. Carausius, following a short journey to review the construction of shallower keeled and faster warships on the coast, reluctantly granted him an audience in his military leather tent swaying gently like sails in a southerly wind. The smell of trampled grass on the floor was damp and sweet yet nothing compared to the merchant's fragrance which announced him far off as objectionable to the nose. This served to irk his protector more.

'Please allow me to offer many valuable gifts to Lord Mithras for your continued safety and good fortune Commander' Septimus stated immediately and bowed humbly.

Carausius impassively remained seated and ignoring him turned the wooden model of the scapha around in his hands instead examining at every angle the detail of the ships he was having built.

'Whilst in Britannia I met your wife' he said bluntly, not looking up or giving any acceptance to the man before him.

'Yet she wasn't the same woman as I had met before, and your daughter was missing, if she is your daughter and your son; are you confident that he is still fighting in Germania?'

'Helena Messalina?' asked Septimus.

'She is my daughter, yes – you know that. Did my wife call herself Faustina? My son I pray is still amongst the legions.'

Carausius chose to remain stubbornly silent continuing instead his examination of the model ship in his hands.

'You see these' and he pushed the small craft across the table towards the merchant.

'They are going to require manning and I have it in my mind to requisition from your kind enough sailors to fill the oar benches. You have sailors enough to man your boats and I am sure that the emperors will look upon you favourably for your generous offer. As from today I am therefore taking four hundred of your men.'

'That's impossible' stormed Septimus without bothering to look at the ship and trying desperately hard to get Carausius' attention.

'There aren't enough of them and you know it! On whose authority have you taken this?'

'Mine!' he shouted back.

'Then recruit' added the commander choosing at last to acknowledge his presence.

'I will be ready for launching my fleet in Maius and I will see that there are more sleek warships afloat than the fattened bloated ships that I see struggling across the water now. You appear to have recovered your fortunes whilst others have fared worse. How is that possible?'

'What are you thinking for you will force trade away and the province will become an outcast to lost fortune? What will you say to Lord Maximianus when we declare you an enemy of our freedom to enjoy such wealth and risk? What answer will the army have for having no one left here for them to shear through taxation? Oh, you are a humble man from a poor family with a simple mind! You have learnt nothing from me at all! I have given you your chances and you reward me like this. You fool with your sword!'

Although raised to anger by the insult Carausius remained seated and called his guard in.

'See this man away from here and march him home. I want all his warehouses checked and I want to know the contents of every barrel. Break into the bottom of each one. Finally I want him to pay for recruiting four hundred sailors and when he has done that he is to pay the navy for protecting him upon the sea. I want his silver and I want his gold. Now get him out of here!'

With that Septimus was ejected from the brief meeting whilst Carausius continued to pick at his model.

In the boatyard the rhythmic sound of constant hammering on nail heads marked the stern resolution that the empire had of clearing the seas, and ridding the coastline of danger. The

Franks, solely intent on destruction and robbery were to be dealt a major blow by the new tactics being planned. All seaborne attacks would be repulsed with renewed vigour, partly because of the commander's wish to fulfil his responsibility to his rank, but also to secretly allow him to ascertain the exact amount of wealth being smuggled across the water. He kept it from everyone that whilst an initiate of Mithras and a trusted soldier there had been a sense within him of the weakness of Britannia's defences to cope with bribery and believed sufficient wealth could buy him the power and the influence that he now dangerously craved. He had been born poor yet his mind was brutally active in securing the best of all resources to ensure that he was going to survive above his rivals. Septimus' money would be forcefully collected, the emperors would supply the ships and ultimately he would risk his life in pursuit of it all. Firstly he had to kill the invaders in sufficient numbers or bribe them to fight his wars thus preventing them too from interfering in his plotting. To engage both sides could prove disastrous. Then when the time was right he would make his move for the island, its wealth and then retire there in safety. There was a great deal to do and Carausius felt confident and in cheerful mood as the centurion led him around the nearly completed ship hulks in their temporary berths. Behind him workshops housing smiths worked day and night to provide the thousands of iron nails required, whilst carpenters sized up the deliveries of timber, selecting with a keen eye those that required the least work to forge into a frame. He felt that his ships would quickly be ready praising the workers for their efforts and to allay the fear of imperial suspicion he made out a false report to be sent to Augusta Treverorum detailing his expenditure and planning. Tullius had warned him not to exceed what was expected of him as spies had openly been asking questions of his real character whilst he was away. There may have been doubts as to his promotion yet the empire was in a desperate state having to rely upon its soldiers for survival, even upon the remotest of frontiers where daily thoughts of death mixed easily with thoughts of life. Major decisions made could often only be made in this isolation and fear without recourse to the future of Rome. She had to stand alone. Men of ambition quickly rose and fell in equal measure. The workmen in the boatyards however, although unaware of the strategy being enforced all along the shores of Gallia and Germania Inferior, were keen to prove their worth as Carausius had a favoured reputation for the seas and the safest way of sailing them. They could see themselves, that in the shallow hulls, the fighting would be inshore and not out in the deep currents of the ocean where to fall overboard was to die. They were taught to swim and therefore stood more chance if close to the shore or up river. The recruitment and subsequent training of more marines in camps close by added to their encouragement especially so as day by day they watched them practice boarding a false enemy ship built on the land behind the beaches. Every effort was being made to improve the fortunes of the Romans in their sea war and Carausius as their leader was pleased. His pleasure was not diminished by reports that a large band of Saxons had been captured by the legion operating across Fluvius Rhenus and instead of slaughtering them they were to be put to use. That included coercing them to take up roman arms against their countrymen and especially so in the navy where they would serve as ideal replacements to fill the rowing benches. Their muscles would be cruelly expended on working whilst the Romans fought. Tullius' report put the available numbers at six hundred. The previous strategy had been to offer them peace terms for resettling the less favourable marginal land from which the roman farmers themselves had fled, but with every passing year the rumour was of foreseeing towns and fields flooded where prosperity was becoming a meagre friend. It was into this region they were being forced to go. Orders though were issued, first to separate the recognisable farmers from the warriors. A fighting man wasn't going to waste warm days waiting for a seed to grow and then labour at reaping a harvest. He was going to offer his life at the gods' calling and seek out fortune wherever he discovered it weakly defended. The farmer could scratch at the soil and if there was ever insufficient reward to feed them the following year then that was his god's intention. A blade was better than a plough and if the tribes were successful then somebody else would laboriously turn the land over for them and provide their living. Carausius' excitement grew at wanting these men, dangerous and hungry for power as they were, for they thought like he did and living on the edge of the empire most spoke the language he understood.

A temporary camp was therefore soundly constructed of double ditches and timber into which the combatants were herded, chained and manacled to prevent any escape. Their guards were well aware of the dangers of allowing them close to their boatyards and in small groups they were taken out and their chains nailed above their seats in the benches they would row from. Then, upon a rising tide, the light scaphae would float level with its pontoon and marines wearing blue tunics, chainmail, long swords and blue shields would board to take their places on the decking above the rowers. At the centurion's calling it would then be cast adrift for a short time whilst checks were made on the seaworthiness of the vessel with all its crew aboard. No provisions for water or food were to be made as Carausius' intentions were not of staying at sea but reacting quickly to sightings of enemy sails from his watchtowers. The speed of the craft impressed its roman crew as the Frankish pirates were forcibly beaten to increase their efforts in propelling them forward. On land Tullius' cavalry would follow the action and quickly intervene if the raiders made for the beaches. The system in place had been tested and had been seen to work. All that was now required were a few more weeks of warm weather to enable the remaining supplies to reach the boatyards and not to attract any intervention by the authorities into Carausius' handling of naval affairs. For as much as he could desire it, he daily offered to Jupiter that the skies above Germania would clear and that the massed legionary offensive would move forward. Every hour spent waiting for the attack was an hour that he had to think about defending his forces from the attention of Maximianus, if ever he returned to the northwest with his troops. In allaying these fears he had reports made out to the emperor of his use of the legions and suggested cordial relations with their commanders. The army and the navy he wrote were to be united.

Eventually the weather did improve and with it came a flowering of sails upon the sea. Trade links again blossomed in the longer days as the rivers of Gallia slowly carried their goods towards the coast to be first stored in the warehouses and then loaded onto available ships to be sent to the burgeoning markets of Londinium. The island was rapidly filling with unwanted goods. Traders there had become sufficient in serving their own needs and items were being made in greater and greater numbers in local workshops. Merchants were losing money and Britannia slowly divorcing itself from the empire across the sea. Carausius though was disinterested and watched from his vantage point as a shower of rain patted the surface of a calm swell outside the harbour at Gesoriacum.

'Will we sail today, my Lord?' asked the centurion of the marines.

'Yes' he replied.

'I have confidence that we will see victory. Have patience.'

With that a horse rider galloped along the military road, halted before handing his despatch to the soldier there and waited to receive the reply. The centurion reached up, took it down and read out...

'It's from the fourth watchtower northeast of here. They report sails coming west and we could soon intercept them and force them away if you choose.'

Still the rain came falling from the darkest of clouds landing upon the greenest of surfaces. It shimmered like fabric as a breeze caught it and playfully moved it about creating patterns upon the water. Carausius was pleased and spoke to the messenger himself.

'Return to Tullius Fruscus' he said.

'Tell him that he is not to move from where he is or give the raiders any thought that they have been seen. His horsemen must remain in their forts and signal stations. Now go.'

'Are we to sail when they come into view, my Lord?' asked the marine.

'If so we need to be free of the harbour now or else miss the opportunity. What are your orders?'

'My orders are that you and your men rest and take their food. Scribe, what hour of the day is it?'

'It is the third hour, my Lord Carausius' he replied consulting his tables.

News of the approaching raiding party at sea infiltrated the waiting boats and although the captives were aware that there weren't sufficient numbers to trouble the roman forces or cause them loss, it was the very fact that they were sailing upon the dominance of the roman water that cheered them. Too far way to be heard and too sensible to risk a whipping for insurrection, they remained in good spirits more so as the roman commander had foolishly ordered his sailors to rest and allow the pirates to sail past unchallenged. Mutterings from his own crew accompanied the slow procession of an enemy fleet, four boats in total seen far out on the horizon and travelling easily with the wind. As the rain came and went in its dance Carausius retired to his bunk and waited for two things. The first was the call of the hourly watch; the second was the messenger to arrive from further along the coast in the direction that the ships were heading.

'This darkness will bring my victory, Lord Mithras' he repeated quietly to himself making things temporarily comfortable by wrapping his cloak snugly about him.

Soon he was asleep.

Somewhat later a voice gently prompted him to open his eyes.

'My Lord, wake up, wake up. There is a report from the coast of Fluvius Sequana. The raiders have left and returned to what they think is an empty sea. Our cavalry have only taken note of their numbers and remained hidden but did not attack as you ordered. The Saxons must know that they have sailed past you without notice and now they are confident of making safely home with their treasures. Shall I order the boats to be readied?'

'Yes, good news!' said Carausius slowly standing up straight and feeling all the better for his rest.

'Has the weather improved?'

'No'

'What is the hour?'

'It is close to being the tenth hour.'

'We need to be quick then.'

Ten scaphae pushed out into the current agitating the seas with the rowers, forty to each boat soundly beaten to get them to obediently work harder and escape the land behind them. Their earlier joy at hearing their countrymen crawling past the idle Romans had now turned to fear as they recognised the trap that had been set and that fear was magnified by the realisation that they would see them all killed at their hands. Desperately they tugged at their chains for freedom; rather they would jump overboard and drown than be responsible for this. A whip came down hard on a man's face and split the soft tissue open. Briefly he had to stop toiling before another lash struck in the same place and caused more damage. A wave washed in as the boat lurched with the salt water chaos adding to their woes. It was only the rain dripping from their foreheads that provided the merest comfort as again lash after lash fell upon their unprotected skin and their muscles burnt with pain. How they wanted it to be over and how the bitterness felt towards their roman captors grew. Theft was part of their culture; it was acceptable. Wealth was mobile and now at the hands of Carausius they were being forced to the end and play a part in their countrymen's demise. They would be there when the boats embraced and they would be powerless to aid the stricken craft as the Romans swarmed upon it without mercy killing them all. A shout from the tiller started to guide the boat onto its target and more speed was required. Therefore more lashes rained down from the deck where the marines waited their turn to join battle. Archers were called to the bow and readied themselves in anticipation of being the first to strike a hit. At one hundred paces the alarm horn was blown from the Saxons, who to a man were almost fast asleep on the decks having only left the crew to man her. With a small sail she struggled for speed against the wind and quickly presented a killing for the archers whose arrows now fell from the sky and struck a man in the back. He fell inwards only to be replaced by another who appeared clutching a shield for protection. Another man joined him and another until the war band was massed on the rear of the vessel providing an easy target.

'Kill them' shouted Carausius.

'Kill every one. Get us in closer.'

In the excitement he forgot his own vulnerability and moved along the boat shouting orders. His fleet were to split and each group take on one Saxon vessel. None of them were to be set alight and all men aboard were to be slaughtered. It's not slaves he wanted, so all were to be thrown overboard and their lives given to Neptune. With a crash the two boats locked, oars pulled in followed by another roman vessel coming alongside on the left. Quickly the marines set about their work tossing grappling hooks into the rigging and pulling down the flimsy sail. That done, a corvus was laid across the gap between the two boats and left foot first the soldiers of Rome slowly advanced cutting their way forward and to the heart of the enemy. Down below the men of Germania Inferior had collapsed with exertion waiting for the cries of their allies to cease and for the inevitable death to arrive. It took longer than expected with the foe defending their lives to the last plank and nail. Those wearing mail and falling into the water were instantly lost without hope. Those not and trying desperately to swim to safety were struck down by arrows. Soldiers returned to their posts wiping their weapons clean and vigilantly looking out into the open spaces of Oceanus. There were only the four ships that had been seen from the shore but out there the world appeared larger and as the day drew towards the twelfth hour it was getting dark and cold. Tired men now longed for the safety and security of their fort.

Carausius first ordered his prizes to be securely tied to the scaphae and a small crew was left on board the Saxon boats as they were towed home. Without the aid of the wind the Romans struggled to pull the weight of both ships and again the blame fell upon the heads of the prisoners below. They were soundly beaten again to increase effort and when it came with a spurt, the tow rope tightened, the roman ship lurched forward and its bow unceremoniously smashed into the head of a dead sailor floating face down in the dark green waters. Easily the bow wave pushed him to one side in its wake with the body becoming entangled in the oars until finally being tumbled out. It was a strange field of death where the souls of men would find no rest and one where no earthly spirit had followed the sails. In bitter silent dejection the rowers below solemnly pulled their stolen wealth home.

Once docked, the foreigners were to be herded back into their temporary stockade until the next time and Carausius, happy that they were too physically spent to rise up once back on shore, waited for the last of them to be dragged to his rest. He quickly praised the marines for their fighting abilities and recommended more practice so as to become even better. That didn't win any cheers and neither did he win any praise from the centurions keen to review the enemy warship in its construction and ability to conquer the seas. Once war had been fought to deprive the enemy of his motives but now it was waged solely to take from him. Carausius, aloof from his men through his own stronger greed walked the length of each ship and with the keenest of eyes pointed to the selected canvas bags to be carried ashore and kept.

These he knew contained some of the stolen wealth of Gallia. With sixteen in total and other storage jars full of spices, wine and incense he regarded the day as a victory and looking at the maker's stamp on the large storage vessel being carried past him telling where it originally came from and thus giving clues as to what it possibly held, he didn't recognise the name or the fact that it would ever be returning to him. He owned it now and by using his Saxon captives again and again he had every intention of owning more. Carausius would share the wealth but in a way that could buy him power and as Commander of the fleet he would continue to grow in influence until his humble voice was heard rejoicing above all others. For the time being though, it would be safer not to show his officers anything of the treasure and to keep it hidden away. He was going to require the confidence of a friend and when Tullius returned to the fort with his scouting reports, then and only then would the secrets be shared.

The fortress of Gesoriacum was well built with adequate storage for it had been necessary to defend itself from attack by land and sea. It was also an ideal place to conceal wealth, although a poor one to then dispense it into the wider lands around. The road network connected it with the Northern provinces and provided a quick route to Lugdunum and beyond, bringing trade, imperial news and the legions towards the coast and Britannia. Many years before, it had brought the Romans to face their fears of the strange island of Albion; those fears being crushed by the dismissive appearance of Claudius' freeman Narcissus who cajoled the troops to cross the narrow sea thus leading to the island's eventual and difficult subjugation. To Claudius, the struggle was worth it and the Divine Julius right in his estimation that the island was rich in metals, although not easily won. Through Carausius' moist hands that same urgent need for monetary conquest surged as he opened the few pearls of stolen wealth he had garnished from the citizens of Lugdunensis. Slowly and carefully tipping open the neck of a bag onto the softness of another he caressed the falling cold silver coinage into the warmth counting it approximately as it fell. There wasn't going to be nearly enough and he cursed the owner for his providence in having probably buried the rest. Carausius had fought the war against the Bagaudae so that stability would return, yet richer men were still continuing to conceal their wealth and a closer inspection of the coins revealed to his dismay that most of them were crude local forgeries or washed with silver over bronze. His anger rose at what he could trade with these and where was the remaining good silver hiding? The answers evaded him as much as the true ownership of these had. Throwing the worthless coins to the floor attracted the attention of the guard outside, who after being reassured that all was well, went back to his duties of keeping others away. Carausius opened another sack emptying its contents into the lamplight where they reflected a burning softness of gold. He had found better fortune and with clutching fingers turned the objects eagerly about in his hands admiring their beauty before the stark coldness of the fort's imperial stone altar immobile and resplendent of military worship in the strong room. There were silvered brooches still clinging to pieces of cloth that had been ripped from the owner's chest and still alive to the very spirit of that person. They seemed ominously dangerous and cursed and Carausius was quick in putting them back into the security of their pouch. What else was there? Reaching in, he recognised the thin expanse of a platter and snatched it out. It too was made of beaten silver and was beautiful. Around its rim danced a zodiac of animals whilst in the centre, Bacchus frolicked with the muses. It yearned to be held and to be displayed as a means of glorifying man's undying conquest over the savages he fought so hard to civilise. Was there another? His hand went back in fumbling through the objects left untouched by his grasping nature – he could feel samian ware bowls and beakers, golden finger rings with jewels or intaglios, bronze bowls and large fibula brooches. He felt the clammy cold flesh of a decapitated hand. The Saxons, in their interruption of a family's life had brutally taken everything. The metals could be melted down or traded, the ceramic tableware used but there wasn't another plate so he tied the bag up and quickly looked at the others which contained all the everyday objects stolen from the house. They appeared to have come from a small single villa. Larger ones existed but they were sensibly further inland and away from the dangers on the coast. Somehow the raiders would need to be allowed access to them before Carausius could intercept their party in the way that he had this one. Slipping on a stolen gold finger ring bearing the winged figure of Victory in relief and admiring it, he closed his haul in its bag and tied it confident of knowing the answer. Saxons would betray Saxons in greater numbers and the Romans would wisely control it all, everything.

With all light of day extinguished, Carausius emerged from his cave-like treasure house and into the fort's central courtyard. Flaming torches in their brackets danced in the night breeze and the sound of regular hobnailed footsteps accompanied the cloaked and speared shadows patrolling the wall. Around him in the dark and without suspicion his men were relaxing by eating their food and acknowledged him warmly as he passed. The day had proved a success for everybody was confident in their leader's military skill and luck but no one believed that the enemy would fall into another trap like the one set today. The captured pirate boats would be missed but the sea mysterious and unforgiving could have taken them despite the calmness of the skies above. The next raiding party sent out would have to be larger and the next after that even larger if they were to return at all or fall prey to the all conquering Roman fleet. The weakest targets had all been plundered and as the cold smoke from them fought to rise any higher, the challenge was now to stand and fight as soldiers against Rome or remain as thieves upon the sea. From their safe refuge in the swamps of Germania Magna and all along its coastline, Saxon revenge in time would strike washing the decay away and again the endless mobility of the seas would play its part in this victory. However, for as long as Mausaeus Carausius held power over the waters of Britannia then the war would be fought as he saw fit and the rewards of such a war distributed in the same way. To him were due the praises of the gods, but in a now fragmented army where response to any foreign threat was suddenly to oppose and immediately counteract it, a more lucrative opening was becoming clearly visible. The Menapian sailor was about to assume the trappings of wealth but in not willing to act or be implicated alone he waited for the safe return of Tullius Fruscus from his patrol. This came the next day with the distant and faint sound of cavalry horns upon the wind and the slow opening of the fort's large gate through which an orderly procession of men passed bearing shields of white and green clutched in their left hands, whilst their long narrow swords idly hung across their left shoulders. Carausius, looking down from the dais of his stone built Headquarters waited as they dismounted by swinging their legs over their saddles. He then called for Tullius to climb the few steps up to his friend. In the yard below horses held by grooms milled about until individually led away to their stables. Tullius shouted orders to the Decurion above the noise that the standards were to be taken to the strong room and that there wouldn't be any inspections tonight. Foot soldiers, keen for any news of anything worth knowing gathered from their barracks to hear talk from further along the coast but with little worth hearing they were soon instructed to clear the way for tired soldiers wanting to rest. In small groups the procession broke up, and as the last rider entered the safety of the fort the gates swung shut behind him to the sight of the sun rays now setting across the sea.

'Commander' Tullius quickly said acknowledging the fleeting moment.

'Look; Cautopates heralds our victorious journey and grants us light enough to see' and pointed to the sky.

'Tullius: my friend. You recognise the sign.' Carausius replied and gripped him warmly before ushering him inside his room to hear the campaign details.

'We shall unselfishly offer our thanks to Lord Mithras and Cautopates on the morning of Veneris, your fate willing. In the meantime we must continue our faith that they serve to protect and guide us and that we too shall be loyal in return.'

With that said he beckoned a waiting slave to take the cloak of his friend and to bring forward warm food to the table.

'We can eat more after I have heard your report' he added, graciously pushing a bowl of warm pork out for them to share accompanied by a little sweet wine.

'You saw four boats?' he asked.

'Yes' said Tullius.

'They appeared to know where to make their landfall instead of having to drift on the waters looking for a lone victim.'

'This is how I want them to be. It appears obvious that there are spies amongst us on the coast that are identifying the undefended villas and these men are responsible for passing messages back to the invaders. I require them to be left alone if you discover any or at the very least I want to capture them without any killing. These are my reasons...' and he went on to describe how fooling the enemy had worked yet the next time it may not.

They wouldn't be so easily tricked and possibly would arrive in greater numbers.

'But we can counteract them' Tullius answered, detailing all the signal stations that were linked along the coast.

'I also have many cavalry units and in time there will be more. If we still cannot manage then there are the legions on Fluvius Rhenus that will come to you. Why are you in support of their treachery?'

The answer was simple and brief. Carausius, bringing out a parchment scroll of the seas that he had been given command of, pointed to the defensive advantages that the Romans had in their fleet. They had the greater numbers, the greater harbours and the organisational authority to counteract any threat.

'We could wage war on these boats as they pass and yet win nothing at all in return' he explained.

'How will that serve to profit us?'

'We are not here to profit. We are here to fight, win and clear the seas. That is what is expected of us?'

'Tullius, listen. Would you rather give to Neptune an empty burning ship of nothing or capture a laden one, fat with treasure for yourself? How will sinking hollow ships be of use to you? It cannot be! Therefore I am going to plunder their shipping for what is truthfully ours, but to do that they have to be allowed to attack the province and to think that they can get away with it. From this day it is going to be your strict duty not to confront them or ask the army for more cavalry units. We are going to work quietly together in bringing these pirates to their knees in submission. Their arrogance will be to provoke us and then to suppose that they can evade capture. You have seen with your own eyes that I have proven the worth of light boats close to the shore in being able to chase them, and if that ever failed then I will command the Classis Britannica to supply Liburna in order to block off their outmanoeuvring us by sailing further out into deeper waters. What they have stolen is going to be our reward. Are you in agreement or not?'

Tullius wasn't entirely sure. Another offer therefore quickly came his way and without any prompting either.

'I was contemplating your own promotion' said Carausius.

'You can form your own militia in your own manner and I will agree with it all, everything. I will find the money for extra soldiers giving you responsibility for patrolling the entire Northern coast and increased pay for doing so. How do you feel, my friend? Is it a good offer and one not made by Maximianus or his advisors?'

'My Lord' urgently responded Tullius speaking quietly and moving closer to his ally.

'Are you not conscious of what you are saying? What about the agents here waiting patiently for news of our plotting this very evening? What about Augustus Maxiamanus? You do not have any of these powers over me, any of them! Let us forget about this conversation please and trouble our ambitions no more.'

Excusing himself he then tried to make for the door before hearing news that could have implicated himself in the plot. Carausius barred his way and ordered him to sit down. He then easily reeled off the names of five men known to both of them in the fort plus a few others unknown to Tullius. These men were the spies of Rome; the poison fluid of the army and now they were dead he reassured him. The time of day momentarily stood still as Tullius took a frightened drink from his cup after which Carausius ordered the door to be opened and for the Centurion outside to come in and then lock it. In his arms he clutched a leather bag and at his leader's prompting opened it thus allowing the contents to fall gently upon the table. There in front of Tullius was his future pay, his reward, the loyalty for agreeing to join the plot. In case he needed any further reminding the Centurion, without warning, quickly withdrew his sword and forced it to the cavalryman's neck. Tullius recoiled staring directly at Carausius and pleading for sense to return.

'Your men will not allow this. You are making a mistake. Release me before it's too late!'

Having first replaced his sword slowly in its scabbard, the officer did as Tullius wanted and with Carausius' permission he returned to blocking the way. Carausius leant against a wall, hands folded behind the neat woollen red tunic on his back.

'Look out of the window, Tullius' he invitingly said.

'Are they your men, those lining up to plunder a share of something from these bags? If so, you had better be quick in deciding about sharing with them before it all goes, because your men will certainly forget who you were or what you ever did for them. I am going to grant you time to think. Then I want you to give me your answer' at which both men turned to leave the room, the centurion guarding the clunk of the key in its lock.

Once outside, Tullius had one more question left to ask through the door.

'Why are you doing this? He pleaded.

'Is it not enough to fight for Rome instead of against her? Look at the failures, the dead and the damned. Are you the same?'

'Rome' carefully spoke Carausius, looking along the corridor and with his back turned to his friend. 'We both know that I've never been there' and he turned about.

'Yet all she does is sow chaos everywhere and what I am doing is taking the opportunity of restoring the lost order.' His voice was direct and clear.

'The emperor will thank me eternally for my efforts I'm certain, so I am in his pay to make the decisions here.' He laughed and before ensuring the room had been locked securely upon his friend the prophecy of Helenea Messalina came back but quickly faded.

'Think about it Tullius' he said confidently and the knife in his conscience turned.

'You are not making me emperor and I am only doing the work that they would be doing themselves. Help me and therefore learn to help yourself. I don't want to be mourning the sad passing of my friend.'

He then quickly walked away and was urgently directed by his staff to the acclaim of the assembled garrison there, silently at first but then with raised voices saluting him even from the rampart in a way unexpected...

'IMPERATOR, IMPERATOR, IMPERATOR' they shouted before Carausius unthinkingly returned with the Roman salute.

'Citizens and soldiers' he shouted before allowing them to fall quiet.

'I offer thanks in gratitude' and he looked eagerly into their faces.

'The rewards for your loyalty are here to be seen yet you have endangered me. There can be more, so much more for us but if anybody knows a man unwilling to join then that man is now free to escape with his life. Today my rewards are pieces of stolen treasure – tomorrow my gift to you will be the barbarian Saxons and their allies, the Franks. Who is to join me in the fight?' At which the chainmail clad mass erupted.

Both far away in the Saxon stockade and even closer in Tullius' room the speech hadn't been fully received therefore it lacked meaning, but for both it could spell their death, as the noisy acclamations continued to rise in the increasing darkness of approaching night. The Saxons would answer for themselves in this open declaration from the Romans of vengeful war, but Tullius Fruscus had but a few hours only in which to decide his fate and time was running out.

The warm moist smell of early morning baked bread had already drifted into the stale prison room air when there was a tug at the door. The guards, polite to a cavalry officer called him out, and Tullius was taken to Carausius' quarters where the commander of the seas was eagerly consuming the warm broken loaf with honey and a few hard boiled eggs. Outside, the day was warming up and the waters calm; it was ideal sailing weather with Aelous playing in the clouds far to the west. The quay too was busy with activity and already three merchant ships had set out for Londinium, although it was unsure as to whether their cargoes would be unloaded to be sold. Numerius Septimus Clemens, despite his loathing of his former employee continued to struggle against the hostilities he was stoically facing but hadn't yet encountered any rumour of Carausius' plans for the sea. In trying to keep a profit and ultimately his respect, he was too busy evading the men sent around to look inside his store houses to worry about the wars. He had chosen to ignore them as best he could but like all sane businessmen he had something hidden away for the troubled times that he knew would eventually return even after this latest purge. Occasional letters sent by his only son warned him of the constant dangers the army were facing although they were often scant in their detail and the papyrus roll too suspiciously clean to have seen miles of dubious travel but nevertheless Septimus didn't have thought to question their legitimacy. He didn't think too often of his mistress Faustina either or whether or not she was dead. Instead he continued his loyal service to the Lord Mithras and paid his dues. Tullius on the other hand, unsure as to how to address Carausius, stood to attention as his guardian finished eating, crumbs of soft bread hanging in his beard. He wiped them away, licked his fingers of warm honey and looked with all seriousness at his friend.

'I will agree with you' Tullius said without allowing anybody else the first word.

'I accept that I have little option and we have known each other a while and borne the same perils whilst winning through victoriously. Naturally I must fear the cruel vengeance of Maximianus yet he is not here to protect me – my lord you are, and therefore I will serve your cause.'

His sentiment had been too rehearsed and the unbroken silence that accompanied it from the other side of the table was ominous.

'It would have been easier for me had you disagreed' said Carausius tapping the table slowly with a finger.

'Then I could have put you to death without further suspicion. Your loyalty is now in question as to my dealing with the problem that I must face, and yet I need you. Your horses are a large part in my planning and without them I cannot secure the communications that I require. Therefore...' and he spoke a little quieter.

'This is what I am going to do, friend. I am going to watch you day and night. I am going to have you followed and your military decisions reviewed. Those orders you make without me being there will be examined and every message that you have sent, will be read. You will be acting for me without me being there and you will respond likewise. No decisions of mine will be questioned and your judgement shall count for nothing. In this way your life will be spared. Tanicius!' he shouted.

'Come in here now' at which a large man entered.

He was wearing a square mail shirt of armour over his chest, skilfully embossed with the bust of Mars.

'Return the Magister Equitum to his duties and allocate these men to accompany him' whereupon he handed over a tablet of names of those he could trust.

'Send in my personal clerk as you go.'

As they turned to leave Carausius added...

'Tullius. Farewell. Mark carefully my thoughts and obey me or else.'

The clerk, a small man who had been wounded in active service, bowed as he approached the taller figure. Framed against the morning light Carausius looked upon him and called him to the window where the glow was pure and unsullied. His instructions were simple. His master was going to visit Vectis where he had thought it safer basing his naval operation in Britannia. The island would serve as a convenient location for the fleet in the Autumnal months to come where there was adequate protection from raiders and where they could reinforce themselves and rebuild. The shore forts of Manilius Albinus would protect and guard the east; Carausius and his ships the west. Therefore there were orders for the commanders he was leaving behind and these orders had to be followed by everyone in his absence. Maps were laid out, inventories of shipping and crews made, weapon stocks, food, horses, men all counted. Battle plans recorded, the most worthy methods of fighting the Saxons written down, coded signals to be sent along the coast in event of attack and more importantly, a chain of command established.

'I don't want to leave with the fight half done' he said.

'Therefore I cannot afford to be away for long. You and you only are in my confidence: Vectis will be an ideal base for me to guard the seas where I will be looking to enjoy my time as my growing years wear on. The merchants and the rich, although they don't realise it, will be providing my comfortable life amongst them whilst I offer them protection' at which he allowed himself a rare smile.

'Now' he continued, picking up a small bronze tablet tied together securely and sealed in wax which he handed over to his scribe.

'Between these pages is engraved a single word. To anybody else who may find it and read it without knowing its significance, the word has no particular meaning. I want you to keep this sealed and in the moment of danger whilst I am away you will despatch it to me with a messenger travelling with all speed. If the navy revolts or Tullius turns a traitor then I am to know immediately. Even if the Saxon host is too troublesome, I am to be told. Now take it and secure it well' at which he passed over the small gift of enormous significance.

Doing as he was told, the scribe and Carausius then went back to the military planning that was in hand.

The months of Iulius and Augustus were good ones, rich in profit. Squadrons of roman ships had done what they were trained to do and losses were negligible. To the Saxon foe the losses were high and in places they had started to negotiate with the Romans, offering to fight for them in return for a share. Their ships and treasure were all missing and the crews of the enemy warships increasingly manned by the captured slaves whilst their decreasing wealth poured into Carausius' hands. He could use it and felt that it was safe now to leave Gesoriacum and travel across Oceanus to seek out a new base where reports from Britannia had led him to believe that the island of Vectis was the most secure of naval fortresses. There were villas there that could be bought with his personal fortune and on a day full of cloud and squally rain he set his sails leaving Gallia behind. Through his mind raced the thought that he too was a thief and that what he was doing was unsanctioned yet the excitement and secrecy ruled this out. He was successful, powerful and was making decisions that would affect other men. In the gentle rocking motion of the waves and the white wake, he recalled where he had started out from and his rise to prominence. Congratulations were going to come now from the grateful Britons in the form of their giving. His journey was to chart a familiar course through time itself and nearly a day and a half later he disembarked with his marines upon the pebble beach of the island where he gave early thanks for his safe arrival. He was approached by a farmhand from the nearest villa who initially would have run away had he not seen the roman pennant flying from the mast of the ship at anchor reassuring him that they were not pirates. To summon help would have meant lighting a beacon and alerting the tiny garrison to the danger so having met Carausius he was hastily bundled forward into leading the way. The path from the beach quickly led inland to a flat expanse of good land where there had been built a three sided house consisting of what looked like a main comfortable dwelling, a simple farmhouse and a store for the villa's produce. Carausius admired its excellent view of the blue waters to the south and to the north it was secured from the land by a shallow expanse of sea. To the east and west there were views of the rising wooded hills of Britannia, some golden with their harvests and lit by the rays of Sol Invictus. He regarded highly the strength of the building and its workmanship with its limestone walls and clay tiled roof leaning into the gentle afternoon breeze that had swooped in from the coast. Stones supported wattle and daub plastered walling and the house spoke of wealth with its strong oak door and iron lock. Rough glass windows without their shutters closed indicated that the house was currently occupied. The labourer was pushed forward to open the door at which the Romans swarmed through quickly securing the house with its surprised occupants prevented from escaping.

'Who are you? How dare you enter like this' the furious owner spoke, rising from his wooden couch and pulling his tunic down across his loins.

Below him a slave girl turned red with embarrassment and tried to cover her breasts.

'Weren't you the one about to enter' pointed out Carausius who then went on to announce himself properly as naval commander of the Northern fleet.

The occupant apologised for not knowing who he was and directed the girl to stand in the corner until this matter was resolved.

'And do you normally announce yourself in this manner? You could have been a Saxon.'

'No' said Carausius unsure of how one did announce themselves under these circumstances.

'What do you want with my house?'

'Are you the owner?' he replied looking about the room they had unceremoniously gathered in and taking stock of the painted plaster walls depicting idyllic scenes of peacocks and flowers. For a soldier only accustomed to the masculinity of a fortress wall it spoke loudly of comfort and privilege and he wanted it.

'No. I pay rent to the Procurator of Britannia Superior. My name is Clodius Frugi.'

'Well, Clodius Frugi, I rent it now and you will be moving out with immediate effect. Have you any ships or transport to the mainland? I want you gone but leave the girl behind. OUT!' shouted Carausius and the half dressed previous occupant quickly fled to the laughter of the marines.

'Follow him' and he pointed to a couple of soldiers to do the task.

'Make sure his family also go with him and if needs be find them a boat. Also find yourself some horses and ride about the island before dark. I want to know what the garrison is. The rest of you make yourselves comfortable in the slave's quarters and prepare some food.'

'Wait...before he goes, bring him here. I have a question' at which the hapless evictee was dragged back. With a glass in hand of the recently poured sweet red wine Carausius stood with his head bowed staring at the floor.

'This mosaic panel' he asked as if knowledgeable of such things.

'What's the meaning of it?' Indicating where he was staring with a hobnailed boot.

Clodius, unsurprised at the ignorance of the uninvited military elite replied.

'It could be Gallus, the cock headed man. Palladius, who suffered banishment from Antioch saw Gallus as such a person and here in exile he could express his freedom to say so.'

With the explanation over and with the slave girl tightly clutched in his grasp at the end of a long day, the newly appointed tenant of the villa saw to it that the previous one was soundly evicted. Jeering accompanied the family dropping their clothes as they hastily loaded a cart and headed away from the farm that had, until very recently, been their home. However it wasn't to be too long before the new owner felt that he would have to move himself as well for in all the commotion that had gone on not one person had seen the sails slowly approaching from the south east or thought that it could be anything but another warship heading for Portus Ardaoni, except in the receding waters of the evening tide it had securely grounded itself and men were rapidly falling out of it. Carausius, walking slowly back to his new domain having seen Clodius Frugi off, stood to admire the farm in all its simple beauty. Taking it had been easy and keeping it would be easier once he had a fleet properly stationed in the sheltered waters around. It was the perfect location to have found, yet a man frantically calling out his name and running from the direction of the beach was to change everything.

'Commander!' he continued shouting as he reached him. The word he spoke almost out of living breath was that bound in the bronze tablet of the scribe.

'You have to return.'

CHAPTER VII
BRITANNIA

The turbulent confluence of two rivers clashed at Mogontiacum where the unpredictable yet impressive Fluvius Rhenus was swollen by the smaller Fluvius Menus. Beneath the bridge much roman blood had been spilt in the constant ebbing and flowing of the Limes Germanicus, an earthwork designed to protect the crossing of the river along its perilous course and where no watercourses existed between this fortress and Castra Regina the Romans feared the incursion of Alemannic hordes being able to seize Italia by her neck. A strike at their heartlands was therefore a military necessity and to be executed in the same manner as had been previously adopted. Caesar Diocletianus, already manoeuvring his armies to attack through Raetia, was adamant that all life resisting was to burn and that the barbarian masses were pushed further eastwards and away from the frontier. In avoiding the wicked currents of the river and the wide banks of their now joint course all therefore appeared to be peaceful with life in the roman town struggling on despite recent deprivations and the fear that the enemy still held in their minds. Renewed conquest was unavoidable and the faithful legions III Italica, I Minerva and XXII Primigenia being selected to undertake the onerous task plus thousands of mounted cavalry in support. With the war horns long sounded and the forests now empty of immediate gathering danger, the crunch of roman boots came stepping from their roads and into the foreign lands beyond. Whispering voices however were suddenly of the emperor's bodyguard having returned early from their campaign. Maximianus couldn't have achieved a complete victory in those troubling warm months of summer following the one thousandth and thirty ninth year of Rome's succession and so rumours quickly spread of the fallibility of roman arms in again being able to crush their foe. The province of Gallia was lately at peace following the defeat of the Bagaudae, and Oceanus under the command of Mausaeus Carausius, now swarmed with roman ships capturing the tall, straw haired men from Barbaricum. That strong sense of security which often accompanied the presence of the emperor, along with his court of advisers, rapidly disappeared as citizens spoke openly of another calamitous war and talk was rife of dispirited soldiers wandering aimlessly through the wild forests of Germania in terrified search of the remnants of their army. Maximianus, aware that two other emperors had been executed in Mogontiacum by their rebellious troops was also mindful of these rumours and as he judged his immediate future he ordered reports to be spread that would crush the notion that it was a defeat that had brought him home prematurely. He would soon be back at the head of the legions but first he needed to consult with his court, the trusted bureaucracy that travelled everywhere with him and now divorced from the archaic Senate at Rome far, far away to the south. What news that his advisors had solemnly greeted him with on the march wasn't what he had expected to hear, but it demanded his immediate response, and as the river currents below the fortress continued to carry with them in their discoloured waters the spirits of the roman dead, Maximianus was angry that more would soon have to join them.

Within the hidden sacred confines of his palace the choice of which campaign to follow was stark and in response two messengers were dispatched; one to reach Caesar Diocletianus with his army in the field, the other more urgently to contact Julius Magnus Aurelius, legate of Legio XXX Ulpia Victrix hopefully still with his garrison at Colonia Ulpia Traiana. His orders were brief and straightforward: With as many men as he could spare he was to abandon any thoughts of reinforcing and supporting his western emperor fighting east of him and was to immediately seek to detain or kill Mausaeus Carausius, who it was now widely reported had been seduced by his powers and was becoming a treacherous foe and a danger to the seas. To have the province of Britannia isolated with her three legion garrisons to the north was a threat no commander could ignore and therefore the court of Maximianus had chosen the only option of brutal extermination. Within the speed of the river's erratic current and a horse's lungs all hopes lay. For Augustus Maximianus, pacing the lonely corridors of his office, the dripping water clock ran as slowly as the river before him had done throughout the Spring. He couldn't choose to abandon the war now as it would expose Diocletianus to the danger of being ambushed and neither could he retreat as this would give the enemy heart to pursue them back to the frontier where the army would doubtless lose their faith in his ability to lead and quickly find another prepared to do so. Fury raged through his every reasoning at the trust placed in one man. It had never worked before, why would it do so now? Where were the controls and the structures to prevent such an occurrence? The answers were predicable...they were there with the emperor himself and whilst he was fighting for his own right of accession other claimants were now seizing their chance. Rough, illiterate men born and raised of the army were bribing the legions instead of the senators doing so and winning through. The only language that they understood was of roman soldier preparing to stand sword to sword against roman soldier and on roman soil as well. It was all a waste of scarce resources yet to give up and not go on wasn't possible. There was no alternative. The war in Germania would have to continue in the knowledge that another threat was growing unabated in the rear and as soon as possible the legions would have to march north and at great speed. A third messenger was therefore despatched, this time to the headquarters of the Classis Germanica. A ship was to be readied at the earliest moment in time and sent across to Britannia to forewarn the governor and his legates of the unseen growing threat. They were to take all necessary steps to prevent the commander of the northern fleet organising resistance against the emperor in person and if Carausius fell into their hands then they were to condemn him and seize his forces. Maximianus called his senior commanders to him. He urgently required a plan of combat in Germania that would enable a swift conclusion to the war and when confronted by an officer forwarding the idea of peace treaties with hostile tribes he had him taken outside and beheaded. If three legions weren't enough then more would have to be raised and if that didn't provide a solution then tribal allegiances would be forged in return for grants of now deserted buffer lands where they could die instead of roman soldiers. Carausius, at all cost had to be brought to justice and as Maximianus dismissed his council of war he could only hate the simple audacity of the man in being able to knowingly alter his policy. To have received the news that the traitor had been washed up dead upon the shores was all he wanted before receiving the equally dangerous news that Diocletianus was heading towards him with his army. In great haste, scribes composing their coded messages were as valuable as soldiers sharpening their swords, and Maximianus more anxious than most to see their waxed scrolls leaving Mogontiacum at all hours of the day. Until a reply was forthcoming and the motives behind Carausius' success in the waters of Oceanus were made clear, it was to be a game of waiting; either waiting to attack in Germania or waiting to be attacked from Gallia. The sole emperor of the west looking at the crowded streets far below his room and in god like isolation could only guess at who it was that would deliver his death blow and began the sequence of mistrust by slamming the door shut upon his court. Far way to the north another man in need of no such guidance urgently began preparing for his growing popularity whilst between them both the bitter reminiscent sound of war horns reverberated in the wind.

The unelected council of war had already met in Gesoriacum prior to Carausius' ship tying up and before he himself, had disembarked. There they had had the suspected culprits rounded up for having passed on information to Maximianus, including the obvious Tullius Fruscus who pleaded his innocence vociferously. He, it was claimed, had more to lose than gain and if condemned as a traitor then why hadn't he already fled to the other side. Up to now that had saved him yet hadn't prevented the swift executions of those closely associated and thought guilty enough of having implicated the commander of the fleet with theft. All acolytes of the Mithraic temple also feared for their lives as the purge looked set to continue and examples made of the rich for their misguidance in not recognising who it was that was actually protecting them. Powerless to intervene, the Persian god of Light watched from his stone egg as his sacred temple was desecrated and robbed of its worshipers and their lives. To most, the worst of times were predicted to return and the name of Mausaeus Carausius one to quickly hate.

'Where is it? Give me the report' Carausius said whilst striding through the fortresses gate.

'Have you discovered who ran to Augustus Maximianus? It's too late to do anything now but I still want his family caught. My plans have been revealed but is an army going to be sent against me? There aren't the men and I doubt it!'

He stopped walking and appeared confident whilst hastily reading the message captured by one of Tullius' patrols and deciphered. Arrogantly turning the page over to see if any more had been written on the other side he laughed at the rhetoric…pirate, rebel and thief.

'Their words cannot inflict a scratch upon me at that distance whilst I protect them from the Saxons and this is how they repay me by demanding my immediate death? Let this serve as a lesson to one and all…' and he turned to sternly address them, his loyal followers gathering to hear the solution to his lone folly.

'If any man desires that his life is cut short in the pursuit of glory then he will have followed me there. You are now implicated in my death by your presence here and if I thought that I could see the face of my assassin before me then I would call him out.'

A drop of saliva fell into his beard, his blue eyes creased a little more and with a raised voice he continued the threats.

'It's useless trying to proclaim your innocence, so stand with me and fight. Together we can resist them both whilst we have control of the seas and they will know that. Soldiers cannot float! We are safe within the timeless beating of the waves and I shall endeavour to see that more of Maximianus' soldiers come over to me from their fortresses inland, so stop the killing of the innocent rich here as I will need their support and their guidance in building anew from the revolt of the Bagaudae. We shall create our own legions, our own navy and our own lands!'

Only this time his speech wasn't met by wide acclaim or applause. Instead, soldiers dispersed to go about their duties but when out of earshot began whispering amongst themselves about their fears of repercussion. Some were for instantly fleeing to Maximianus before the stealing became an insurrection and no mercy was offered to them. Others were all for the adventure and if it ended badly for Carausius then they could simply melt away as deserters. If they were condemned to die by another man's actions then it made sense to take whatever they could before the end came and ignoring his threats they went back to quietly looting the innocent along with the dealing of their kind of justice. Those actions hadn't gone unnoticed and rumours again spread in the towns of an open revolt. Carausius was taking his share and now his men were for taking theirs. It was a rapidly deteriorating situation that was to bring Numerius Septimus Clemens once more to the secure hideaway of the fugitive rebel. Dressed against the cold winds blowing from the north and fresh off the surface of the sea he approached the guards on duty at the main gate and revealed his identity, up till then well hidden within the oily fleece of a stout cloak clasped to his face.

'You know me' he said, pulling the heavy cloth to one side, now looking older and speaking slower in a tired slur.

'We may do; filthy creature. What do you want, for the orders are to admit nobody?'

'I request an audience with the commander, Mausaeus Carausius. I have important messages for him' at which he discreetly brought out a couple of weighty silver coins and handed them to the first of the soldiers.

He looked at them, turning them about in his hand before passing them to the other guard who likewise fumbled them around in his.

'There are two of us...' and more reliable coinage appeared.

'Stay there and don't move' said one of them before slipping under the arch of the gate.

The other soldier went back to leaning on his shield trying hard himself to keep out of the wind that buffeted the heights above the harbour below. No words were exchanged. After a considerable time the first soldier reappeared and ordered that the gate be briefly opened, through which he led the merchant, growing tired and already numbly cold. The barracks inside were alive to the sound of preparations for war and through open windows Septimus could clearly see the evidence of such as blacksmiths hammered upon orange iron to forge new weapons. In noticing his interest the guard pushed him hard in the back telling him to keep his eyes to himself. There was nothing for him to see. Furthermore, there wouldn't be any questions answered either and at the locked door of Carausius, he was handed over. A tall well built man in his early youth now took charge and hammered hard on the wooden panels, so hard in fact that his chainmail armour reverberated with the demand that it be opened at once. The sound of a latch dropping and the spoken password led to an open door through which Septimus was pushed. There inside Carausius sat at the head of his table with his most trusted advisers.

'Well, we have Numerius Septimus Clemens...' and he taunted him without rising.

'Have you willingly come to hand yourself over as a traitor before being condemned? Search him!' and one of the men abruptly took charge looking for evidence of a concealed knife, but there wasn't one.

In disappointment he pulled the merchant's left arm tightly behind his back forcing him to collapse face down upon the table where he could no longer see his assailants. A few moments later Carausius rose from his chair pacing around in thought before ordering that the man be released. Struggling for air Septimus tried to regain his composure and staggered briefly to remain upright where his former friend faced him.

'I began to wonder how long it would take you to find the courage to admit your crime. Is it your daughter's seedy reputation, is it the money that I have taken from you to build the fleet up or is that my faith is stronger than yours in both our fortunes to come? Are you jealous of me? If there was any man alive here in Gesoriacum who would have reason to see my capture then it would be you' at which he punched him hard in the side of the head.

In falling to the ground, Septimus failed to get up expecting another blow to quickly follow.

'Stand him up!' ordered Carausius, 'and to think that I was once controlled by you. Now what do you want before I hang you for your stupidity in being here?'

His table of colleagues remained seated, watching the event.

'Noble Lord' Septimus spat out of a bloody mouth and his head throbbing.

'I have no loyalty to the emperor. My loyalty is to my god alone and the protection he offers which even now I begin to doubt. You and you alone have seen my farms burnt to the ground, my wealth stolen and those that I love dispersed throughout the land. Oceanus has vowed to swallow my trade and storms flood the harbours where my old buildings fall into ruins beneath the waves. Am I to run to Augusta Treverorum? What can be done there that Lord Mithras alone cannot do and will the emperor repair the damage? Will his army march here to provide for my security and give me sanctity that I may live in peace? That is in question: Therefore I come to you willingly from all peaceful men to seek a truce between us. I speak for them all in saying that we are prepared to finance you, if it is that which you require, and in return you agree to leave us alone; you and your men. In this way there can be trust again' and with that said and bowing low he once more appealed for clemency and an end to the fighting.

'Only the army can save us, Septimus. Remember that. Pay them well and they look after our security but fail to pay them at all and they will take twice as much from you!' Carausius warned.

'If you are keen to help as you say then my scribe will take you to where you can dictate the names of the wealthy I expect to donate to this new peace. I shall establish the town where taxes can be rendered and these will fund the army against Maximianus, if and when he chooses to fight us. Now lead him away and make sure that he is not making a fool of himself!'

With that said the door was unbolted and without having learnt anything of the impending rumours of Augustus Maximianus far away, Numerius Septimus Clemens was bundled out leaving the leaders of the rebellion behind to discuss amongst themselves the dangers they yet had to face.

Carausius who was glad to see the back of the merchant cursed him openly drawing a favourable response from his allies. They too had had their share of trying to placate the wealthier towns into remaining faithful towards the army whilst they continued to openly rob and steal from them. Without an appointed financial procurator no recording of goods was being kept and people were again reverting to silently burying their wealth in the deep soil. Against strict orders this had been forbidden, yet it continued. Less and less would be coming into the treasury now building up at Gesoriacum and a worried Carausius drew his friends closer to discuss the idea of using Rotomagus as the financial base instead. It was away from the sea he argued, and therefore wouldn't be vulnerable to pirates and also being inland it would make the collecting of taxes easier. Furthermore it would serve as a centre from which he could redistribute the wealth back to his men. Tullius Fruscus would be appointed to oversee the transfer of monies from the two treasuries and would also take responsibility for employing die cutters able to reproduce fresh new coinage. Silver plate and old copies of imperial antonianii were to be melted down for this purpose and although having demoted his friend, Carausius wanted to trust him with this onerous task. He also felt a surge of confidence in trusting those with him that day and wanted to share amongst them the dangers of being implicated by the authorities and so had food sent for them all. A knock at the door allowed the junior officer to enter carefully carrying in his arms a large pot of warm pork stew strongly scented with cumin and from which he divided the portions equally amongst them in samian bowls. Before allowing the food to be eaten it was thought prudent to have it tasted by the officer who brought it in but Carausius waved this away stating that greater dangers waited for them other than from his own kitchen. Again everybody laughed and one man fell to the floor in mock death only he didn't rise again to the sound of applause. In a choking fit he struggled to breathe clutching at his throat until his final convulsion arched his chest out and he stopped moving with warm food flecked across his chin. Charon had had his man. Immediately all others threw their bowls down and spat out the contents of their mouths onto the floor and clothing before waiting for the cruel death that had unsuspectingly taken the first of them. The junior officer backed away into the corner and loudly swore his innocence before being grabbed by one that hadn't taken a mouth of poison. Carausius, realising that he could be alright too, ran for the door where he shouted that all the cooks be detained immediately and that no one was to eat anything under any circumstance.

'Bring him!' he yelled, pointing to the scared white faced individual desperately wanting to go to the aid of the dead man on the floor as if in recompense for some crime that he hadn't committed.

The guard did as he was told and dragged the terrified soldier after Carausius now rapidly making for one room in particular before the poison took him as well. Without warning he burst through where a surprised Septimus Clemens looked up from having just completed his list of names.

'Is this your work?' Carausius swore, and taking the captive off his guard threw him towards the merchant where he fell at his feet. The two men unrelated looked in disbelief at their dangerous new alliance.

'What's happened to him?' asked Septimus unwilling to rise to his feet along with the accused.

'Who is this man? I don't know him.'

'You two have plotted against me and he is the twin acolyte of your silent plans, is he not?'

'I still don't know what's happened, Lord Carausius. Maybe you can tell me...' he further protested.

Yet, without any explanation forthcoming they were brutally pulled to their feet and hurried along the veranda of the fort's main building before being taken out into the street that ran alongside the barrack block. From there they were dragged up the steps to the rampart struggling to follow Carausius as he leapt excitedly along in front.

'Stop there!' he called out and the two men were carefully turned about to face the growing crowd of bemused soldiers below.

Poison had already been the word on their lips and all felt that retribution was going to be as equally swift and taste as bitter. Without lawyers or court approval; without trial or appeal and after a few loaded words Carausius had the two men pushed to their instant deaths, arms spinning as they tipped and fell through the air.

The clumsy attempt on his life provided the talk of the barracks and for the remainder of the day it served to remind his soldiers that their revolt had now been acknowledged by Maximianus. This was to be only the first throw of the dice in his suppressing of rebels where to richly reward a single man for his bravery in poisoning another was better than having to raise an entire army, and in a province ravaged by internal strife there would be no end of those poor souls prepared to try. The decision was taken therefore that before the winter storms closed the sea routes Carausius would retire to his villa on the island of Vectis where he could hide from the emperor's wrath and continue overseeing the use of the navy. With word possibly having already reached the governor of Britannia Superior the small island would be easier to defend and with slave quarters it could house his bodyguard too. A flotilla would be added and one strong enough that could provide a deterrent against any incursion across the shallow waters between there and the mainland by the Romans. Finally, an envoy was to be raised and sent with a treasure ship far to the north of the wall of Hadrian where he was to openly encourage war between the Pictish tribes and the Romans in the promise of future support from Carausius. This would serve to divide his enemies and stall them in hunting down the Menapian now quickly preparing to flee on the next tide.

Only Carausius didn't make for Vectis.

As far as it could see the watchtower on the mouth of Fluvius Thamesis had reported nothing unusual in the comings and goings of the shipping that afternoon. It had been three days since the attempt upon Carausius' life and as his pennant flew proudly in the easterly breeze snatching in the sail it gave the soldiers on the low hills beyond no cause for alarm. They watched from their ramparts as the warship slewed past accompanied by two others; their destination the port of Londinium. Against the darkness of the November sky it faded away before coming back into view and then faded away again until it was perceived to have been closer now to the city than it was to them. A spear of ash wood and iron was idly leant against a wall and its owner called down to his compatriot auxiliary that they probably wouldn't be seeing another ship that day and therefore the evening meal could be prepared. When the messenger arrived to gather the daily reports there would be nothing new to add except the passing of the Commander's small fleet which obviously posed no threat. They all knew that with winter getting closer in the falling temperature soon no ships would be at sea and life in the small signal station reduced to chores and boredom only where danger was but a distant dream. No crowds lined the banks of the river either in Londinium where it narrowed to accept a wooden bridge across its murky waters and with little attention from the slaves huddled inside their warehouses the ships quietly settled at their tidal berths as if not wishing to stay. Nobody would have seen the marines quickly climb down from the decks whilst the commander himself strode with a purpose at their head and anybody witnessing a troop marching towards the far side of the bridge would have been forced away as they watched. Finally, in the near darkness of night the sound of boots reverberating across the sky as if heading for the Forum signalled that something unusual was going on. A servant pushed to one side in the vast hall of the governor's palace by the river knew it was true but he had little time to shout the alarm as he was picked up and then pushed in.

'Do not lie. Where is he?' demanded Carausius of the brazen official coming to meet them.

Quickly following behind were the first of the cloaked marines who having endured a bitter crossing of the sea were not entirely oblivious to the warmth and comfort of their new surroundings and looked embarrassingly out of place in such a sumptuous room.

'Who allowed you in?' Came the nervous reply from the more than secretive head of the palace staff.

'Search all the rooms and stop anybody trying to get away' Carausius ordered and his men dispersed, their damp flat soled leather boots taking an easy grip on the palace floors.

In preparation he had had them remove their hobnails in the time available sailing across the sea.

'I'll ask you again' he said to the official, 'where is he? I want the governor to come out and answer to the plot of trying to assassinate me, for you will recognise me as the commander of the northern fleet. I also want Manilius Albinus for the same charge. Where are they or will your death suffice as I hunt for them?'

Withdrawing his spartha and walking a lot closer, arm raised above his waist to strike hard he was stopped by an educated voice coming from his right at which point he slowly dropped it again.

'Wait,' it requested.

'Or would you simply kill a man for his loyalty. We knew that you would come. See how this one shakes, as his own mortality is revealed to him. You don't need to kill him so allow him to go free and I will reveal the governor's whereabouts.'

The clenched sword turned to face the traitor.

'Who are you?' Carausius demanded to know.

'I am Allectus and I am in the governor's financial staff. I can show you where he is travelling to if you will allow me. Now please, let this official go.'

Echoes of returning boots rang out from the corridors radiating from the hall and before long all had regrouped from their pointless search. The emptiness of the vast building itself suggested that nobody was hiding there and that if they had been they had long gone although almost innocently for there didn't appear to be a plot to be running from. Nevertheless, Allectus was given over to the marines after being allowed to quickly dress appropriately for the weather outside which, following the darkest of days, had now started to rain. A messenger too had safely returned from the city garrison and reported that following a suitable bribe their prefect wouldn't be calling out the guard and he silently welcomed a change in circumstances. His family hadn't forgotten the last bitter attempt at shaking off the roman yoke and without being too obvious in their support Carausius could be guaranteed a silent majority of new powerful political allies, for Britannia, like Gallia was rotten to its core and prepared to bring the sacred eagle crashing down to earth. Where one commander raised his sword in defiance others would quickly follow the signal and the insurrection spread. Yet as he appeared there on the brink of war and monumental changes Carausius knew that the head of Britannia Superior needed to be found first for he was the vine connecting Maximianus with the island and either he was going to feed support to the new ways or he would be cut down to wither then die.

Collecting his thoughts and trying to ward off the effects of tiredness was proving doubly difficult. It would be easy to allow his men the luxury of ransacking the palace for a night's rest before setting out the next day in search of their quarry but he knew that the messengers from the coast could be reporting having sighted his small squadron earlier that day sailing for Londinium. He couldn't predict the loyalties of men prepared to march against him for they belonged to Maximianus. Therefore he needed the wit to stay ahead of them whilst ambitious officers, having no doubt read of the emperor's edict that the fugitive be caught and tried for taking the navy for his own gains, would be imploring their men to venture out in the darkness of a wet night and ride as hard as they could to raise more troops. If the rebel was indeed on board the ship bound for Britannia then this was their chance to seize him for the advantage they had was that this was their island and they knew where the roads led.

A light mist of rain blew under the colonnade and columns of the palace's entrance and Carausius cursed it. In front of him the river smelt like any other and was familiar in every sense and how he longed to be at safe anchorage in a friendly harbour, warm and dry, and without reason to be fleeing from danger. His mind all too briefly wandered back to Septimus' losses at his hands and the barbarian thrown into the silent currents as revenge before regaining the sense of what was happening in the present. This wasn't the time for regret with his men requiring leadership and so taking his leave of the restless nature of the river he focused again on Allecus and his promise to lead them to where the governor could be found. To the southwest where the roads aimed for Glevum and the safety of the fortress a little further on at Isca; headquarters of the Second Augustan legion. That's where the loyal financial official had him running to. With torch in hand and impatient to leave orders were sent to the fleet still at their berths. The ten men without military boots were to return to their posts on board with the message that the three ships were to make for the small settlement of Clausentium on the south coast. There, they were to wait off shore for the arrival of their commander roughly a week later. If he hadn't arrived by then they were to sail for Gesoriacum and report their loss after which it was going to be every man for himself.

Now in the light drizzle each one steeled themselves for further discomfort in search of their prey out there in the cold rain squalls of Britannia. One man called out that Aegyptus would have been a better capture and his humour quickly spread warmth amongst them. Then a slave pulled an unwilling horse forward to the bottom of the flight of steps, saddle ready to mount with the superstitious noting its lack of enthusiasm at being called upon to work at such an hour and in such weather as a bad omen. However, without hesitation Carausius accepted the offer of being helped into his seat from where he could better view his men. With water droplets running across their peaked iron helmets and with scutum and spear in hand they shook their clothing and stamped their feet readying themselves for the order to march. Another horse was pulled alongside at which Allectus acknowledged that he was to ride it and lifted a leg ready to be thrown securely into the vacant place. Seeing this, Carausius stopped him immediately saying...

'You know this land better than we do therefore you can walk across it!' at which the beast was offered to a favoured officer instead who gladly accepted the gift.

Then looking behind, he saw two hundred men forming their ranks against the damp imperial stonework of the governor's palace and heard the rain drip from its roof onto the road below. Without wanting to look upon the faint glow of Londinium any further he slowly led their way out of the city as miserably dictated by Allectus walking at his side and to the amusement of the city dwellers watching through gaps in their shuttered windows. There was to be no further conversation between the two men, yet as Carausius struggled with the responsibility of where he was going, where his enemies were and how well his ships would escape the confines of the tidal Fluvius Thamesis without becoming ensnared on a sandbank in the morning light, one doubt surfaced more worryingly than the others – where had he recognised the financial officer from?

Torches gave off a dim light but there had been sufficient to see them through the long hours of walking that they endured and even saddles provided little relief for the riders suffering cramped thighs. However, the straightest road again proved its worth at not allowing them to stray from its borders and waste valuable time wandering about in the darkest of woods. With every step Carausius felt his freedom stretching ahead with the rays of a better start heralded by the morning sun and upon reaching Pontes allowed his men to rest in a field upon the boundary of the town. Soldiers were sent into the streets to wake the occupants of the few shops where food could be sought. A butcher, dragged from his bed was offered far less for his livestock than he wanted but wouldn't rise to an argument. The army out this early meant one thing and that was trouble. How could he know that he was unwillingly feeding that threat to his livelihood any more than the beaten up tavern owner was? A huge fire was lit around which men gathered to cook and to allow the water to rise in steam off their cold cloaks, heavy with the night's weather, before scouts reported back that there was a barn that could be used full with winter forage for the beasts of the farm. In their turn they were allowed to sleep a little before having to regroup and march on a second time. Too much idleness could lead to being surrounded and then captured which would have meant certain death or enslavement for everyone involved, including Allectus who it was assumed had now sided with the rebels.

'Where next?' he was asked before the column marched off and the reply came back.

'Straight on.'

With his ignorance, scant knowledge of Britannia and few maps, Carausius could only trust the somewhat uncertain guide hoping favourably that they were travelling parallel to the sea and if needs be it could be an escape route to the coast that served to protect them. With Sol rising behind and then setting before them at the end of the day he deduced that south was to his left and given the straightness of the road they were heading in the right direction; west. If the road erred to the right for any reason then they were travelling north and away from safety. Two hundred soldiers no matter how loyal were no match for the island's garrison and although the emperor's men were stationed on the coast in their forts how many would be willing to abandon them in search of a fugitive leaving the way open for Saxon pirates to attack behind their backs in a trap? Every hour suddenly became the game of chance that he had grown accustomed to. Your enemy desperately needed to know what you weren't doing rather than what you were. To this end the walking resumed in the late cold sunshine of the day and whilst there was sufficient light to ensure nobody had deserted, Carausius had them all counted. Nobody had and therefore the small force moved on confident that the silver face of Diana would guide them and not betray them to the forces of Maximianus surely now aware that the Palace had been searched with the head of Britannia Prima missing and silently hunted down.

Calleva Atrebatum was the next approaching town although it was feared there would have been more resistance to unfamiliar faces marching towards it dressed as marines of the navy. With due warning, and in alarm, the city magistrates may have ordered the shutting of the five gates to stop them gaining access to the temptations inside. Civil war and roman soldiers had sown desolation many times before and it was the population at large that ultimately suffered at their hands. Had anybody seen them spreading panic and fear then the gates could already be shut and without sufficient time or men to launch an attack, the town would have to be left impregnable whilst hungry men filed past its walls. Revenge for their evasive actions could wait until the island was ultimately his. They trudged on as dawn broke across the hollow out of view of the town's ramparts and with a milestone recording the distance that they needed to march as being another five, Carausius had no other option other than of resting his footsore men. Allectus was summoned. Was the governor likely to have been inside the town? Yes; there was the likelihood of that as it possessed the comforts required for a man of status boasting a grandiose house and its baths. Where would his bodyguard have been? Unsuspecting of any attack upon his person then they would have set up a temporary camp outside the town walls and in alarm retreated inside. That was the answer then. Scouts would be sent to quietly advance the next five miles without military dress. They were to establish the whereabouts of any bodyguard and return as quickly as possible. Even dressed lightly and able to move at a swift pace Carausius knew that they too were cold, tired, hungry and may not have the courage to do the task properly reporting back early that all was well. Taking them aside he promised a reward for their due vigilance, warning them also of their responsibility which they solemnly acknowledged, and with the road being too exposed to wait upon, it was cleared of the remaining soldiers who retired a discrete distance into the fields finding shelter in thin scrubland. Being early winter meant that no labourers were at work in the fields for there was little to do and therefore the countryside was silent except for the dancing Furies of breeze that washed in from the east. From their hideaway the men watched as four of their number, cloaks pushed into their legs by the wind, march off towards Calleva Atrebatum whilst in the opposite direction four more were sent, their cloaks billowing out behind them east to provide an early warning of cavalrymen from Londinium riding towards them. From his vantage point chosen for providing views in both directions Carausius settled down to the hours of waiting ahead. What was it that would wake him from his shallow sleep first? With the rhythmic metallic sound of horse's mouths gratefully tugging at the opportunity of what grass there was available through their bits; with the silent transit of Sol in the heavens and with the deserted road before him, the fate of Britannia and her population couldn't have appeared less important to mankind itself.

It was late and his hands were numb with the cold at having to prop his head up. A solitary cart trundled past on the road but its driver hadn't seen anything and carried on at the same speed travelling east. Carausius, head jerking wanted desperately to fall sound asleep and envied the simple life of the wagon driver now rumbling home for a bed. A short distance from where he was it suddenly stopped allowing four figures to roll off the back. A brief conversation followed after which the wagon was allowed to continue then without ceremony or disguise the men climbed the small hill to where their commander was and brazenly announced their mission a success. In fury they were reproached for their lack of thought. What if the wagon was to be stopped and the driver questioned about strangers? Had they considered the risks? This wasn't Oceanus where the vastness of the deep waters offered protection against the limited numbers of vessels sailing upon it. For all they knew the island garrison could be closing in looking for them. They had to begin to think like soldiers! His men protesting their innocence tried lying that the wagon driver was a mute slave knowing that they couldn't be proved wrong and were ordered to collect the other four from their outpost further along and bring them back. Slowly and angrily Carausius, prematurely having been awoken, called for Allectus. In a state of raised alertness it was now important to try and make the right decision about where to go next. The scouts had reported that there was no activity at Calleva to suggest the presence of the governor so where could he be heading?

'Nobody would mourn over your death here' Allectus was told.

'Why do I trust you? We have been chasing hard for days now and there is nothing – NOTHING!!'

The raised voice attracted attention but nobody challenged it.

'Bring me a map, quickly!' Carausius ordered at which one was spread out before him, Allectus being pushed to his knees before it.

'Show me where we are going because at Calleva the road splits five ways. Which is our road?

'Lord Carausius, I have faithfully told you that Isca is their destination. We may be hours or even days away catching up. At Calleva the military could assume that you have been unsuccessful in this revolt and have made to return to the sea via Noviomagus. Therefore as we look for the governor, they are looking for us. I suggest the road towards Durocornovium for another day after which it may be wiser to abandon your attempt.'

However there was no future other than the present and no day closer to when Carausius could declare it finished. In Gallia it wouldn't be long before Diocletianus and Maximianus started to prepare an army against him in the same way that the Bagaudae revolt had been jointly crushed. At the head of their forces would be the men desiring the death of Carausius most of all; in particular Julius Magnus Aurelius. If he was to succeed then it had to be now as to fail was to die. A hasty but thoughtful plan was therefore drawn together. The horses that they had were to be given over to the scouts that they may cover the roads quicker and the rest of the invading force were to follow on in the same laborious way marching at night, but only for another two after which the plot would be declared a failure. Evidence of where the man was that they sought would only be found in his bodyguard and their camp. Off the scouts were sent leaving Carausius to gather his tired men and explain the way forward, whereupon they declared to give their utmost in this mission silently demonstrating their loyalty with raised swords. Then it was back to the road and the short journey around Calleva in an attempt at not being seen. Not long into the renewed boredom of marching a cry came from the rear that horsemen were approaching from the east behind them and that the road needed clearing. Marching in two abreast order made this easier as the two columns rapidly filed away left and right, into the relative safety of the land around. Two horsemen thundered past at speed and were quickly gone. The marines, waiting for the order to reform, then went about their business with renewed heart whilst the men at the back were implored to again keep their eyes and ears open. Not having yet made Calleva would prove a stroke of luck as the town would have nothing unusual to report and the horsemen, although full of dire warnings, would soon have passed through. Keeping his thoughts closely guarded, Carausius could only trust that the Londinium garrison had been true to their boastful words of loyalty and that his own ships had escaped capture. Desiring everything for himself was one thing but he couldn't achieve it without armed help and if his own men were ever to sense a weakness of plan then they would soon abandon him. Their sworn allegiance along with the blessing of his personal god was never more required than at this moment.

Negotiating a path around the town was complicated by the dark, the location of the amphitheatre and by the lack of anybody's knowledge of the immediate countryside. However, by stealth it was achieved and the party crossed the north road without being seen to reform a little further along the road that made for Spinae and the west. The last remnants of cold meat and bread were shared out the best they could with nobody taking more than their need. Water, now in short supply, was rationed and the men forbidden from filling their bottles by Carausius. Every neck and shoulder muscle aching from chain mail fatigue and the constant marching was rubbed into accepting one more effort whilst helmets were removed before being repositioned to try and gain the most comfortable fitting. Fingers that had spent three long nights gripping a shield had seemingly lost their touch and were close to being claw like and blistered. Legs, which had stumbled over numerous obstacles throughout the dark nights tingled with cuts, and feet sore from the flat soled boots throbbed upon their iron nails. To have given up now and to have returned to the perils of the wind and tide wouldn't have been a disgrace for disciplined toughened men except that the more they were pushed, the more the fire burnt within them to do their duty. In the faint glow of the morning and with hushed voices they waited for news whilst trying to prevent their eyes from closing in desperate sleep. That news came from their scouts and it was to be beneficial. They reported seeing a column of horsemen with a carriage turn off the road and head west along a track. Keeping a discreet distance they had followed it without being spotted although in riding back they were challenged themselves and could only reply that they were looking for the best road to Aquae Sulis. Allectus, again quickly brought forward was questioned.

'Why would the governor choose a lesser road like this? Is it the road to Isca? Where is he going to?'

The questions coming at him like an arrow storm led to him sensibly trying to avoid them and so were left unanswered which angered Carausius.

'Patience...' the finance official pleaded, 'I can only answer the one question. You can get to Isca by Aquae Sulis but I doubt that the ferry will be there in this season to cross Fluvius Sabrina. You can also ride to Isca but that is not the quickest way. As to why he has left the safety of the fastest road I cannot say except that it must favour us. He cannot be aware of this plot and therefore is planning to visit friends, for that is not a well used track. If you were quick then to catch him now would be best...' and at that he stopped talking.

'It's a trap! This is all too easy and you're leading us into his arms. No sooner do we approach then we will be surrounded and taken. How can I trust you any more than I can the two challenged riding back? Anybody knowing the arrangements of his bodyguard will suspect that it is wrong: two lost soldiers looking to travel to Aquae Sulis and at this season?'

Allectus had his answer ready.

'Lord Carausius, the wild hunted beast full of sweat and short of breath would demand an equal and swift death from you. Would you have enjoyed the chase to let it go? Now is your time to strike.'

The words sounded almost familiar yet Carausius, bitter at his avoidance of the questions, attacked him.

'Why did you say that?' He asked.

'My apologies if I have offended you, my Lord. I am also here at immense personal risk and you can guess my reasons. I am no longer as free to leave as you are!'

'Answer me; why did you mention the hunt? Your face: where have I seen you before?'

Time briefly stopped whilst men took stock of their situation. Three days of tired marching had led to a personal feud between their commander and the suspicious traitor Allectus yet it couldn't continue. The two protagonists could answer their quarrels elsewhere but here on unfamiliar ground and at a point where it was necessary to decide quickly the course of action the marines chose to intervene.

'Push him to the front!' and they shoved Allectus forward.

Carausius, taking back the opportunity of regaining the initiative, could only agree and rapidly organised the men into two columns again left and right upon the road only this time he was going to be bolder in risking being seen. If approached by anyone brave enough then they were moving inland from the sea in response to a threat and Carausius the usurper, without his bust upon any coin would remain incognito except only to the governor and his staff. Finding him quickly was now imperative. Allectus, head bowed in half guilt and submission led the force onwards and to the point where he indicated that the road made its diversion from the main carriageway and headed south west. This was where their quarry slept soundly, ate and bathed as their pursuers ground their hobnails down in forced marches. The order was given for a quick pace of run followed by walk in the attempt to make up the distance and with increasingly tired eyes the low hills on Carausius' left side drew his gaze knowing that over them could be his ships and safety. The temptation to retreat from this course of action tugged stronger as every man there watched the next for signs of weakness that could foretell that the game was over and who it was that was going to run first? However, the road went on in its relentless course following close the smallest of rivers that fed the fields either side with rich soils. Farms were few and settlements even fewer in their dispersion of the population and it was such that Carausius feared having been seen with every able bodied man now running to defend the ramparts of the nearest town. He needn't have worried. The countryside, although rich in its harvests was poor in its rewards and large estates resulted, their opulent owners choosing to reside elsewhere and leave farming affairs to their bailiffs. The towns fortunately were widely dispersed and therefore few but only the hardy were at work in the fields and forests that bounded the road. The approaching group of returning horsemen from the west even served to cause little alarm on a day that was turning out to be agreeable for fighting. A cool breeze that ran along before them wasn't enough to be chillingly cold but more than enough to make the warm blood of insurrection slow to a tempered thought at the next move whilst the riders, pulling to a halt, delivered the desired news – the governor was no more than four miles away with only a small escort, which considering the times that they were living in, surprised Carausius. He would wait until dark, which tonight could be late given the clear cold skies of daylight supplying Sol Invictus with time to settle in his fiery bed. First though the riders had reported the need to ford the small river which was best done now, and as the governor of Britannia Superior unwittingly relaxed upon his travels, the trap was being set by men accustomed to conquering deeper waters than those.

Through the lowest branches of the oaks the sunlight tried to make its way desperately reaching out to illuminate the dark before having to die away. Angular blocks of flint in the sturdy walls of the grand farmhouse off the road reflected this orange glow shimmering like the thousand small fires about to burst into life at the merest waft, yet one by one they went out having unwittingly raised the grey walls seemingly higher in the light green night sky. Every man there hiding in the woods watched as the windows of the twin storied building were warmed by the soft glow of oil lamps, and Carausius, happiest that without ramparts nothing of the outside meadows could be seen by a sentry guard. A pan pipe's mellow note flew towards them ahead of its applause and the smell of a strong meat cooking languished in the light cold air teasing their nostrils. It was as if their prey was playing with them, always aware that they were there before striking the fatal unseen blow that would end it all whilst having been so close to the pleasures they desired. To a man they were now desperate for the attack to commence whilst their commander fiercely urged caution. There was a plan which they would follow because in the small fields surrounding the building and slightly to the south away from the river, the camp of the bodyguard was set up. There, bodies moved slowly against the merest faint glow of a fire and sparks, like the falling stars fell to earth at their poking with a stick. The horses, which were kept slightly away from the tents, were occasionally raising their heads and looking up but in the darkness it wasn't easy to count them. Carausius thought about twenty with a few oxen required for the carts carrying the necessary possessions of an important man on the move throughout his province. None of the animal's sensed danger which augured well for the attack was now underway. Occasionally the large oak doors beneath the main arch would open slightly and a figure walk out clutching beer for the escorting cavalry before idling back through them. There didn't appear to be too much care taken about their closing and at the next opportunity a small detachment of men forced their way in leaving the gates slightly ajar as they did. Silence hung in the river valley as Carausius had ordered, before the assault on the main bodyguard began, relaxing before their warm fires and expecting nothing to be delivered but another amphora of beer and scraps from the kitchen. Instead, iron swords rusty with inaction tore into them with relish and in the dark killing was easier without the guilt of an unready man looking you directly in the face. A few managed to get to their feet withdrawing their own weapons and helplessly unable to identify who it was that was attacking them. There were too many for this to be the work of simple bandits and far too well organised. Therefore without hope for their own salvation they tried to escape into the villa or the woods where they were met by Carausius' second line of men cutting them to pieces easily as they blindly stumbled forward to their deaths. Allectus, who had been told to stand well to the rear, had shed his own guard galloping wildly down the slope to share in the glory of that night's action and unwilling to be remembered for having not participated in the dangers therein. Silently another shadow of a figure took his place emerging from the gloom and clearly lost.

'Spare me' it said from its terrified mouth and seeing Allectus standing motionless there, its legs wanted to run but feared the doing so.

'I don't want to die' and it sobbed as it fell to its knees.

'Get up. Are you the bodyguard? Where is your courage now it is called for?'

'My sword...take it' the coward said.

'You must raise the alarm. Now run! Cunetio is to the west. Cross the river where you dare and head north first. Nobody will follow you. Go, and don't surrender your life or your sword again.'

Quickly looking about him and making sure that no-one else had seen them together, Allectus then helped the man to his feet giving him his sword back before pushing him behind. As fast as he had appeared he had gone. Below and before him the ransacking was following its usual course with soldiers calmly picking over the dead yet in the calm mid hours of the night and to the sound of owls and the occasional wolf calling, the villa itself fell silent. Purposefully the building wasn't set ablaze as it would serve as a beacon for its own alarm whilst inside men began to bargain for the greatest prize known to them all; complete ownership of the provinces of the imperial court of Britannia.

In one room alone heavy incense and plots hung in the air almost thick enough to prevent the golden ring inscribed with clasped hands upon the governor's finger pointing to Carausius and demanding the meaning of his attack? Behind him cowered the owner of the sumptuous building obviously unaccustomed to violence himself. By his side the remnants of the pathetic bodyguard found themselves pinned against the wall by the intruders whilst slave women tried desperately to cover their nudity lowering their heads in shame and wanting embarrassed to slip away. The pan pipes had stopped playing abruptly and the painted figures upon the hypocaust heated plaster wall no longer danced in the light from the sooty oil lamps. Half eaten rich food had spilled from upturned silver plates and cushions, scattered across the mosaic floor led to trails of red blood where the eye focused upon a silent figure comically slumped at his death. Carausius' time to reply for his treachery had come.

'Be silent!' He shouted at his prisoner whilst turning about to give orders.

'Count them all, the dead as well. Has anybody escaped?'

Withdrawing his sword he walked towards the man he recognised as being the military Decurion of the mounted escort pushing the tip into his throat and demanding that he reveal the numerical strength of his guard. When the reply failed to come through disobedience and not through cowardice, Carausius pushed his weight into feeling it pass easily through the warm clammy soft tissue and then knock against the bones of the spine before exiting. The man collapsed and instinct took over with the weapon being wrenched free of its grip before the blood sprayed upon him. He fell like a stricken oak in a coiled pool of blood. To a man fists tightened at witnessing this and the very breath in their bodies became shallower whilst their hearts beat faster. Dry mouths desperately wanted to utter their curses in defence of the dead but had to remain resolutely shut. To Carausius, tired, irritable, but elated nothing now was beyond his cruelty and he felt the supreme authority to act like a god surging throughout his limbs dispensing justice at will. Mithras, his guidance but unable to exert any physical control in the affairs of mankind, was certainly now forgotten in war. All earthly fortune was to be his as were the fortunes of those under his control. The governor realising quickly that this was the flagging end to his legitimate authority boldly spoke out without fear hoping to encourage others to their heroic deaths and bolster his fame.

'Look,' and he again pointed across the void between them.

'There is no mystery. Our protector, Lord Carausius has himself chosen unwisely to raise the banner in defence of the Saxons by taking me. You act as if an agent of these very pirates and must have had Saxon eyes in my palace. None of you shall escape the roman justice and Maximianus will crush you without mercy. I alone begin to pray for your lingering deaths and listen for the trumpet calls throughout this land bringing the garrison swiftly to my aid. There will be no escape and you shall forfeit your worthless lives ensnared here.'

Any excuse to have killed him there and then would have been acceptable but he was going to be important to the rebellion; a hostage for what Carausius wanted and therefore he was tied up before being bundled down the flight of stairs to greet the waiting cold outside. In the crisp night a frost was forming except where the dead lay across the ground and as the wagon was clumsily brought to the main gate the prisoners were loaded with the final orders given. Those men who had set out from Londinium and who had marched without rest were to follow as best they could the mules and cart towards the coast. A boat would be waiting for them at Clausentium and even if it wasn't then they were to wait. One would arrive eventually. It was important that Carausius escaped ahead of them and for their waning loyalty he promised much. Behind him lay the scattered remnants of the struggle; slaves with no loyalties, dispossessed soldiers of their weapons and a villa empty of its guest. By whatever light was available and through the folds of the leather canopy over the cart's frame the man who had up to then been powerful throughout his province looked on for witnesses to the crimes committed. No face came to his attention except briefly that of the finance minister – Allectus. Why was he there? He called out momentarily attracting the man's attention but then was ignored. He was certain that it was him but as the wagon jolted to its start he never gained a second chance. With as much speed as was possible the rebels left the valley heading for the south and the road towards Venta Belgarum. Behind trudged the rebellious remnants of the small army trying to convince themselves that they too would be saved for it would only take two days by horseback and three on foot without stopping. The warships of Gesoriacum would then rescue them all.

Footsteps across the sand filled quickly with water behind them and it was good to have the smell of the sea in their nostrils. What wasn't needed was abandoned on the shoreline by the vanguard, weapons and chainmail included to make the short wade out to their ship easier where one by one they were dragged aboard and saluted as heroes. The prize for Carausius, the governor of Britannia Superior, looked nothing of the sort as he fought to combat the feeling of being sick upon the waves. No slave leapt up to offer a bowl to accommodate his throwing up and no man there could have imagined that this was how he would be viewing his province now: from the deck of a roman pirate ship. He was a beaten man, his province lost, yet as the sails unfurled and the calling voices rhythmically matched both the rising oars and the breaking waves he cast a glance along the ship to see Allectus looking back. Although his face was filthy and red with the effort of being there his eyes still shone brightly with their ambition. With a slow deliberate dip of his head he acknowledged his part and then discretely looked the other way. Along the shoreline rode horsemen from Portus Ardaoni raising their spears pointlessly to the sky and unable to provide any other chase than where the ground that supported their horses' weight led them to and where the waters that broke upon their horses chest's became too deep. Out and into the narrow channel towards Vectis was where they last reported seeing the pirate sails heading for. The raid upon Britannia had been a success and with his prisoner now with him it was intended to overwinter on the island fortress. When possible more ships would be brought over from Gesoriacum to fend off the island's meagre navy and in the following Spring negotiations that would cause Maximianus to rise in furious anger could begin as to who had real control of the West. Satisfaction spread throughout the army at the news of this victory only tempered some weeks later when the fate of the rearguard was learnt. To a man they had been ambushed and cut to pieces easily without mercy, their severed heads deposited silently in the waters that lapped against the usurper's lavish home where gently they bobbed to and fro until eventually succumbing to rotting beyond recognition. Not one effort was made to bury them and the ground thereafter avoided in shame.

CHAPTER VIII

IMPERATOR

The time for rejoicing now came to its end as Carausius was still unaware that the war in Germania had run its course with victory for the loyal troops of Maximianus. Gathering thousands of prisoners and the spoils of war, the emperor had temporarily led his men back across Fluvius Rhenus which stubbornly remained as the barrier to incursions from the east and into their forts where they gratefully acknowledged the mighty gods of Rome, Jupiter and Hercules. How the province rested in its uneasy peace allowing the dice of fate to spin out of control between two men before eventually having to tilt and roll face up or face down.

Far away a squadron of ten ships had arrived with efficiency off Vectis to accompany their victorious commander to Londinium. There, the servant of roman administration fearfully awaited its new orders whilst east and west of Oceanus more warships prevented the movement of shipping. All throughout the relatively comfortable months of winter Carausius had had the time to interrogate his prisoner about the financial and military strength at his disposal and it was an uneasy Allectus, as financial envoy, who had to sit and watch the man opposite squirm in agony wanting to openly identify who his true supporters were. Albinius' name was already on the list of proscription and it was widely assumed that he had already chosen to run away. As the scribe's nib scratched at its wooden page men's lives were being forfeited without them knowing for the greatest weapon of all blind fear like the plaque was already doing its work. Once pressed for its knowledge the intention was then to simply discard the useless wrinkled carcass like one would the sweet grape or the sour olive because for him Maximianus couldn't have been any further from saving his life than he was. To Carausius, the old governor was an inconvenience and his death close by. It would serve no purpose to have taken him to Londinium and nothing was to be gained from bartering with his life. In the island prison he was granted no freedom in case he bribed the guard to escape and thereafter fomented resistance against his enemies. Allectus, formerly in his paid staff was suddenly forbidden open access and constantly searched for evidence of messages passing to and fro, but that would have proved dangerous to both men. Instead there was to be a sudden unannounced change in the legitimate imperial policy and it was determined to be ruthless in its birth beginning with the drowning of the bound and gagged ex-governor quietly at sea. Allectus now had to watch his own back fearful of giving off any signs of mistrust towards the new regime and as Maximianus was seething at the news of the loss of his province, the previous governor's name would be quickly erased by its stupidity at being caught out with his bodyguard in a villa. Suddenly Rome's mood could violently swing and with bellicosity and awe, a new name be announced with which authority be given to win back the lost coast of Gallia along with the island provinces of Britannia. Between these two competing courts stood the man of money and commerce cautiously watching his own personal fate evolve.

With a cloudless sky compliant to mankind, and Neptune today willing to serve the fragile naval ambitions of the world, Mausaeus Carausius rode the short distance to board his ship looking frozen against the shimmering backdrop of the horizon. Dismounting and handing the reins over to his groom he reiterated all instructions for the next few months to those there promising that a stronger force of soldiers would be sent over to provide a guard for the villa and island itself. In the warmth of the day it would be easy to forget their reason for being there and once the sails of the fleet had disappeared into the eastern sky they could be forgiven for relaxing. However they were warned with dire consequence that not all ships sailing from the south were potential allies and that Maximianus would be doing his utmost to remove them from their post with every means available. Therefore daily vigilance was going to be crucial in retaining the island yet once Carausius' own imperial message of forgiveness had spread west from Londinium along the southern coasts to reach the harbours opposite Vectis then they could all relax in unity. To see raging fires at night or smoke throughout the day would symbolise that resistance was ongoing and that nobody was to be allowed to land on the shore. The fate of the old fighting men of Britannia would be theirs too if they failed. On good days their watch would ensure their continued survival; on stormy days no-one would be as foolish as to send over an army and at the very least the coastline of Gallia was in strong hands with weak legions still willing to be seduced with bribery. Carausius could do no more: As the loud cheers of his bodyguard reverberated around the shallow hills of the small harbour he gathered up his cloak climbing into the light patrol boat rocking gently against the waves where he took one last look at his villa and then across to the haze laden mainland. Allectus, unused to sailing struggled to get into his boat whilst on the far side of the island and out of sight the governor too struggled to board his although few were there to witness the tragedy as he was legged aboard without due ceremony. As all boats left, the tide lapped equally around the island and in its active voice was the whispering of 'IMPERATOR, IMPERATOR' although nobody listened or heard it call.

The journey to the mouth of Fluvius Thamesis over three days was uneventful for no fleet on the seas could rise up to challenge the might of Carausius. His Saxon allies were warned to stay in their harbours and not to interrupt the new transition of power across the narrow channel for it mattered greatly to them who ruled. Their own lands were shrinking with the increasing pressure from the east and if powerful alliances could be forged then so much the better. They could always be broken again like a wolf shadowing a shepherd and then joining the ferocity of other wolves at their moment of attack. Trust nobody. For the time being they were needed and that need came with a price; the freedom to strike at the empire where it was weakest and in disarray. Yet Britannia was too strong and about to become stronger. Ten warships turned for the port of Londinium followed by another four sent out from Gesoriacum and as they entered the estuary the order was given to first sail, then row in pairs keeping away from the shoreline where missiles could be thrown; Carausius, constantly imploring Aeolus for his continued guidance and benevolence at providing a flat calm sea ensured that sacrificial offerings of food and wine were passed overboard for the benevolent journey complemented by a bright moon that had risen and set with them with its guiding constellation before the work of subduing the province began. Then once at anchor all faces strained towards the quays looking intently for the delegation of imperial recognition to humbly row out and accept their fate yet none came; there were no citizens on the shore and the quietness of the city led Carausius to believe that they had chosen to abandon it before retiring inland where a counter attack was waiting.

'They weren't expecting us' his navarchus said.

'That isn't the truth! The city garrison would have known that I was to return; yet it seems that the bravest of Maximianus' agents has had time enough to warn the province by risking the winter storms and get across. We don't have the men to invade!' Came his anguished reply.

'Perhaps we ought to have brought the governor along.'

Carausius cursed the ignorant remark before laughing out loudly that he was swimming with Neptune and wouldn't be attending. The man failing to grasp the answer immediately asked for his orders in an attempt at redeeming himself militarily before he too risked being thrown overboard.

'They will soon know that I am their saviour from beneath the Roman yoke!' Carausius said.

'How can I have failed in not having been recognised as they would have followed us along the coast with cavalry and their beacons would have shone across the land? It is now the seventh hour and nobody sleeps in the city. The river too is laden with bloated shipping and yet no-one unloads it? Is this what the Saxon thieves find when they come looking for prizes and songs to sing at home? The cowards are out there and we will call them to us like birds into the netting. Now row upstream and fire upon the shipping at its berth with your ballista. You are to set ablaze as many as you can. I shall then reward the accuracy of your men. Remember, do not turn around in the deepest channels for they are unknown to us but if the river begins to empty then drop your anchor and stay there. Do not fall back upon me. If I have to then I will order the rest to retire and resume the landing on the next rising of the water. Now go!'

A boat was immediately lowered and the man climbed skilfully aboard setting about transferring from one ship to another at the head of the column. With as much ease he scrambled up the side of the leading one and in moments a drum beat boomed out across the river at which oars fell from its side into the water only to lift again lugging it slowly forward. Then once in position white traces of fire arrows began to curve across the sky, some falling short into the river, others bouncing harmlessly off the tiled roofs of the warehouses and tumbling unevenly to the ground. Eventually the correct tension in the bowstrings was marked and thereafter arrow following arrow thudded into the ships' decking causing them to eventually catch fire. It took a great effort to start the blaze but soon a breeze lifted fanning the heat towards the timber sheds causing smoke to be seen across the entire city. A cheer went up as more darts followed and vulnerable vessels succumbed to their fate.

Eventually people were spotted coming to the water's edge to salvage their goods but were quickly forced back again by the ferocity of the fire and by the arrows flying unpredictably towards them. Comically, some could be seen falling to the ground clutching their chests or being lifted from their feet by the impact of soundless death. Very shortly afterwards a small pilot boat was launched from the shore heading directly towards the main force at which point a horn crisply sounded two notes to order the cessation of firing. On board was the messenger from the province of Britannia Superior. As it closed in upon the main fleet a clear but shaking voice without any script called out before the assembled bowmen on the decks:

'To Mausaeus Carausius, commander of the northern fleet. We say this is our surrender. The city gates are open to you. Spare us from death.'

A pennant idled in the breeze from its mast and the smoke from the fires drifted across the rooftops of Londinium. Amongst the weathered reddened faces of the assembled army the greeting wasn't entirely to his liking.

'Let it be known that I am coming to you' Carausius replied shouting down 'and any attack upon my force will be met by the end of you all.'

Without reply the small boat turned about and rowed back.

He took his time in selecting the best landing place considering the river's flow and the potential for being attacked once ashore. It appeared too hazardous to have followed the messenger from where he had embarked for nobody could have guessed what ambush was hiding amongst the warehouses. Eventually, and in consultation with his centurions, they chose a spot a little downstream where the marines could disembark on a gravel beach without fear of being surrounded. It took effort to assemble the force that now eagerly fell from their warships riding at anchor in the changing motion of the seas but the signal was given to aggressively row the landing craft towards their prize. The first men to wade ashore quickly formed up in a wedge behind their shields and man by man this expanded until it allowed the new emperor the security of landing himself. Once on firm dry ground he immediately set about the task of winning power. Archers were sent out wide to scour the rising ground and give warning of cavalry that never came to threaten them. Following these, lightly armed auxiliaries scrambled into positions of height where they could foresee the way ahead, but there was still no sign of a response as more soldiers filled the beach increasingly fearing an attack at their most vulnerable point. Suspecting a trap, Carausius glanced out to sea where he thought approaching sails would herald a response from the island but none came. Instead, his ships and therefore his salvation continued to rock quietly at their post against the most peaceful of skies with afternoon drapes of cloud pulling across from the horizon. With a quick council of war convening the order was given to form up in marching order for he wanted all with him together this time and not to become detached. A small force was then left to guard the landing craft. They were told that if attacked they were to try and escape with orders for the ship's commanders to spread havoc at will upon shipping, people and property. Their vengeance would be understood by loyal followers in Gallia if the enterprise failed and thus rendering the province further isolated from Maximianus. The furious army would turn to face the legions instead in bitter retribution and then return again to the island once victory had been firmly secured. It was better for all that the garrison capitulated now as it said it would. Feeling that they had everything to gain by being there the invaders moved quickly towards the north east gate of Londinium and away from their river sanctuary.

A clarion call of twin bronze horns rent the sky from stone towers either side of the open gates and with fragile nerves every man's hand tightened its grip upon his sword handle ready at an instant to withdraw it and then begin fighting for his life. The column instantly halted at the perceived alarm with shields quickly raised against the walls before them and stood its ground. No man gave way or dropped his guard whilst Carausius' heart thumped at the waiting. The sound of sandals scuffing across the cobbled and gravelled road surface reassured him slightly although his men refused to lower their shields and instead peered through the gaps between them. They watched intently as a delegation of toga clad elders crept forward, clothed in chains and holding the symbols of office in their arms. The leading elder was the first at offering his submission in an attempt at drawing Carausius out by spreading his empty arms before him and as he did so a commotion followed behind leading to the old man unceremoniously being pushed to the ground. The others scattered in fright as through their rank ran screaming men, shields tightly clutched about them and swords raised high towards the heavens. Circular red shield clashed hard against circular blue shield as an archer in the rear quickly brought a trumpet player crashing down from the gate and then reloaded before stepping back, next arrow at the ready. Confidently the battle scarred men of Carausius' defended themselves before thrusting and cutting their way forward stepping over the dead on the road as they manoeuvred until above the clash of weapons a man bravely rode out splitting the warring factions aside with his mount.

'Peace, stop!' he shouted as loud as could be heard.

'I am the prefect of the city garrison and these are the governor's men and not mine! Peace, and return your arms.'

He gave a clear signal before kicking his reluctant horse forward and from behind the walls more soldiers streamed out looking ready to repel the invaders before they too stopped short of engaging. The marines reformed their line across the wide expanse of ground hemmed in by neither building nor boundary and waited again. Between the two armies the dead men of Britannia lay save for one and as he attempted his last sword thrust with nothing to lose the prefect charged impaling him with his spear causing him to stumble to the ground in a mass of chain mail. Every man looked up in awe as he pulled his horse around and he looked down in the silence of that afternoon upon what had arrived. Nobody without authority spoke a word allowing the men in white togas to reappear, carefully helping the elder to his feet and wiping his garment down with their hands. Another order was then given at which the garrison of Londinium aligned themselves parallel to the road dropping their shields and forming a wall.

'Lord Carausius...' the prefect said upon his spinning horse, 'the city is yours. You have my protection.'

Unsure at first of the protocol of usurpation, the commander of the northern fleet left it to his own centurions to rearrange their order before regaining the dignity that the situation offered to him whereupon he slowly followed the city magistrates to the basilica, the largest structure in the city. There, a sea of many curious faces had washed up and jostled around. Another horn sounded at which all men twitched again but it was a call only to announce the gravity and seriousness of the predicament that those imbued with the province's security had suddenly now found themselves in. This hadn't been the first attempt at ridding the island of the onerous roman authority and with every new plot came the risk, that Rome, which had ruled for so long now would want revenge. It would only be a matter of time and to preserve one's life and property it was better to co-operate. The older, wiser men of the council knew this to their cost. They led Carausius and his party onwards and up the wide shallow steps of the imposing three storied building and into the massive hall flanked on either side by smaller offices. At the eastern end stood the tribunal where he was directed yet to a man not one citizen offered true subjugation by bowing low. His marines quickly asserted their authority by standing tall behind him and whilst the shuffling for places seemed to endlessly go on, Carausius took the opportunity of surveying his new province at close quarters. The ill fitting mortar and unlevel masonry of the basilica still spoke with the magnitude of a great building suitable for his purpose and he was impressed. Then, after a lull, order was restored and those with no reason to be inside were pushed out and the doors slammed shut. Proceedings could now begin.

'My Lord, Mausaeus Carausius' spoke a noble with the acknowledged authority to do so.

'You must forgive....' whereupon he was stopped in mid speech and pulled away from saying any more.

It was time for them to listen.

'Are you not treacherous and disloyal citizens of Britannia?' said Carausius.

'I have not been sent here as an envoy to govern you by your schoolmaster Maximianus or to offer you his protection from the Saxons whom you loathe. I arrive here as Emperor of the West: Caesar Augustus Mausaeus Carausius and you will fall to your knees surrendering to me as Gallia has.'

He stepped back signalling to his guards to gather together those thought as being men of some importance. Barely able to comprehend the address that had just been given some of the braver spoke out after first repeating their words in their mind.

'By what legal right do you claim the purple?' One shouted for the many before receiving his answer from the newly occupied dais.

'By the right of Jupiter given to me! There are warships in Gesoriacum and a legion ready to sail. There are more to come from the barracks of Fluvius Rhenus ready to mutiny for silver against the reign of their oppressor. I have Saxon allies poised to plunder your estates and fight for me in return for their freedom. You are and you will serve as slaves...' and there he stopped.

Although completely aware of the illegitimate claim to rule, above the rising whispering tide before him came the face of Helena Messalina standing, having been rescued on the beach and the burning Saxon pirates drowning. Carausius, tired and surprised at himself pulled his iron helmet off for comfort yet couldn't stop himself becoming embroiled in a bitter exchange of words much to his centurion's annoyance.

'My Lord, you are inflaming them to rebellion again' he said.

'Remember your plans.'

Yet he couldn't. Having to shout to be heard had already marked him out as unruly but the anger continued to rise and with a pointed finger he stretched his arm out towards them in accusation.

'You cowards have known of my intentions. You have seen the smoke of my villa throughout the winter and have kept your distance hearing by rumours that I had captured the province. Where are your mighty three legions begging for the honour of repelling my attack? Where has been your planning? Has not Maximianus thrown to you his idle promise of salvation and sent amongst you the means for my destruction? Well has he...the man who has never come to offer you comfort from your peril? Answer me!' at which point he pulled the nearest man to his chest and looked hard into his face.

'My husband' a woman's voice shouted.

'Please, he has done nothing wrong. He is an honest man. Leave him, please!'

Carausius' stare wasn't returned by the man who wisely chose instead to look at the tiled floor in revulsion.

'Go back to your wife, I fear her more than you' he mocked and then pushed him away.

'Clear the hall, but if they are here, I want all people named on this list to remain. Nobody is to leave without my permission' and he summoned a soldier forward to shout the names out, many of whom were the wealthy landowners of Britannia Superior and known to be close to the deposed imperial court.

The parchment role had been the harvest of his winter captive; the ex-governor and now was the time to reap it. One by one the named were drawn forward and ushered through into a smaller more intimate ante room where Carausius had the door pulled tight behind him with two enormous guards stationed outside. The remaining populace were drained from the building where they chose to either mill about waiting for news of their loved ones or slunk off to spread rumours of the day's events to those yet unaffected by the new changes. Inside more detailed plans were being formed.

'Where are my legions?' The new emperor asked.

The answer was that they were in their barracks, the cavalry and auxiliary too in theirs or on patrol. No measures had been taken to repel the forces of Gallia and they had little to match their naval strength either. It made no sense therefore to abandon their posts and leave the province vulnerable to attack whilst roman fought roman to the death. This pleased Carausius immensely. His military strength with which to fight Maximianus had grown considerably and the elders of the province selfishly aware of its rich independence were happy not to sacrifice such wealth in the folly of Rome. Their punishment, if it was to come was a long way ahead giving them time to either hide their treasure from the new usurper or spend it. Protection always has its price and it didn't take Carausius long to talk about money and where he could immediately seize it. At the revealing of Allectus as his new finance minister there were few signs of discontent as eyes met, heads lowered but not all people sighed. He would be responsible for seizing tax revenues due and securing the treasury building from where he could begin to pay the troops. The magistrates would be accompanying the marine commanders to the legionary bases over the coming weeks and in the meantime they were to provide for their needs whilst still in the city. For this they were given an armed guard to locate provisions necessary to feed them until a new base could be established and they could supply themselves. A few men immediately stepped forward offering their support for favouritism in awarding contracts to the army. The opportunity wasn't to be wasted yet the emperor, loathing their greed was non committal.

'Remember that I have power over you all' he said to the merchants there.

The interrogation of the province finally concluded with the desire and orders to see the country house of the wife of Numerius Septimus Clemens burnt to the ground and its family evicted before the whereabouts of Manilius Albinus was to be determined. Calleva Atrebatum was also to be thrown to the torch. These choices were purely acts of spite. A knock at the door requested that it be opened and a soldier forced his way in throwing to the floor a captive in a brown tunic and leggings. It wasn't Albinus.

'What's the meaning of this?' Carausius barked.

'This is the agent from Augusta Treverorum found hiding amongst the crowd outside no doubt waiting to harvest news for his master's ears. He was pointed out to me, although he denied any association until I made him speak' at which the burly soldier grinned.

The figure curled up at the emperor's feet and waited for its miserable fate to be determined but he was curiously unable to pass an instant judgement. Instead, in his mind Carausius remembered the Saxon slowly swirling around in the red river current of blood long ago in Ganuenta.

'Pick him up' he ordered.

'He is to be released but make sure that he is part of the goods bound for Gesoriacum and once there then let him loose to run. What can one man do alone to the ambitions he has witnessed here?'

Facing the worried multitude, he added...

'See my clemency, Britannia! From this moment I shall live in peace with our enemy and may my example give courage to you all. You are all now free to leave' at which the small room emptied to the chatter of bewildered voices.

Carausius, with three new legions although the loyalty of the VIth was suspect due to its remoteness in Eboracum, auxiliaries, cavalry and ships felt the confidence at his boasting and as he watched the wealthy walk away he requested that the prefect of the city garrison be brought to him at the governor's palace by the river.

Later that evening and after having eaten a little food, the orders for the remaining daylight were issued with a watchword for the guards on the gates given out. The city was calm and without riot towards the new authority imposed upon it and there was little need to arrest any culprits for insurrection. All soldiers could be safely billeted until their permanent accommodation had been secured. However patrols were maintained on the streets and the following day would see armed scouts riding out to the nearest towns to listen for talk of rebellion which they were to report back immediately if overheard. Carausius was advised not to leave the safety of the palace and its riverside escape as there was little to be gained from visiting his provinces so early on. He was reassured that in many ways they resembled Gallia and there would be time enough in the years to come to look them over and make improvements at his leisure. The larger towns enjoyed the protection of their walls; the coast had its forts and the countryside was bursting with riches of every kind. No man could have wished to have taken such a prize for himself and won it so easily. What was required now was to reward those loyal supporters who had instantly learnt to salute the name of Imperator Caesar Augustus Mausaeus Carausius. For that the Procurator was required and Allectus, who hadn't taken part in the seizing of the city, was to be summoned the following day. Until then, the view out over the darkening palace gardens across the falling river and towards the stars on the horizon couldn't have been more satisfying, for without a fleet of his own Maximianus it appeared, had lost the island forever.

The following day of Martius dawned cold. Gone were the damp warmer winds from the south west that had given the fleet a safe passage from Vectis and they were now replaced by a crueller and harsher breeze from the north east. Albion, the older name for the white island seemed appropriate at a time when everything was still winter dull and awaiting for flora to awaken. Sword like steel ripples of cold reflection danced across the river's surface where they soon disappeared from view at the water's edge and hunched figures pulled at reluctant draught animals crossing the exposed timber bridge. In midstream the fleet remained where it was save for a few warships that had returned to Gesoriacum to gather extra men and to spread the jubilant news that isolated Britannia had fallen. Charred wrecks remained at the wharves where they had been tied up; their owners unsure as to what to do. Nobody had mentioned compensation. Throughout the palace, stirrings of heat could be felt beneath the mosaic floor as slaves worked hard to rake out the night's ashes and then rekindle the furnace to warm through the many flues, the smoke adding to the other early fires throughout the city. Business it appeared was continuing and administration going quietly about its work.

Temples were being opened by the priests, markets traded early before the coldest part of the day arrived with its flurries of snow and the law courts prepared to hear their cases. A large part of dutiful civil life would have been unaware of the change in its fortunes except for an early delegation of business men pleading excitedly for the protection of the fleet in resuming trading with Gallia if and when the weather improved. The people they explained would welcome a return to buying the imported goods recently unavailable to them with the piracy on the seas but their enthusiasm was met with a need to save the navy for its real purpose – maintaining a watch over the island and keeping its emperor in power. The Saxons, in agreement for their support and promises of not attacking the rebel bases also needed placating and the merchantmen were their pay. Trading could resume but at its own peril.

Little by little the floor warmed and the prospect of a day inside relaxing appealed, but what was really needed was an envoy to conduct the tedious business affairs through to their final appropriate paperwork. With the morning stretching on Carausius began to grow impatient demanding that Allectus be summoned for this meeting not so much out of a desire to become embroiled in facts and figures but out of a desire to experience what being an emperor meant. To be kept idly waiting by another was dangerous. However, to maintain that the meeting would be to his advantage he asked to see the bathhouse ensuring that it was going to function correctly at such an early hour as this. Normally they would have been lit for the afternoon usage and prior to the evening meal where guests could relax in their unseen privileged comfort. Admiring its painted wall murals of ocean creatures and mighty Neptune, the emperor acknowledged the artist's skill, joking that the sea itself had never been that warm at the few times he had chosen to embrace it. This time he looked forward to his exercise cajoling them towards more effort at producing plenty of heat and steam. This, the slaves did willingly as it meant little in the way of hard work at the day's end as the bathhouse would then be shut; both sides appeared comfortable at the agreement. With beads of sweat gathering upon the cooler limestone columns and then running to the flagstone floor in tiny veins of moisture Carausius left happy that it would serve his purpose of interrogating Allectus, self made financial minister of the previous occupant. Even to him the warmth was now becoming a burden that most sensible men would seek to avoid and he left.

'My Lord' said the steward of the palace approaching.

'Your guest has arrived and is waiting in the atrium.'

'Good. Fetch him.'

And he obediently turned to escort Allectus past the guards on the door to the main living room where a warm brazier gave off its welcome glow complemented by the soft furnished chairs and richly painted decorations. Through the floor and walls the endeavours of the household slaves at keeping the building's hypocaust channels warm were slowly being won.

'Allectus, welcome! You are now my guest in the house that you must know so well' Carausius said gripping him firmly by the arm.

'I hope that soon we may be able to accommodate you likewise, as befits your status in this province. Unfortunately I no longer relish the barracks or the harsh bed of a fort and I will rule from here! Have you rested?' he asked, directing him temporarily towards the warmth of the brazier at which point the treasurer went to remove his heavy woollen cloak pinned at his shoulder with a brooch.

This was however denied on the grounds that the emperor had something that he wanted him to see and donning a light cloak led him through a door and into the garden where a pale sun struggled to fight through against an increasingly cloudy sky filling from the north. Two guards followed keeping their discreet distance but their hands too shivered as they gripped the pommels of their swords trying desperately to wrap them in the folds of their cloaks. Both men were growing increasingly keen to be inside and wondered at what was taking so long for the emperor to say to his minister of finance. They could only watch as the one man raised his arms high and spread them across the sky like an eagle whilst the other politely agreed at his side. Finally their private conversation came to an end at which point Carausius beckoned the two soldiers to come closer before again returning to his guest.

'Will you eat with me?' he said.

'I thought of concluding the day's business early as I have plans for you that I need to discuss and we can do that in some luxury, can we not? The bath house is lit as you may have noticed and the sweet aroma of dry wood burning wafts across the empty flower beds of my garden. Never have I felt this cold as now! It must be the river. Come...' and with that he led him into the apodyterium where two powerful slaves were waiting, but at an agreed signal they quickly grabbed the weaker man from behind forcing him into the caldarium and still fully clothed.

The emperor then signalled that he would be back after having taken a cup of warm sweet honeyed wine brought out by a slave. Upon his return he was happy to witness the pained anxiety spreading across the younger man's face. Wiping the early signs of moisture from his own, Carausius bent lower and between the taut arms of his bodyguard that were forcing the increasingly worried body against the hot floor where he beckoned Allectus to have the opportunity of speaking out.

'I have been completely faithful to your cause' Allectus spluttered.

'Have I not, and have I not also led you here at extreme danger to myself. You will find that I am guilty of nothing. Let me go if I have given you no reason to be suspicious' yet that elicited nothing in the way of a response and instead the guards were ordered to now kneel upon his chest thereby making his already laboured breath harder to win.

With great difficulty in breathing and a reddening face, Allectus began to lose consciousness at which point one of the assailants released him dragging him upright where he could lean seated against the whitewashed wall running with damp. There they maintained their stranglehold as once again Carausius peered into his face.

'Do I behave like the emperor?' he said slapping him gently but unsure as to whether he could hear him or not.

'I witness changes, small changes which in you are noticeable. I have to account for such things. You hair is longer than before' and he touched it.

'Your face is unshaven' and he stroked it 'and you avoid my company. For a man wanting favour you act alone and that only serves to alarm me. Yet above all I know nothing of you. I have one question for you – who are you? Tell me that and you can be free.'

The warm sharp iron knife was scraped skilfully across his throat digging out the hairs that hadn't complemented his full beard and after which a strong perfume was gently applied and stung. The man on the bench with his head upon a soft pillow felt more comfortable than he had done so for many a month deprived of care by the rush for power but the rush was over now and he could think of relaxing. He wanted to sit up but the slave pushed firmly but kindly upon his bruised chest indicating that he had to co-operate and to remain prostrate a little longer. Only his unruly hair required attention and then he could dress. In the corner another slave waited patiently with a clean laundered blue tunic and a pair of white woollen breeches. An elegant embroidered cloak hanging up spoke of his status. Then a door opened at which Allectus panicked expecting the immediate intrusion of two more bullies to finish their work and the warm iron knife bit into his flesh drawing blood. Silently the door was closed again as the intruder left a sealed parchment roll that was for his attention only on the table. He was conscious of the fact that he was bleeding, only by the slave trying to stem its pulsing flow but soon it had stopped of its own accord and Allectus was allowed to sit up holding a cloth to his neck.

'Where am I: and where is the emperor?' he asked, not recognising the room that he found himself in or even the time of day.'

The slaves couldn't comment on their master's whereabouts but no doubt he was interviewing another potential rival in his own way. The folly of accepting such an early meeting as had taken place slowly began to sink in and Allectus, unsure of what exactly he had said during his time in custody broke out into a cold sweat and shivered. A slave stepped forward to fuss over him but was held back at arm's length.

'Pass me the roll' and he did so.

High on the wall facing towards him the smallest window shed enough daylight to read by and opening the bound case he began to mumble to himself at some speed. His orders were simple. Using all imperial authority he was to secure at once a passage to Gesoriacum. There he was to ask for Manius Tullius Fruscus responsible for gathering taxes into the treasury and to compile documents into his success then return. Carausius feared that very shortly the occupants of the island would be again hiding their wealth and much more would be required with which to pay off his followers. Allectus was then to instigate the founding of a mint in Britannia that would strike its own coinage and therefore deprive enemies from trying to denounce and deny the emperor's military successes up to now. In between, and if he was loyal and true, he could have possession of the country villa that he had asked for as a retreat from city life. Therefore there was little time to lose and rapidly recognising the madness that could threaten his life at any moment he quickly dressed in the clean warm clothing provided. He then left, without seeing or meeting Carausius on his way out, but was stopped suddenly by the sound of a man's high pitched voice pleading for its life somewhere in the palace. He was sure that it was the voice of Albinus, once prefect of the Classis Britannicus, but tried to dismiss it from his mind.

In fleeing himself, it was now imperative that he managed to warn his mother as to the danger she could be in and in the light breezes carrying with them flakes of snow from the far north, came the nagging loneliness of a following arduous journey to Gallia Lugdunensis. A journey he wasn't entirely for making to meet with Tullius Fruscus.

CHAPTER IX

FRIENDS AND ENEMIES

To have been offered power and then shun it would have been an immediate sentence of death and denunciation for any man. The Procurator of Britannia with its loyal guard, regalia and the assumption that he was quietly filling his own account carried with it an authority not to be challenged by anyone, yet Allectus was finding it difficult being that person. Following Carausius' accession he slept in clammy cold sweats at the anxious thought of the emperor despatching his agents at the merest suspicion of plotting and every lonely day only grew longer without the reward of being safely at home. Even in the occasional company of Tullius Fruscus, the taint of fear stalked him at being found out through carelessly revealing the merest truths of his past. They were friends, Tullius and Carausius, and were known to be temple followers too. Tullius could be an influential man and the procurator felt unable to cast his shadow fully over him so throughout the weeks following his sudden arrival in Rotomagus the two men discretely circled each other like gladiators in the hot sand waiting for their opponent to lower his guard at which point, the other with or without approval, would have to strike. The contest resumed during a visit to the coin mint that had quickly been established to pay the troops.

A well guarded one storey building resounded with all manner of noises including the clanging of various ingots being dropped on the floor to the coin striking coming from a lighter room and away from the filth and grime of common metals skilfully being broken down. Individual precious objects were idly being accounted for by the clerks, although following smelting, some of these were being separated but most destined for another mint that was being established elsewhere; rumour having it that it was to be Britannia. Here though in Rotomagus old bronze coinage along with tin and copper were being weighed then melted along with silver to provide a currency to rival that of the true emperor. Gold coins were scarcer but were still produced in sufficient numbers ensuring that the taxation of wealth was successfully being enforced by a strong detachment of troops. Forge hammers crashed loudly down again upon the warm metal sheets as they cooled causing them to spread and thin before the next stage of cutting the blank dies could begin after which the fresh coinage was stamped out by men with thickly built forearms. Every complete wooden chest of five hundred new coins bore the mark D and PR before being weighed, hammered shut and taken immediately to a strongroom. There they remained in the darkness under lock and key until required to ensure that the rebellion continued to grow which it did like a seed searching for light. The greed of all men is tangible although nobody succumbed to its temptation dutifully going about their tasks with the boredom that repetition brings with it. Allectus attempted to appear interested in what they were doing despite having never seen a fabrica before and appeared out of place by asking questions. His tax official Tullius remained seated in the office with his abacus recording the day's work and whispering with his slaves about the figures written down, thus allowing the procurator the freedom to roam at will. Occasionally he would get up and walk to the door where he could watch the man sent to report upon him whereafter he would sit down again annoyed by his presence and the lack of any real accusations. In his hands he toyed with a round heavy iron stamp cut out from its flat face and used to strike the softer plain flans. Gently he rocked it to and fro in the dust upon his desk until at last the inspection ended and Allectus returned. The guards ushered his authority before him and every man rose to his feet as he entered the office. The procurator who warmed to the show of respect then reciprocated, by allowing those who had been seated to return to their positions. The power of his rank was altogether instantaneous and he quickly applied it again by demanding a drink to quench his throat of the fumes he had taken in and putting the beaker back upon the desk he picked up a bronze silver coin looking carefully at the emperor's head stamped upon it. He saw the die that Tullius had been rolling in the dust picking it up and trying to match its figure with that on the coin held tightly between his fingers. Everybody watched him do so waiting for his scolding at a poor copy of the imperial family.

'It won't flatter the emperor' he said dourly, 'and I am suggesting the face looks older. The legend too is off the edge.'

He then turned about slowly to look them all in the eye expecting the man who had struck that particular coin batch to speak up and beg his forgiveness, eventually turning the observation in Tullius' direction. Pinching the coin between his fingers and tapping it on the wooden desk he patiently waited for his answer.

'Well?' he motioned, laying the offending tiny coin flat in the palm of his hand and stretching it out before him. With increasing confidence he closed it again and grasped the coin tightly as if to be used in evidence at some point in the future. Tullius, knowing that his visit was all about gaining the advantage withheld from defending the accusation.

'A feature well seen' he carefully replied.

'You have to understand that my craftsmen who engrave these, do so without the presence of the emperor who must be entirely committed to ruling his island, is he not, for he graciously sends his procurator to comment in his absence? Perhaps you would reveal the best features of his bearing being only recently separated from him? Maybe you could also show us the correct angle of his face, the one that the emperor would enjoy seeing for all we have are images of Diocletianus and we alter these to give Lord Carausius the wisdom that age would suggest. He must not appear too young as that would tell of innocence and inexperience in such a victorious general. People must sense that he was born with good fortune and is therefore favoured by the gods.' Tullius was smug with his answer and furthermore amused at Allectus' rejection that he be entirely responsible for the features upon the coin.

The first blow had been struck by him although poor workmanship would be punishable if it degraded the imperial house causing people to mock at the integrity of its personality. Even worse was to follow: With the desire to open a mint in Britannia skilled men would be drawn from Gallia and if this was an example of their work then it wouldn't bode well. Tullius therefore promised a closer scrutiny of the fabrica and would be shortly attempting to win disenchanted men away from the southern city of Lugdunum to compliment the rebellion in the north. The coins needed to be clean, unsullied and freshly crisp in their appearance; everything else to the wary soldiers who had up to now followed the emperor would be recognised as being cheap copies and their value suspected of not being worth the metal they were made from. In their thousands they would be discarded and discontent would also require that they be quickly replaced before supporters of the emperor deposed him. Nobody wanted to receive poor money – soldiers or merchants alike and the lesson in finance delivered by Allectus was a warning to them all. At that very moment, outside the confines of the room, a rebel legion remained defiantly at its post but to Diocletianus and Maximianus these men were nothing but traitors. What would it take for them to change their allegiance overnight, he asked? Being cheated! More and more legions were required to desert from their forts but they wouldn't unless flattered by Carausius' direct message appealing to them that his cause was a righteous one.

'Being a friend of our Lord, Tullius, I am surprised that you do not share in his ambition for us all.'

The insult struck firmly home creating in the mind of him the intention of deserting just to see Allectus tried and condemned to death but the idea quickly faded in its complexity of execution.

'I will expect better things from you' the procurator concluded ensuring that his staff were witnesses to the warning and thereafter couldn't deny ever having heard it.

'The message from my noble Lord is...' and he took a little time before announcing clearly what he thought it was.

'There is to be peace. I come in the name of that surrender to warfare and whilst we are vigilant to the approaches from Germania Superior we must not fight amongst ourselves. Tullius Fruscus, I now offer you that treaty in the name of the emperor himself. Dine with me tomorrow afternoon that we may forgive these errors in more pleasant surroundings. Will you accept?'

It was said without any admittance to weakness appealing to Tullius to show contrition himself which he humbly did, accepting the invitation to a private audience with the emperor's trusted official.

The accommodation set aside for Allectus was not ostentatious as the city hadn't received imperial recognition, always lacking behind Lugdunum in favour and fortune although it could lately boast an amphitheatre and public baths being provided for under Diocletianus. Carausius had raised its worth in locating his mint there as it lay on Fluvius Sequana, possessing excellent trade links with the coast and beyond. However, what had been hastily provided in the form of rooms was to prove adequate for entertaining and it was on a cooler afternoon than of late that Tullius arrived for dinner. The streets of Rotomagus, following the customary closing of the law courts and markets for the day, were quiet and in the near distant horizon the sails of the amphitheatre could be seen stretching in the wind although today no festivals had been planned and its doors remained shut. Nothing but the sound of the distant bath house resonating with laughter and the bumping of carts along the road could have disturbed the delivery of the imperial edict. Inside the villa the food was being prepared in a timely manner and a guest poet sought to recite verses of the Aeneid for pleasure later on. A dancing girl had also been procured for the evening showing that Allectus had an ability to lavish treasury money easily upon his entertainment. Away from the mistrusted security of his isolated Britannic life he needed to relax and sensing that Rotomagus was complemented with a mixture of pleasure and business he declared himself approachable yet guarded in what he could say of his news to strangers. Therefore under a cloud of sweet perfumed incense be beckoned the slaves to open the door to the first of his guests, a wealthy merchant and his wife who had returned to the city. These were quietly followed by Tullius, who clutching his napkin and trusting his nose made for the triclinium where the food was being readied. Being a single man he usually ate at the street bars that served supper in a manner that was adequate for him although he could have chosen to take a villa for himself with slaves and not squatted in the barracks. After the fall of the Bagaudae there were many half abandoned buildings available but their sad decay spoke of the fragility of the current usurpation preventing him from ever wanting to become settled. All around the spirits of rebel emperors whispered in the wind of their failed attempts at creating a new empire, whilst illiterate men in command of far off legions took what they could before they too died in their turn. To see what Allectus was morally taking for himself was therefore of great interest to his guests who had gathered around the dining table and were quietly introducing themselves. An apology was soon brought in for the absence of a magistrate who had rudely accepted another invitation and would be away, leaving just the four of them. In the awkward silence that followed the slave's message the brazier spat out a small flame deflecting everybody's stare towards it until Allectus, as host, chose to address them. As he spoke he looked perplexed at the snub to his office so early into his visit and tried at laughing it off declaring that his seafood would be fit to eat and his wine stronger than any other man's. At the back of the room another slave smiled broadly behind his back waiting for the order to bring such wine to the table because there wasn't much of it left. The revolt, the rebellion of Carausius and the uncertainty of the future had now left the cellar close to empty. Trade routes with the southwest vineyards had temporarily closed as merchants could no longer trust that they would ever get paid and good wine was therefore becoming daily harder to find. The dinner guest, a trader himself tried to offer an explanation on behalf of his like, but the procurator knew about the price costing of supply and politely waved away his excuses.

'You see, Tullius' he said.

'This is my message to you; the quicker you mint the emperor's coins then the faster I can spread them into people's hands before taking them back again in tax. If the amphora runs empty tonight then we can kick your backside and blame you!' at which everybody laughed and turned to mock the absent magistrate for his hunting elsewhere for scraps.

Tullius however, had chosen to drink beer.

In playful mood the first course was demanded and silver plates were efficiently brought from the kitchen brimming with warm pickled beetroot served with a dressing of mustard. Another attractive plate held mussels lightly covered in a thin sauce of sweet wine, cumin and fish sauce whilst the largest plate contained snails fried in oil. It certainly wasn't the feast that Allectus had desired and as he looked despondently towards the door to the kitchen he was met with a simple shrug of the shoulders from the cook.

'Praise to Mercury! Is this menu from Britannia?' the merchant laughed whilst poking at a snail with the sharp end of his long thin silver spoon.

His wife, happy at not having to speak her opinion of the food joined in the efforts at securing a mouthful of something tasteless. There weren't even sufficient spices to hide the bland chewing of the meat in her mouth and the conversation dropped to a struggle to finish eating. More wood was demanded to fill the brazier as Allectus had noticed his guests shivering slightly. In the warm glow that settled them down before the next course Tullius wanted to return to the matter of Britannia as he had only scant knowledge of Carausius' flight from Gallia and asked of his whereabouts. The rumours were that he was in Londinium after having conquered the island without a struggle. The gates of the city were thrown open to him and the crowds rejoicing in seeing off the austere distant rule from Augusta Treverorum. At long last they had sensed a liberator sent to free them and accepted the new emperor with great enthusiasm.

'What about the old governor of Britannia Prima? What ever happened to him?' Tullius asked.

'I saw him alive and being kept a hostage on Vectis' knowledgeably answered Allectus.

Unable however to provide too much in the way of a commentary upon the invasion as he had been prevented from landing alongside the soldiers and had only fully come into Carausius' trust following the capitulation of the city.

'Had you known the emperor before? Where had you met him?' Tullius pushed.

'No, I hadn't. I came to my post via...' and he didn't finish but instead rose to herald the second course which consisted of braised chickens cooked in pungent ginger sauces and accompanied with chick peas and boiled eggs.

Again its simplicity let the host down and as the merchant took a small mouthful of cold egg he promised to look into providing the market of Rotomagus with a wider choice. Tullius grinned at his offer knowing that it wouldn't be achievable without profiting somebody and then he repeated the question of Allectus' rise to favour wanting to know why his old friend, the man he had sponsored for Mithras would choose him. The procurator looking over the rim of his wine beaker and towards him threatened complete silence with his stare.

'You ask too many questions of me and not of my guests' he replied pointing towards the merchant and his wife who were busy devouring the less than impressive meal.

However with a change of heart his wife was asked her opinion of what ought to be available to buy in the market, and once she had finished her list the talk again quickly returned to the rebellion and its consequences for them all.

'What's wrong? What have you to fear?' Allectus asked, citing the two new island legions that had sided with Carausius.

'In Germania the army has an impressive history of supporting rebellion and whilst I was there...' but unsure of himself and what he was saying he stopped talking of his past, again snatching an opportunity instead to signal the bringing in of the final course which consisted of wrinkled soft pomegranates and dry smoked cheese.

These could not be served any colder than they were and the joke that it was therefore the best course of the evening. It was the cook that required his backside kicking, they all agreed.

'Germania' Tullius quizzed whilst chewing over a piece of sweet cheese.

'That is a long way for you to travel on imperial business with the army? How did you arrive in Britannia and what experience have you had in financing the palace?'

His questioning grew more dangerous for at any moment the guard could be called in and the evening suddenly declared over with himself being dragged out into the street and beaten up without any remorse. He had been quick in throwing the question for nobody had forewarned him of the procurator's unannounced visit and Allectus could be anybody's spy. The merchant and his wife, nudging each other and warming to the infighting between the two men, signalled for their beakers to be refilled whilst Allectus gathered together his thoughts.

'Who are you?' Tullius dared to ask.

An angry scowl now filled the face of his host as he struggled with the answer. Nobody was to ever know of his bullying at the hands of Carausius on that day, so recent the memory, and the humiliation still fresh. Secretly, only he knew that his rise to promotion had come from sacrificing the ex-governor to the rebellion and little more. There were many more lies waiting to be found hiding in the darkness of his past and that was where he intended them staying.

'My father is a rich man' he boastfully said.

'Much like yourself and following my revulsion at the endless wars in the east I managed to escape and fled towards Ganuenta to be near him. I therefore know the soldier and the tax collector although I would prefer to be the latter. Does that satisfy you Tullius, that I have both the confidence of the emperor and knowledge of the army? What about yourself?'

Tullius knew the army all too well and in embarrassment admitted that his service ambushing and killing Saxons had only led to this meagre command, commandeering the bitter wealth of rich families in order to manufacture coinage with the emperor's bust stamped upon it. From that first moment after being dismissed from Gesoriacum every coin that he touched stained his fingers; every coin that he inspected led to a loathing of his former friend. Unlike Allectus, he was forgotten and could no longer seek favour destined instead to this life of servitude. For that reason alone he hated the man who controlled him and without recognising it Tullius was becoming dangerously full to the brim with a damning false loyalty with secrets that he would wish not to be divulged. Yet the procurator, in sensing more exploitation by Carausius in his rise to power felt sympathy towards him and having heard his tale tried to reconcile their differences. He raised his beaker, praised his guests for their stomachs and then offered to write an excellent account of what he had found in Rotomagus. In that way Tullius would never have reason to see the emperor again allowing his anguish instead to manifest itself elsewhere.

Putting the drink down the poet was then called for so that he could speak and others listen for their pleasure without arguing. When asked from where he came it was a surprise to be told that he was local and had only taken up literature to avoid military duty but he was proficient at it. He had recognised quickly the roman vanity and appreciated fully their love of their gods in sanctioning what they alone had achieved, even amongst the smoking ashes of rebellion. Every worthy man it appeared declared a lineage stretching back to Romulus and Remus and as the dinner guests comfortably lay back to hear Virgil's tale of the flight from Troy they each imagined their own greatness, all except the merchant's wife, who having drunk too much had fallen asleep. Aeneas would again sail without her.

The tale of the Prince of Troy was in its shortened version to allow the guests to picture the escapades his family endured in fleeing the Greek destruction of their city and eventually being guided towards the shores of Italia where his son Ascanius finally secured their dynasty. Artfully raising and lowering his voice where appropriate, the poet masterfully told the sad tale of Dido's death and the struggle to cross the ocean at the god's bidding. In the low oil light of the room and the gathering dark outside he respectfully led them through Hades in the search for Anchises, his father, where he revealed the semi living effigies of past and future heroes. To a man they all shivered a little more at the description of Phlegothon, the burning river of Hell in Tartarus and then basked in relaxation at the description of Elysium, the land of Joy where the chosen ones drank from the River Lethe again before being reborn. It was an excellent recital of the story and all throughout Allectus saw on his future coins the imagery that could be used to appeal to many other proud supporters. In his mind he began to foment the legends that would please Carausius' own vanity; the sailor having set out on the treasonable course to Britannia and winning against the odds. In Tullius' mind alone rested the violent death of Turnus and the taking of his lands, but once finished, all applauded the young poet vigorously before he opted to take his leave.

'Thank you' said the merchant.

'An interesting evening' and he shook his wife gently to wake her.

With renewed thirst she looked into the bottom of her cup and saw the bitter dregs lying there like sand washed about on a drying beach. A slave offered to pour more but she declined suspecting that he hadn't strained it properly and the next mouthful would be just as coarse and bitter. What she didn't know was that they were all now drinking from the bottom and that the supply was running out. Embarrassed by this lack of thought, Allectus called for the dancing girl to perform hoping that she could divert their attention for the remainder of the evening but they had had enough and politely asked for their leave too which was granted. A slave was therefore provided to see them safely back to their own rooms in the town leaving just the procurator and his mint official to watch the lithe girl sway about before their table of cold food, rough wine and beer to the doleful piped notes of a musician. Eventually though even she stopped, detecting no spark of enthusiasm for her skills and clutching a small reward of bronze silver coins departed into the night. There was nothing more to come. The evening was over.

Allectus stretched out on his couch and then rising yawned loudly to signal that Tullius ought to leave as well.

'Tell me' he asked of the man obediently rising to his own feet and wiping his mouth.

'Do you fear me or are you afraid of the months to come, fearing instead that Maximianus will attack?'

'I feel safe enough' Tullius replied.

'I know what loyalty is and how the garrison protecting me mistrust Rome. He will not risk an attack until he senses a weakness, a split, and so far there is none.'

'Good. I can have confidence in returning again. However, I feel that you and I share that common foe.'

'Diocletianus or Maximianus?'

'Neither' replied Allectus without needing to explain.

'Be careful.'

'I will. In my turn be warned not to invite merchants to dinner or attend the temple of Mithras with them in the presence of the emperor; he loathes them. Your father came from Ganuenta? Lord Carausius had somebody from there cruelly thrown to his death out of mere suspicion.'

'My father wouldn't follow such a man, Tullius. I am told he is stronger than that but did you know the name of the dead man?'

'Yes, we both knew him and unfortunately he was proved innocent' Tullius replied with his back to his host and tightening his cloak about his shoulders making ready to leave.

He politely stopped what he was doing, turned and looked the procurator directly in the face.

'But you fled to Ganuenta you said and yet somebody is telling you about your own father?' he irritatingly asked.

'Perhaps another day Tullius, another day' answered Allectus avoiding his stare.

'It has been an evening of small secrets, you must agree. The dead man's name? What was it?' he repeated only this time looking forcefully at him.

Without guilt or the intention to harm in a time of unrest and disappearance, it was easy to speak the man's name as it meant nothing personal to Tullius except that he had simply long lost the opportunity of social advancement and dinner invitations.

'His name was Numerius Septimus Clemens, a kind man' he remembered, briefly adding a description of a person whose stature hadn't changed over the years.

'Would your family have recognised him?'

'No, not at all' replied Allectus trying to conceal any sign of emotion before following his guest to the door and out onto the quiet street where a slave waited patiently to bolt it upon his return.

'With the god's protection go safely, and thank you' he said before the squeal of a hinge and a clunk of an iron key in its lock separated them.

Tullius, taking an interested last glance at the villa and its temporary occupant, knew there were to be difficult future decisions ahead for them both. Friends they could never be as the strong bond of a soldier's trust through adversity had never shone through and the procurator had constantly appeared the influential weaker man. However, in Allectus' collusion with his old colleague, there could still be a chance for an escape from the drudgery of Rotomagus and back into the ebb and flow of military politics where Tullius could contribute something towards the rebellion. Everything now depended upon the report being read by Carausius within the distant fortress of Britannia, for everything concerning the future was to lay in his hands and his hands only.

CHAPTER X

THE DARKEST LIGHT

The quietness and religious light of the small temple offered Carausius all the sanctuary he momentarily required, a place to contemplate his crushing thoughts. He still believed the loose limbed flame behind the relief of his god Mithras would proclaim to him a favouritism, but it mocked no more than it had done to scores of followers before and now served as a trick of the eye, an invention only of mankind's making. There was to be no triumphant victory of light over the gathering force of darkness in his war and in desperation, to find strength and renewed vigour, he had run from street to street seeking out the companion gods of Londinium discovering them as scathingly remote, disinterested. In his bleakest hours they had abandoned him too. He rubbed his eyes of their selfish tears wishing that time could repair the damage inflicted by his decisions but now had to rise and vigorously defend the events rapidly gathering to break his reign. Outside and scared for their own lives in the uncertainty of impending invasion the citizens had chosen to abandon him no longer afraid to point their fingers at the defeated wretch responsible for another calamitous war with Rome. Only slavery and retribution would follow the fall of the rebellious sailor. A new name to fear had suddenly risen upon their lips instead: Constantius Chlorus and he would ruthlessly return the Roman law to the lawless Britons.

The unforgiving stone temple floor scraped against his knees whilst his own ageing frame was more apparent to him through the contrite position he had adopted whilst having crawled there. Muttering, bowing and pleading to be answered he promised, without compromise, great rewards to the Lord Mithras in return for the destruction of the enemy forces now perilously gathered in Gesoriacum. Only four years previous he had celebrated great Neptune and Oceanus swallowing up a relieving fleet despatched from Fluvius Rhenus and in their own belief everybody assumed that the rebel emperor's fight was just, witnessing its destruction. What had now changed? In their remote fickleness why had the gods abandoned Carausius to support Rome in this renewed bid to bring his empire to an end? Outside he could hear the hobnailed boots of his guard fidgeting about on the steps as if he expected the answer to be forthcoming, yet being of insufficient rank to enter he was excluded to the divine will. He epitomised that confidence had vanished due to a series of defeats, only remaining loyal to the emperor through bribery, but once the money had stopped coming he would run away like the others had. From the hidden darkness Carausius nervously called out to him.

'Guard, guard, is there any more news? Is anybody seeking me?'

'No, my Lord' he truthfully replied.

'There is nothing to fear outside when you wish to leave. The city is quiet and you are under my protection.'

Reassured of his immediate safety, he returned to repeating again the incantation that the priests had long ago taught him, carefully avoiding any confusion in stating what it was that he wanted and closed his eyes firmly shut out of some respect. Looking abandoned by its own followers Carausius had the sacred void to himself yet he was unable to feel the intimate presence of the saviour bull slayer by his side. It was as if the Persian had elected to leave and no longer resided in the province soon destined to fail him. A quiet loneliness therefore accompanied his thoughts in which he mortally recognised the need to act was now. An urgency to secure the province; gather up arms to defeat Constantius Chlorus, and in thinking that he could meet the dangers alone, Carausius had no option other than leaving his god to that empty temple.

'Guard!' he shouted again up the small stone flight of steps and no longer concerned by the reverence of the sacred place.

'I am now ready, protect me as I leave!' and he did as the emperor commanded resolutely watching for any sign of a gathering crowd or trouble.

Carausius, in complete trust, brazenly came out looking up into an overcast sky anticipating that rain would arrive by the evening brought forward by a southerly wind. Tying his helmet tightly beneath his chin and ensuring that his sword wouldn't impede him he called for his horse, raising his left leg in readying himself to be thrown into the saddle. He settled gently upon the soft leather and again felt the surge of being able to control the affairs of man through the force of military arms. Surrounded by a small escort of round shielded cavalrymen he then kicked his mount into a canter and rode off into the city. Jupiter's lightning bolt failed to fall from the threatening sky and he felt sanely vindicated. All Londinium was now aflame with the rumours that Gallia had fallen and the fleet of Constantius Chlorus would soon be rowing towards them whereupon they would supplicate themselves and plead to be spared his vengeance. Carausius, angry in his belief that nothing was lost, called the troop to a halt where the crowd was perceived to be deepest and, when assured of silence by a few men riding down the loudest objectors, hailed out...

'For seven years citizens of Britannia I have given you my protection and that of my armies. The loss of Gallia is harsh to bear but does not fatally wound us. There is Oceanus, the fleet and the loyalty of Legions II Augusta and XX Valeria Victrix. There are also many forts and walled towns that would have to crumble in front of the invaders before we decided to ambush them on a battlefield of our choosing. This island province is not my homeland yet I will sacrifice myself in fighting to save you. Therefore do not hesitate... send your sons to the army that they can fight too and together we can rule victorious! Salute!'

A rousing, swollen chorus of 'Imperator, Imperator, Imperator...' filled the market place leaving Carausius to trust that he may be a living god and adored by the multitude that could turn against him.

'Reading of the divine Marcus Aurelius' struggles against the Marcomanni has strengthened me and it is now towards my own vigil that I must turn' he quietly spoke to the more senior amongst his rank, whilst adding...

'I believe Tullius Fruscus will have brought reinforcements from the six legions with him before he fled. I am also told he is in Portus Dubris and it is there that I shall organise the forces against Constantius Chlorus, so ride on quickly and away from here whilst the people still believe in me.'

The troop, obeying its orders, gathered together in lines of two abreast making for the wooden bridge across Fluvius Thamesis where stragglers in the road leapt aside at their approach. Whilst crying out for gossip they were unaware themselves of the true alarm. Their anxiety however was increased by seeing the armed horsemen in a state of readiness for war and where roads crossed smaller parties with permission broke away heading towards the furthest outposts unaware of the dangers that they could be in. All of Britannia Prima south and along its coast now looked out into the falling darkness of the evening and wondered what tomorrow was going to bring. Where the rumours that Gallia had fallen were yet to break slaves ignorantly lit the oil lamps waiting for their master's return and children fell asleep, whilst along the empty roads of night the emperor's guard clattered, the rain in their faces. A day's exhaustive riding along with much of the next and the imperial escort trotted without ceremony into Portus Dubris where a few soldiers were seen milling about in their customary drunken state. Carausius, with much on his mind and intent on making for the fort close to the harbour hadn't spread his troops out in anticipation of ambush, choosing to ignore the advice of his more experienced officers. Neither had he taken any notice of the soldier's military dress heavily disguised under dull woollen cloaks. Too many it appeared were mimicking their fallen comrades in a belief that tomorrow would see Constantius Chlorus' forces thrown about on the uncertain currents of the sea and destroyed before landing. They would laugh out loudly at the destruction of Gesoriacum before disappearing into the darkest corners of the town where in silence they waited for orders.

A recognisable trumpet blast signal led to the opening of the fort's gate with the garrison inside resolutely standing still to greet the emperor. In dismounting he could smell the proximity of the sea above the warm flesh of his horse and hear its wild call in the birds soaring overhead and saw in all the faces there the complexion of their salt worn lives. Against the quay a bireme's mast rebelliously rose above the stone rampart and in the southern sky the coast of Gallia could not be seen across the idle water from the watchtower. Quickly taking control he ordered the shutting of the gates and a doubling of the guard. Had any fresh sails been spotted at sea? At first light scouting vessels were to be rowed out depending upon the weather and a ship full of silver to be sent to buy more mercenaries but they had to respond quickly to win it. Desperate not to make any mistakes through tiredness, he then called for his bed early before demanding that all men there in Portus Dubris capable of command were to meet with him in the fort's praetorium at first light. Those that came forward willingly would be well rewarded. Those that didn't would be flogged until they reluctantly decided to do so. All men with any news from Gesoriacum were also to attend and he would reassure them that they needn't fear blame for the loss of the province. A scribe was going to be required to record eye witness accounts of Gesoriacum's destruction and any man with knowledge of the numbers of enemy cohorts climbing over the fallen ramparts was to speak without fear. The emperor had prepared well and amongst the hills and cliffs of his refuge he slept soundly that night on his mattress of straw with the stars silently navigating their course above. At the calling of the first hour of daybreak he awoke dressing immediately in a red tunic and heavy bronze scaled mail shirt that required the help of his most trusted slave to buckle up. Slinging his sword over his shoulder and customarily ensuring that its blade would come free easily, he turned to play with the gold ring upon his finger. The eagle, this silent effigy of Jupiter was about to strike for him and he felt the resurgence of powerful confidence. Through his window he could feel the sea breeze and hear the daily commands being shouted out as high on the hills he witnessed a small column of horsemen followed by a group of soldiers slowly struggling for the best ground where they had been posted to scan the distant horizon. Then there was a knock at the door and the guard reassured him through an open crack it was a friend arriving early to meet with him before Carausius was due to address the garrison. With his face to the door he watched it open to the sound of a familiar voice and relaxed. In walked Allectus.

'Greetings, my Procurator of Britannia. What brings you here for I am warmed at your courage? Are we to console the province together in this day of our reckoning?' and he slapped him hard about the shoulders with a simple message.

'Answer me that you have brought with you gold and silver for I need to buy more soldiers, more allies to the cause. Where are you camped and when did you arrive?'

Carausius seemed relieved at Allectus joining the fight and not at all threatened although their embrace lacked the strength of true friendship.

'I arrived last night, my Lord' he barely whispered, 'but out of weariness my path to you was closed. They told me to return this morning. Where has my authority gone?'

'It shall return' laughed Carausius, 'once my brother emperors, Maximianus and Diocletianus have conceded that the wasteful effort to capture the province back is ill fated and dangerous. Constantius Chlorus will fail them. They will then overrule their advisors and leave us alone to fight amongst ourselves! Then you can have the tax on what is left although you will be reaping a smaller harvest. Your country estate may have to be sold to fill the treasury vaults. That is the new value of your worth to me. Would you comply with my wishes to continue serving me or do otherwise?'

The threatening tone had suddenly returned and along with his next question, which was more direct he asked...

'Have you brought any coinage with you or not?'

Allectus, struggling with saying 'No' wanted instead to shout out a password he had treacherously agreed whereupon help would instantly flood into the room from outside but his courage failed him at Carausius' rejection of his abilities.

'Silver is a seed, Allectus. I need to throw it to the wind where it will scatter and harvest my legions. Without legions we are nothing!'

Carausius stopped abruptly as if the mention of a legion stirred a thought.

'Where's Tullius Fruscus? I was told that he was waiting for me here. Go and find him and we can hear the account of Gesoriacum ourselves. Order some food to be brought here as well.'

'No, my Lord, I will only bring Tullius to you' and he briefly left the room desperate for it all to end returning with a leather bag clutched tightly in his hand.

'Tullius...' he surprisingly announced, throwing the bag towards the emperor without fearing his retribution and whereupon it bounced across the floor before spilling out its sad weight.

Carausius poked at the bag firmly with his toe and the head rolled out before settling to one side; it was grey cold, smashed but still recognisable through the veneer of dried blood. The emperor stared into the dark dead eye expecting it to talk back yet feeling nothing demanded the meaning of it.

'Tullius was disloyal all along to your cause, and you ought to have known it before he deserted' the procurator announced.

'How do you know this' Carausius said, intrigued by his intimate knowledge.

'Why would you receive news such as this before me?'

'My villa is closer to the coast than Londinium and they sought me out first.'

'Who sought you out?'

'The remnants of your army; they did. They fled the bitter fighting but not before Tullius' head had been thrown over the walls of Gesoriacum as a warning to all there to open the gates. He had been missing they said for a while, but before they ran away they collected this token to prove that the town has been taken and the fleet there along with it. The forces of Constantius Chlorus had succeeded in blocking the harbour mouth by the construction of a breakwater thus preventing the ships from escaping. In panic at their entrapment all discipline broke down and...' But he didn't need to reach any conclusions.

The putrid fleshy ball of Tullius' head was evidence enough. A boatful of soldiers was all that remained from Gallia.

'I Minerva, VIII Augusta, XXII Primigenia, XXX Ulpia Victrix, VII Claudia' Carausius repeated, as if intimately knowing them all.

'It was you that gave me false reason to reinstate him from the dismal yet responsible rank that I thought he deserved in Rotomagus. All these men lost and where shall I replace them? From the cesspit that is the garrison here in Britannia? To think that I, Marcus Aurelius

Mausaeus Carausius, could trust you! Who are these soldiers here in Portus Dubris then? Where have they come from and who do they belong to?'

'My Lord, I shall find out.'

'You do that quickly' he asserted angrily calling for a guard to enter the room and sensing an emergency.

There was no reply from outside and in panic the emperor stormed to the window to see what was happening to have enticed his men away. In the courtyard a heavy wagon drawn by two oxen had stopped. There was something unusual about it as men were gathering around it like fish in a tightened net. An argument rapidly broke out between two of them attempting to get to the front line and very shortly all discipline had gone, with the remainder joining the fight. From the sides of the cart handfuls of coins were being thrown about in the air from chests marked in paint with the letter 'C' and landing amongst the crevices of the cobbled surface. Carausius called out for somebody to stop what was happening but nobody looked in his direction and he went ignored. He turned to leave the room where he could personally intervene and restore order yet no sooner had he taken the first of those steps towards the door than Allectus cried out 'Nunc!' and in rushed a stranger.

'Get out of my way' Carausius threatened and making to withdraw his spartha, but he was too old, too slow and the man easily overpowered him throwing his sword into one corner of the room where it settled with a metallic ring next to the cold eyes of Tullius.

'You traitor!' he shouted as his arms were pulled tightly behind him in the struggle.

Allectus finding renewed bravery in the company of one braver than himself, took the initiative, rapidly binding the emperor's hands and when finished he stepped warily back and alongside his colleague. After regaining his breath the man introduced himself with a purpose.

'I am the legate of VI Victrix legion from Eboracum. My ship sailed from there a week ago to land at Durobrivae where I met with the procurator and a merchant ship laden with hidden silver from Maximianus to secure our loyalty. We have been hiding at Allectus' villa before eventually receiving the news that Gesoriacum had fallen. His mother Faustina; you had met her, was very pleasant' he added sarcastically.

'You cannot hope to wish that this plot will succeed, you fool. My generals will hunt you down like game and then rejoice over your bloated carcass.'

'No, emperor' came the measured response.

'Your generals have fled, run away. They also have families of their own and fearing retribution having supported you their cause is lost. Your army can be bought for a cart full of silver and is currently without leadership or motivation. Your rule is now over.'

'You have been sent to murder me, is that the reason for this? Why can't I offer you something? You can have the warehouses in Londinium as a prize to sack if you desire. We negotiate...' but as he looked darkly into Allectus' light face he realised that his trust had been badly misplaced and there wasn't another gamble to bid for.

'Be careful of him; this spineless official he will let you down' Carausius said, but the legate wasn't for listening.

'You knew all about me!' wept Allectus in pent up frustration and now grasping the opportunity of vengeance that he had so long thought about exacting.

'The bath house in the Palace of Londinium...you extorted all the information that you required to know then as to who I am but you have never spoken a word. You have had your chance!'

He felt the shame of that day lift from him in his revelation as the steam itself had done so in a cold sweat, many years ago.

'Then who are you Allectus, for you never gave away any secrets as you passed out with fear but I've kept a hold over you ever since. Tell me now for we can be colleagues, co emperors if you wanted and forget our differences. Order the guards in and arrest the legate.'

He sounded convincing but Allectus suddenly spat out the only three words that could cause Carausius' skin to rise in irritation.

'Numerius Septimus Clemens' he said slowly to avoid a repetition that would have undermined its impact.

'You must remember him because Tullius did. I am his only son and you may recall hunting at my mother's house with spearing the wild boar. Many has been the day that I have hated you after discovering how my father died and now the day has arrived for me. I will claim my prize.'

'Kill me then!' threatened Carausius.

'Kill me if you can. You are as incompetent as your stepsister was' and he laughed at her memory.

A furious brother rose to defend his family's honour.

'I have kept you in power. I have paid wise men to follow you against their own judgement to see them killed and I have given you the finance to buy silence from loud men. Without me, without my knowledge and without my help you would have been dead a long time ago. My sister made a mistake.'

'Then what are you going to do?'

Outside the window orders were being given for the first of the ships to leave as the sea had risen. Everybody could hear that they were being provided against the emperor's advice. A scouting vessel would be rowed out upon Oceanus but mustn't stray in the currents and become helplessly stranded around the coast. Instead it had permission only to record the strength of Aeolus, the rise and fall of Oceanus and then return immediately. A detachment of men in the lighthouse above Portus Dubris had been given the task of extinguishing the flame and instead start fortifying the building to watch diligently over land and sea. As for the ship of silver, that wasn't to sail. Once news of Carausius' defeat had spread to the Saxon and Frankish shores then they would cast off their allegiance, immediately returning again to attack the province at will when the fleet would be needed to fight off Constantius Chlorus. Why pay them when the dwindling resources of Britannia would struggle at grasping anything back? Carausius, with hands still tightly bound strained at regaining his command. A lack of ships' carpenters and timber on the other side of the sea would hamper any attempt at the Romans coming. Everything had to be planned for and he knew the thoroughness that Rome was capable of. Their wars in the east must have been settled for them to be able to spare the legions for this undertaking. In being provocative, he had aligned himself with the legitimate emperors but they had spurned his overtures again and again plotting instead to rid their lands of his influence. By any means, by any hand Carausius was to die. What was going to be accomplished by arguing now? All military knowledge had to be shared in the common danger and he returned to bargaining for his life.

'We're not going to kill you' revealed Allectus.

'Too many men may be hiding their loyalties to you that we may be uncertain of. This revenge needs to die, and die now. You have to leave and they need to forget about you and concentrate instead upon the task before them. The VI legion will soon require its commander back in the north before the Picts sweep south behind our back and over the wall of Hadrian.'

'Then you are going to assume the purple, Allectus; the merchant's son? You are going to rule without knowledge? You cannot buy the army. The province will be lost. Are you mad? This province needs a far stronger man than you.'

The legate, who had quietly judged the two adversaries, now felt that his work was done. His presence had brought an air of calm authority over the fort and at his calling a soldier arrived at the door. The gatehouse that had remained shut was to be opened and his cohort in the town was to march in. If the bodyguard of Carausius, still feasting on the silver thrown to them were to put up any resistance, then they would be killed. Once Allectus was firmly established he could then leave a strong force behind as well as procuring more help from nearby coastal forts. The fleet he recommended moving to Vectis for the time being, and the use of mercenary Saxons he would advise against. New military commanders would be raised, men with experience of the island and sent to where they were needed. He solemnly promised to return to Londinium before the onset of the winter and when confident enough that all fighting in the north would have ceased. Allectus, he firmly told him, had to quickly cure the Cursus Publicus of its spies and communicate any invasion plans rapidly with him. Now militarily governed from the north, Allectus was to wear the radiate crown in the south under its protection. To this Carausius' heart thumped in furious anger.

'You will not last a year.' He warned.

'He governs in your name and if all fails then you will die as he proclaims that his true loyalty was to Maximianus all along. He will soon abandon you. The fortress at Eboracum will give him all the protection he needs whilst you fear everyday the sight of enemy sails getting closer. You do not have thick walls to shelter behind and whilst he can patrol his battlements you have hundreds of miles of coastline and few men. He cannot be trusted. Release me now so that I alone can restore you.'

For a moment Allectus' logic wavered and he looked at the man about to share power with him. He looked trustworthy yet the procurator couldn't be sure and with time running out there wasn't going to be any returning to the past. To have freed Carausius would have led to his being dragged up the stone steps of the rampart and flung to his death like his father had been. The legate too would have had no other choice than to have taken his own life before Carausius' imploring gaze. The decision was therefore made and Allectus would be the new ruler of Britannia and its provinces.

'When the scouting boat returns, and if all is well at sea, then we can carry out our plan' Allectus said.

'But it must be today regardless.'

'Yes, my Lord' the reply came, his confidence rising at hearing his name spoken in such elevated tones.

'We need to secure him, but first I'm going to go outside to look upon the fighting' at which the legate withdrew his sword and with care opened the door before slipping out.

'Allectus' whispered the emperor.

'Listen to me. Where has it all gone wrong? I've successfully defied Rome for seven years, made you wealthy and established a calm influence upon the Britons in this island. How long do you think that you have got before they build a fleet and set their sails to finish it? Quickly, untie me and live' but his voice was barely audible in the commotion that was flowing unpredictably towards them.

Carausius, hearing his name being shouted outside struggled with renewed vigour at his entrapment and rushed towards him; between them the sword still lay on the ground and along with it the future of the man who could handle it first. Upon snatching it up, its blade was thrust with all determination towards Carausius' chest without wounding him.

'Sit down!' shouted Allectus.

'It's over.'

'Legions of Britannia, I'm in here. Rescue me' yelled Carausius in hearing the clash of iron upon iron outside the room.

With an audible grunt however and the heavy dull sound of a lifeless man falling to the ground, it all went quiet. Then the door opened and in stumbled the legate only this time struggling for breath.

'There are no more. He is the last' he said with some difficulty and pointed to their joint captive.

'The scouting vessel I saw is also back. Pick him up; I'll help you.'

When outside the door, the three men stood witness to the rebellion at its end. In the near choppy waters of the falling tide Sol Invictus had cast his light upon mankind and like a polished mirror it reflected all hope back to the sky. Then with a kicking struggle the old empire was dragged to its conclusion, past the lifeless bodyguards still clutching their silver pay in death and towards the quay where another scouting vessel had been readied. Chained to its timbers were the men Carausius recognised as being Saxons and unable to free themselves by any means, they looked at him helplessly. This was to be his final voyage and they his crew. Being bundled aboard, he himself was also tied securely to the planking and then the orders given for the first of the boats to take up the slack rope between them and to start pulling. Allectus had his final words ready and spoke them with all clarity and bitterness so that there would be no misunderstanding him.

'You are now being cast upon the sole mercy of Oceanus,' he said,

'Where all the shores and rivers of Britannia remain hostile to you. The waves may mistakenly carry you to the warring armies of Constantius Chlorus or with Neptune's protection you may land upon a new Roman shore and establish yourself again but you are destined never to return! Look upon this island for the final time. It forgets you!'

Then stroke by stroke, the two vessels slowly exited their harbour sanctuary with those of sufficient curiosity remaining at their posts long enough to witness the collapse of another imperial victim. There was no audible salutation of horn or voice. Others quickly went about the profitable business of picking over the fallen for their possessions whilst the more ambitious sought out the new emperor's favour. When far enough out to sea to ensure no assistance was ever possible upon the day's tide, the rope was severed by axe leaving Carausius' followers to curse their probable fate. No Roman beacon would tell of their departure or any cohort signal their safe return. One day later and in the rising salt swell that spilled upon the boat of pirates causing their lips to burn with thirst, all Carausius could hear was the slap, slap, slapping of the wet hand of Oceanus Germanicus against the wooden side of his boat and stare through half open eyes to where it was that he thought he had left Britannia behind in the last faint rays of the mocking sun.

GLOSSARY

AUGUSTA TREVERORUM	Trier (Germany)
ALBION	Earlier name for Britannia
APODYTERIUM	Changing room of a bathhouse
AENEID	Virgil's epic first century AD poem relating to the founding of Rome
ALAMANNI	Hostile Germanic tribe
ANTONINIANUS	Silver and bronze coinage, heavily debased and bearing the bust of the emperor wearing a radiate crown
ATRIUM	The central courtyard to a villa
ANDERITUM	Pevensey
AQUAE SULIS	Bath
BAGACUM	Bavay (France)
BRITANNIA SUPERIOR	That part of Britannia containing two legions, most of the important towns and the richest agricultural lands as opposed to Britannia Inferior. The island was divided by Septimus Severus late in the second century AD.
BALLISTA	Roman heavy artillery engine firing large arrows or bolts. It could be dangerously unreliable. Sometimes mobile and moved about on carts
BAGAUDAE	Motley army of peasants and military deserters roaming throughout Gallia
BRANODUNUM	Brancaster
BARBARICUM	Regions outside the known civilized roman world
CLASSIS GERMANICUS	The German imperial fleet

CARACALLA	Roman emperor responsible for creating all men equal throughout the empire. There were to be no citizens and non citizens
COLONIA ULPIA TRAIANA	Xanten (Germany)
CUNETIO	Mildenhall (Wilts)
COLONIA CLAUDIA ARA AGRRIPENSIUM	Cologne (Germany)
CAUTES	Acolyte of Mithras with torch up symbolising sunrise
CAUTOPATES	Acolyte of Mithras with torch down symbolising sunset
CLAUSENTIUM	Bitterne, Southampton
CALLEVA ATREBATUM	Silchester
'C'	This could either denote the coin mints of Clausentium or Camulodunum
'D'	Quingenti – five hundred
DUROCORTORUM	Reims (France)
DUROVERUM CANTIACORUM	Canterbury
DIANA	Goddess of the moon and hunting
DIVINE JULIUS	Julius Caesar
EBORACUM	York
FLUVIUS THAMESIS	River Thames
FLUVIUS SEQUANNA	River Seine
FLUVIUS RHENUS	River Rhine
FLUVIUS MENUS	River Main
FORUM	Meeting place to be found in the centre of any large roman town
GESORIACUM	Boulogne
GALLIA BELGICA	Northern France/Belgium

GANUENTA	Once an important trading port on the coast of Germania Inferior but long lost to the sea
GERMANIA	Like Britannia it was split into two provinces – Inferior was the barren northern coastal region; Superior to the south.
GLEVUM	Gloucester
HELINIO	Roman coastal fort in Germania Inferior. Long lost to the sea
HERCULES	A god famed for his strength. Depicted carrying a club
ISCA	Carleon
JULIOBONNA	Lillebonne (France)
JUPITER	Mighty roman god associated with the eagle and thunderbolts
LUGDUNUM	Lyon (France)
LUGDUNENSIS	Large roman province of central France
LIMES GERMANICUS	A roman defensive system that followed the course of the River Rhine incorporating watch towers and a good road network
LONDINIUM	London
MENAPIA	A region of Germania Inferior
MARTIUS	The month of March
MITHRAS	Persian god with similarities to Christianity and symbolising the victory of light over dark
MOGONTIACUM	Mainz (Germany)

MARCUS AURELIUS	The philosopher emperor who spent many lonely years away from Rome fighting on his borders and who recorded his thoughts in writing
MERCURY	God of merchants and communication
NEHALENNIA	Germanic river goddess
NAVARCHUS	Senior roman naval officer
OCEANUS	The body of water surrounding the known roman world
OCEANUS GERMANICUS	The North sea
PROCURATOR	The leading financial official in the roman administration
PONTES	Staines
PORTUS DUBRIS	Dover
PRAEFECTUS CLASSIS	In charge of the Provincial fleet
PORTUS ARDAONI	Portchester
PR	Prima Rotomagus (the first mint of Rotomagus)
ROTOMAGUS	Rouen (France)
RAETIA	Roman province taking in Austria, Switzerland and parts of Germany
SOL INVICTUS	The unconquered sun. Closely aligned to Mithraism
SAMAROBRIVA	Amiens (France)
SATURNI	Saturday in the Roman calendar
SPINAE	Speen
TUBICEN	Horn blower
VEXILLARIUS	Standard bearer

VESTA	One of Rome's earliest gods. God/goddess of the hearth and without personification
VIRBIUS	A roman god of the forest
VECTIS	Isle of Wight
VENERIS	Friday in the Roman calendar
VENTA BELGARUM	Winchester

Printed in Great Britain
by Amazon